GLIMP$ES
by
Almondie Shampine

www.almondieshampine.com
author@almondieshampine.com
www.facebook.com/AlmondieIncorporated
www.facebook.com/AlmondieShampine

Printed in the United States of America

www.almondieshampine.com

DEDICATION

For Martin Bargabos

PAUL
CHAPTER 1

Dr. Paul Stevens pulls at his greying temples with his fingers, allowing his burdened shoulders to droop. He's the only single man he knows that has to endure incessant nagging, shrill complaints, and floods of tears without the reward of a home-cooked meal and a partner to share his bed. He does get paid for it, achieving mild financial security, but no security of meaning and purpose. Like the tides return the boat to the shore it is trying to escape, he deals with constant regression, which tends to increase feelings of helplessness and delineate hope.

He sighs into the Dictaphone. "Ms. Johnson seems to have suffered a set-back and has fallen into the throes of her generalized anxiety disorder and PTSD . . . again. Omit again in dictation please. The antecedent appears to be that her son was accepted into college. Ms. Johnson appears to suffer excessive worry and anxiety. Quote, 'Lots of bad things happen at places like that. He could be drugged, mugged, beaten, and raped.' Prior sessions up to and including most recent have revealed that Ms. Johnson was date-raped in her second semester of college approximately 25 years ago. Since her son's acceptance, Ms. Johnson has spoken of flashbacks and nightmares regarding those traumatic events, except now her visions show her son being victimized versus herself.

"Ms. Johnson is requesting I meet with her son to convince him, quote, 'College is no place for a good kid', unquote. I have agreed to meet with him during her next appointment to assist with the resolution of her concerns. She has been referred back to Dr. Snyder to reevaluate her medication levels and psychotherapy sessions will be increased to twice a week for a period of no less than 6 weeks to provide increasing support for this transition. Nancy, please pull up statistics on the frequency of male druggings, muggings, beatings, and rapes at Florida State."

Mechanically, Dr. Stevens presses stop and rewind, removes the tape, and labels it.

At the blessed beep of his watch alarm, he stands to retrieve his coat. He bypasses the mirror, head down, and exits his office. "Going to lunch," he tells his ever-faithful assistant and administrator, Nancy.

"We got another cancellation from Mr. Weedling. It's his third one," Nancy tells him. "Should I send him the notice?"

"No, no, he doesn't follow procedure. That's the nature of social phobia. Consecutive cancellations?"

She nods.

"I was afraid this would happen. One step forward, three steps back. Schedule a home visit. Baby steps. All over a matter of public incontinence. At his age, no one cares."

"Dr. Stevens, are you okay?"

He looks up at the concern in Nancy's voice. "Fine, why?"

"You seem . . . upset about things."

"Nancy, are you sure you want to get into this career field? It's not what it's cut out to be."

"With all due respect, Dr. Stevens, what do my career aspirations have to do with your being stressed and negative?"

"I'm not being negative. I'm being realistic." He begins pacing the floor, pulling at his temples again. "I wanted to help people. Not sit in my office everyday with chronic hopeless cases."

"Wo! Stop right there. Chronic cases?"

"Yes. Helpless. Hopeless. Regression the signature of their pathetic lies. These people don't want to get better. They need their illness like a crutch."

"Stop. I won't listen to any more on this subject. You are the only hope they have. That's why they keep coming back. Because you help them."

"Help them? How long has Ms. Johnson been a patient of mine? 10 years?"

"Exactly. And it's loyal clients like her that keep your business alive and thriving."

"I didn't get into this for the money, Nancy. It's not about the money. I mean, is this all there is? Is this what they call living? Waking up every morning and –."

Nancy picks up the ringing phone and swivels her back to him. "Dr. Stevens's office, this is Nancy speaking. How may I help you?"

Paul slumps his shoulders and exits the office. He spends 40 hours a week listening to people talk and complain and question life's purpose. He has no one to listen to him.

Paul is rammed in the shoulder by a passer-byer. He turns, but they do not look back or offer an apology. Paul steps into Coffrey's and walks to the side table in the far corner and sits, while needlessly poring through the menu. A coffee/sandwich shop, Paul comes here five days a week for lunch and orders the same thing. Tuna Salad sandwich with cheese, no tomato, on wheat, and the soup du jour. He waits 10 minutes exactly, just like every day, and then gets the attention of the waitress.

"Sorry, didn't see you there. What can I get for you?" She says this every day.

"My usual please."

She looks at him expectantly, and then her eyes brighten. "Martini, straight-up. BLT, no mayo."

Some men walk through life and can't be missed. Others? Who knows? Who cares? Paul is the latter. He tells her his usual and has her read it back to him."

"No tomato," he repeats.

His virgin bloody Mary comes without a cherry. He peels the tomato off of his sandwich with distaste, and leaves her a .50 tip.

"Look at that. Right on time," Nancy says dryly.

"Glad you noticed," he says, strolling toward his office while purposely trying not to understand her implications or think about the four remaining hours. He feels a little tipsy from the alcohol mistakenly placed in his drink. He closes the door to his office, calculating the time it takes for alcohol to metabolize. Well, at least the first 30 minutes of the next session will be tolerable.

The 4:55 pm alarm marks the closure of another day's work. He grabs his coat and paperwork and joins Nancy in the outer office as she closes up her end. "I'll see you tomorrow, Nancy."

"Dr. Stevens. When I'm not feeling well, I take a bath or do yoga. It really helps ease the anxiety that unbalances us and our thinking processes. A negative attitude is not going to help these clients, and they'll stop coming back."

"I don't think you understand, Nancy. They'll stop coming back when I *do* help them, because then I'll have succeeded in the healing process."

"There is no cure for a cold, but that doesn't stop doctors from trying to alleviate the symptoms, take them out of work, and order them to rest to build their immunity. Goodnight, Dr. Stevens."

Well, Paul certainly wasn't the only one acting strange. Nancy had never spoken to him with anything but the utmost formality, hardly even seeming to notice him most days. But then he has never been one for striking up conversation over, what he considers, mundane things. He knows firsthand how frustrating it can be constantly hearing others complain.

Perhaps she's getting burnt out as well, or she's beginning to like him and he's getting under her skin.

Paul considers this on his short walk home. He's only had one girl in his lifetime while in graduate school. She had been the salve to his wounds following his mother's suicide, but his grief had thrown him face-first into his graduate study and work. He hardly acknowledged her and had little time for her. Her chipper attitude and exciting lifestyle drained him, so unintentionally, he had dragged her down to his level, turning that beautiful smile into tears. Boredom replaced excitement. She had called him cold, unfeeling, without emotion, heartless. She had diagnosed him with Major Depressive Disorder and Obsessive Compulsive Disorder because of the anxiety he would feel if his routine was disrupted.

In the beginning, she had talked about marrying once out of grad school. In the end, he didn't even turn his eyes away from his studies as she walked out the door for good. He'd hardly thought of her thereafter, hardly thought of any woman in face of there being greater things in the world that needed his attention. He could never make a woman happy, because his ambitions, his overwhelming need to help others overrode anything else considered of importance.

Paul unlocks the door to his small single family two-bedroom home. One foot in the door and she is there to greet him. She rubs her body against his shins, purring happily. Missy is a better companion than any woman could be. So loyal and faithful. She relies and depends on him and awaits patiently day after day for his return home, always trusting that he will come. He doesn't have to impress her or try to prove his love. She loves him without question, appreciating that he is her bread and butter, or cat food and water, rather.

He'd found Missy 12 years ago on his doorstep. Love at first sight. They needed one another and didn't try to hide that fact. It was right after his transition from graduate study to real life, when he'd never felt more lonely. Missy works her life around his, which for some reason is deeply satisfying for him. Not one night in 12 years has she not greeted him at the door, one foot in, with a grateful Meow.

Paul bends and strokes the long-haired balding Calico before hanging his coat on the hook, and removing his shoes and placing them meticulously on the shelf. He enters their small kitchen with Missy at his heals.

"So what's on the menu tonight, Missy?"

Paul has the TV dinners in the freezer stacked so that whatever is on top is what he gets. It allows him a moment of the element of surprise, which is about how spontaneous he gets. "Oh, processed chicken parm and penne pasta. My favorite." He places it in the microwave, then opens the cupboard door next to the fridge where Missy's cans of food are stacked, "And you get Tuna with bits of Salmon." She purrs against his shins. "Yes, I know, you love your fish."

He opens the can and places her food in her silver dish, then refills her water dish. "Chicken Parm. Red or white. White is good with pasta." He pours himself a chilled glass of wine. His mother had loved a glass of wine with every dinner. He had acquired the same taste.

Balancing the TV dinner and cat dish in one hand, and holding the wine with the other hand, he moves into the modest living room that entertains a beige couch, dinner stand, side table and lamp, and TV and TV stand. He places the cat's dish at his feet, then plops down on the couch and clicks on the TV, just in time for the 6 o'clock news.

"So, how was your day, Missy? Anything exciting happen? Yeah, mine was pretty much the same. Same thing, new day. Ms. Johnson regressed again because she doesn't want her son going to college. I know, I know, what parent does not want their kid to go to college. Parents will kill – or kill themselves – so their kids can go to college. Yes, I've been thinking of Momma today, missing her. Yes, I know. I always do that when a patient goes backwards. You remember how much progress I was making with Mr.

Weetling, getting him out in public again? Well, he's back to holing himself in the house. He's so petrified of being incontinent again, but he's adamant against wearing Drypers. Nobody notices. That's what I said. Who looks at old men's butts anyway to notice the extra cushion? I told him it would decrease the likelihood of his breaking a hip. I was trying to be funny. He didn't get the humor.

"Ms. Lawson is getting nervous because garage sale season is coming soon. She says the compulsion is so bad that she's salivating excessively and her hands are twitching again. I reminded her that there's nothing wrong with her buying something, but to carry only 10 dollars on her at a time, and before she can replenish that 10 dollars, she has to get rid of an old item that she doesn't really need. Oh look, this guy must just *love* bad publicity."

Paul focuses on the screen of a John Whitman, son of the multi-billionaire Bill Whitman, all accumulated through the holding and selling of stocks in America's most thriving enterprises, including 67 percent of his own. The reporter reveals that John had engaged in another best-party-of-the-month and created yet another huge mess and scandal with the daughter of Welch Portman, billionaire, who was engaged to be married to another man. Footage shows them entering a bedroom together, holding hands.

"Miss Portman is innocent. There has been no scandal. We simply talked all night and picked out themes for her up and coming wedding." John's mischievous grin says bullshit. Another shot shows John leaving his father's office angrily and telling the camera man in not so nice words to leave the premises.

"Sad they call this news," Paul says, lifting the remote to change stations.

"Rumor has it that Bill Whitman has fallen ill and has started cracking down harder on his only heir that play time is over, though this has yet to be confirmed."

Paul smacks his lips at the last drop of wine and stands. "Missy, what's wrong? You hardly touched your food. You love fish. Yea, I know, my dinner wasn't all that great either, and it's supposed to be my favorite. I don't know what's gotten into me. Even Nancy notices that I'm acting strangely. Are you getting tired of the same old thing, too? She told me to take a bath. Imagine that. I don't do baths. I take showers. That's what I do."

Missy follows him into the bathroom as he gets the water going. She loves sucking up the steamy heat. Paul showers, washing his hair and face, then his body, and steps out. He brushes his teeth, shaves his face, then moisturizes. He uses nasal spray, cleans his ears, rinses his eyes, and blows his nose. Just like every night, he puts on the striped white and blue pajamas his mom had gotten him for his 21st Christmas. He'd had to cut strips on the sides of the elastic to fit his broadening middle.

He cleans up the dinner mess and washes his fork and glass, then checks his phone. No callers, as usual. He tries to will it to ring. It doesn't. The silence bothers him tonight. With a cup of chamomile tea, he finishes his research grant proposal and seals it in an envelope. "Kiss it, Missy. Bring it luck. If this goes through, I'll really be able to make a difference."

He moves into his bedroom and clicks on the TV. Missy waits for him to get underneath the covers before jumping in beside him. He watches George Lopez and finally falls asleep to the Nanny. Just another Monday marking just another beginning of just another week.

XXX

It was Paul's mother that had indirectly encouraged him to get into Psychology. She had suffered from Bipolar Disorder with occasional psychosis for as long as he could remember. His father had remained with her, thick and thin, highs and lows; that is until Paul moved out. Assured that Paul was grown and could care for himself, his father had left his mom after a period of mania that left them in debt once again. It was the sixth time she had blown through Paul's college savings that his father had managed to save on some kind of business-venture scam.

Paul had returned home from his first year at college to find her in a severe major depressive episode, unable to care for herself. She'd stopped eating, stopped taking her meds, and stopped getting up to go to the bathroom. He had found her soaked in urine and feces watching a soap opera with unblinking dead eyes. It's the worst he'd ever seen her, and Paul had blamed his dad. His return triggered another manic state. She cooked non-stop, day in and throughout night, sleeping impossibly little, and sharing that sleep-deprivation with him. She'd come into his room all hours of the night, talking about how she was going to own a 5-star restaurant. "Try the food, Paul, try it. Just one bite. I have to go shopping. I have to go shopping, get more food," she'd say rapidly, her subjects changing just as quickly. At 3 in the morning he'd tried stopping her from leaving the home in the state she was in and wound up having all the china whipped at him to shatter and splatter against the wall.

Resisting her attacks, he had reminded her the food was gone. As soon as she left the room, Paul had called his father. Mom was returned in hand-cuffs, screaming shrilly. According to the authorities, she had piled up a cart of food and walked out of the store without paying for it.

"These idiots don't understand that I can't pay money when I don't have it. I told them I'll have more money they can ever imagine once I finish building my 5 star restaurant." Paul's father had cautiously approached her, staring intently into her eyes, and asked her if she'd taken her meds.

"Those things? I haven't taken them in months and look at me? I feel great! I'm throwing a party. I got shrimp and cake and a meat platter. Everyone's invited. Look, we already have guests," she had referred to the two police officers."

"She needs to be hospitalized," Dad had said somberly. When they moved to remove her cuffs, Dad advised against it, because as soon as she heard the word *hospital* she went into rage, kicking, biting, screaming, spitting.

"Don, I don't want to go. I don't want to go. Don't let them take me. Please, Don, I'll be good. I'll be good."

It took four full-grown men to get her in the back of the squad car. Dad's soothing, yet tired voice reassured her that it'd be just for a little while, long enough for her to make the menu and the plans for the 5 star restaurant. Dad was the only person ever to be able to calm her in such a state. She had looked at him adoringly, "Did you get the eggs?" she had asked.

"What?"

"When you said you were leaving, I told you to get eggs. How could you forget the eggs?"

Dad had been gone for six months.

Once at the hospital, she'd been dramatically brought down from her high. Paul and his father had thought her asleep when they had their hushed conversation about their choices and their future. "Paul, you can't quit college, you can't," his dad had told him.

"Dad, she can't take care of herself. She needs someone to be there with her and make sure this doesn't happen."

"I can't," his father had cried. "I can't do it anymore. It's too hard. There's no help for her. But I can't have you leaving college, Paul. I didn't put up with all of this all these years just to have you ruin your future and say goodbye to your dreams as well."

"Then what are we supposed to do? We can't just leave her. Dad, are you forgetting who she is when she's not going through episodes? She's not always like this."

"That's what makes this so hard, son. She'll do so good for so long and I'll remember the woman I married, the woman I love. Things will be so great, so wonderful. Then . .

. I'm not a young man anymore, Paul. I just can't do it anymore. It's killing me."

"We'll take shifts. I'll come back on weekends and all my school breaks."

"Listen to yourself, Paul. Even you can't handle her."

"She loves us. She'd never - ."

"She doesn't know what she's doing when she gets like that. It's all so real to her. It's getting worse."

"So we just abandon her?"

"No, not abandon her. We'll visit her all the time. There will be trained professionals who do this for a living."

"You're going to send her away to a – a - ?"

"It's okay, Paul." Mom's voice had surprised them both. Tears flooded her eyes. "It's okay. Everything's going to be okay."

She had rubbed his head as he rested it in her lap. Her fingers so full of love and nurture. Her voice so gentle and kind. "Tell me how college is. Tell me everything. Talk to me, Paulie, just like we used to. Stay up with me all night and talk to me. I love hearing your voice, such exciting tales, your experiences. Tell me everything, Paulie."

He had been the sunshine of her life. No mother could ever love a child like she had loved him. He talked and talked for hours that night while she rubbed his head and hummed softly.

She was sent home the following day, provided 10 different scripts to stabilize her moods, once again, with a whole combination of horrible side effects. She had once told Paul that she hated taking them because they changed her, and made her feel drugged all the time, like a walking zombie or a robot without her soul. It was that night, 16 years ago, when Paul was 22 years old, when she'd killed herself. A selfless act so that she would no longer be a burden, Paul knew, for it had only been for Paul and her husband that she'd gotten out of bed each morning wondering if today was going to be a good day or a bad day. She had praised God endlessly for those good days.

Silently, Paul knew, she would pray for a cure, because for most of 22 years, he had seconded those prayers. His mom had been ill because no one could cure her, and in the end she had taken her life because there had been nothing anyone could do to help her. The medications just simply hadn't been enough. If she were alive today, things would be different, due to advances in treatment methods for those suffering from manic depression, but it hadn't been available to her then, and just another beautiful soul had been forever lost to mental illness.

Every client is his mother, pleading with him to help her, please help her. Each case is personal. And every week they return and every time they regress, he feels like he has failed, just as he had failed his mom.

CHAPTER 2

Six a.m. Friday, Paul is really struggling for the first time in the 12 years of his practice. He thinks about calling in sick. He can. He owns the practice. But in 12 years he's never missed a day of work, arrived late in the morning or left early in the afternoon. He feels a type of dread he isn't accustomed to. The day feels strange.

He opens his curtains and finds the day downcast and dreary, perhaps instigating his mood. A lot of people struggle on such days. Grey is the color of misery and rain the signature of tears. His coffee pot gives a hiss, a pop, and dies. Stepping out on the curb to cross the street to the coffee shop, he gets sprayed by a mud puddle from a passing car. He stops at the dry cleaners and changes into the suit he'd worn yesterday, now wrinkled and baggy, and hands them the muddied suit. The door jars as he's heading out and he drops his coffee cup. He arrives at the office 10 minutes late, hoping Nancy brewed coffee. She isn't there. He heads into the copy room to start the coffee and the phone rings.

In this flash moment, he finally understands why Nancy has been pestering him for a cordless phone for several years. He'd told her it was an unnecessary expense.

"Dr. Paul Stevens' office, how may I help you?" he answers. The guy on the line is hysterical, saying he just lost his wife and child and his about to blow his brains out. "Calm down, sir. There are other alternatives." Paul has to pull the phone away from his ear, the caller yelling so loud. He frantically searches the desk for the black appointment book. "Yes, yes, I'm listening. I'm sorry. My secretary hasn't arrived yet and she takes care of the scheduling. Sir, don't do that. Please. I want to see you. Can you come in - ." The line goes dead. "Hello. Hello. Sir? Are you there? Dammit."

Nancy arrives. "Now you're cursing at our clients? Give me that. Now look what you've done. You made them hang up. Who was it?"

"Some guy. He was asking for you. I told him not to call here." Paul doesn't even know where that had come from or why he'd even said it.

Her face visibly pales. "Rich?"

"I'm kidding. I wouldn't do that. I don't even know why I said that. It was a highly suicidal prospective client with whom I was trying to arrange an appointment, but couldn't find the appointment scheduler, and he hung up before I could tell him to come in immediately. Now he's probably blown his brains out, as he was threatening to do, because I do need to remind someone that this *is* a place of business and reliability and professionalism is expected."

Nancy looks at him, dumb-founded, then bursts into tears. All this and still no cup of coffee. "Why are you crying?" he demands.

"You've never yelled at me before."

"I didn't yell at you. Stop being so sensitive. You've never been late before. You concern yourself over my negativity, but all this week you've been snapping at me, giving me an attitude, and telling me what's best for my clientele, when I'm the Doctor and you're the secretary."

She becomes rigid, her tone cold. "You're absolutely right, Doctor. I forgot my place. Some very bad things have been occurring in my personal life. I thought you of all people might actually understand, seeing as how it's your profession and all."

"Personal matters stay at home, where they belong. Not at work. You want to make it up to me? Get me some coffee. I've had a hell of a morning and I need coffee."

"Personal matters stay at home where they belong. Not at work," she murmurs mockingly.

"What?"

"I said I'll bring it to you."

Paul walks to his office with a grin, suddenly feeling much better. He likes the banter. The pure professionalism, yes doctor, no doctor, was getting old. Reminds him of his times with Claire when they used to bicker. He'd make her cry. She'd make him want to yell. There was a very real human quality in seeing Nancy cry. Maybe Nancy likes him after all.

Paul goes to his usual place for lunch. With gritted teeth, he endures the too-long wait, explains his order in detail, doesn't bother this time in asking for a Virgin Bloody Mary, but gets it anyway. While peeling the tomato off of the wet soggy bread, he feels his face heat hot. He throws the sandwich on his plate, causing the china to clatter loudly.

"You finished?" the waitress asks him, seeming oblivious to his distress and uneaten sandwich.

"I have been coming here for the eight years since you opened, Monday through Friday, at precisely 12:10. Every Monday through Friday, I have to wait 10 minutes, jump up and down like a monkey in order to get service. Every Monday through Friday, I order a virgin bloody Mary, soup of the day, and a tuna salad sandwich, with cheese, no tomato! Every Monday through Friday, I have to peel the slimy tomato off of my sandwich and this leaves me to question, who is the bigger idiot? You for providing lousy service or me for coming back every Monday through Friday?"

She throws his bill on the table and walks off. As he's retrieving his coat, management, a kid no more than 21, confronts him. "Sir, I've got a waitress in tears telling me you harassed her. We do not tolerate such behaviors here at Coffrey's. I'm going to ask you just once to pay your bill, and leave, and reflect on your actions."

"Reflect on my –? Your waitress sucks, and if she can't handle constructive criticism for her poor services, then it will reflect in her tips and all the customers that never come back because all they want is a tuna salad sandwich with cheese, no tomato. No tomato! Is that so hard to ask for?"

"Mistakes happen and I'm sure she would have been more than willing to apologize had you not confronted her in the manner that you did. Now, if you'd be willing to apologize."

Paul shakes his head and turns toward the door. "Sir, your bill."

"Shove it," he says angrily.

"Then I'll ask that you not return here until you pay your bill."

"Oh, don't worry. I won't be coming back."

Good guys don't get noticed until they deviate from their norm. Then they're not forgotten.

Paul crosses the street and walks a block to The Cave, where he orders a mixed drink and a slice of pizza. Whereas Coffrey's is laid back, low key, an older crowd enjoying a quiet lunch, this place is loud, full of outgoing conversation and energy. Paul finds a booth furthest from the bar. His drink is strong. The pizza is greasy. The stimulation is intoxicating. The clientele ranges from kids, students, to their successful model lawyers, realtors, journalists, and executives. The wanna be successful and the successors. Where does he fit in? They all seem so confident, so alive. What is their secret?

Paul's phone goes off into his second drink. "You're late," Nancy says. Paul can't tell if her tone is patronizing or if she's enjoying this moment, like she's been waiting for this very moment in all these years to say those words, especially after his treatment of her this morning.

"My next patient isn't scheduled to come in until – ." He looks at his watch. Two hours had passed since leaving the office. Tipsy and dazed, holding a cock-eyed grin, Paul returns to the office to his waiting clients. He apologizes for the delay and starts the session off with Ms. Johnson's son, who appears to be as fidgety and anxious as his mother.

"Dude, you gotta do something. I gotta get away from her. She's crazy. She's driving me crazy. She's got herself convinced that the moment I step on campus, I'm gonna be raped. Come on, how realistic is that? I'm a guy. Some girl wants to rape me, then I'm all about that, you know what I'm saying'. So you're the Doctor. How do I get her to stop bein' so crazy?"

"A mother letting her only child go off into the world is like a child getting on that bus for the first time for kindergarten. There's separation issues. All parents experience a great deal of anxiety when their child is ready to leave home. Most have evolved their lives around this child and aren't yet ready to let go. It's very scary. You want this transition, to be a part of the big world and move out from underneath your parents' wing. She doesn't want the transition of having to live a life for herself that doesn't completely evolve around you, because it's very scary. It's unfamiliar. You understand?"

"So should I start, like, being bad and making her life a living hell so that she'll want me to leave?"

Paul chuckles. "No, no, no. That's not what I'm saying. Doing things gradually one small step at a time can make such a transition easier. Your mom wants me to tell you not to go to college, because she's very scared, but if you gradually wean yourself away from her, it will become easier for her. What are ways you can think of to wean yourself away?"

"What, like, maybe staying at friends' houses a couple days a week, so she can get used to me not being around her all the time?"

"That's a start, yes. But when you're away and she's afraid of something bad happening, what can you do to ease her fears?"

"Call her, tell her I'm okay."

"Good, good. So say, at first, you call her twice a day, then after a couple weeks once a night, then after another month, you call her every other day, right?"

"Yeah, yeah, I can do that. And I'll tell her I'll come home every weekend and after a while every other weekend and for vacations."

"You got it." Paul smiles.

"Hey, man, you're pretty cool, you know, for being a shrink and all."

"Thanks, man," Paul feels genuinely complimented. "So I'm going to bring your mom in now. She just needs reassurance. She loves you and just doesn't want anything bad to happen. Nancy, please have Ms. Johnson come in," Paul says over the intercom.

Ms. Johnson enters and sees her son's relaxed smile. "So is it all set? Have you decided that college just isn't a good place for - ."

"Mom, I'll call you every day, twice a day, to let you know I'm okay."

"What?" She stops moving forward. Her face an image of devastation.

"I understand now. I thought you were trying to ruin my life, but you just love me so much, you don't want to let me go. You don't have to be afraid, Mom. I'll come home every weekend for a while. Everything's going to be okay. You'll still be my mom and I'll still be your son."

"No, no, no, no, no! This wasn't – You were supposed to tell him not to go. It's in his best interests. Momma knows best," her voice grows shrill, her respiration difficult.

"You said she'd be okay," the son shouts. "Mom, breathe. Count to ten. Chill. 1, 2, 3, 4, 5 – she's not breathing!"

"Go into the waiting room. I'll take care of her," Paul says calmly, but the son is already on the phone, calling for an ambulance.

"She's having a heart attack!"

"Let me handle –."

"No, stay away from her. It's all your fault. Mom, it's okay. I don't need to go. They have colleges online now. I'll go to one of those. She's having a heart attack. Oh God, she's having a heart attack!"

"She's not having a –."

"Shut up. Just shut up! You don't know nothing'. My mom's sick. She needs me. Can't you see that?"

My mother killed herself so I could stay in college and have a life. That's how much she loved me. She knew I'd give up everything for her, so she killed herself to keep me from doing that. I do know. I do, Paul thinks.

XXX

Last session of the longest day of his life, Paul glimpses at his watch, though the alarm is set to go off at sessions end.

"And how did it make you feel to learn that your sister had an abortion when you have been trying so long without success to have a baby?"

In his head, his voice sounds monotonous, like a tape recording, just repeating their words back to them without the emotionality. His existence is not his own. He is merely the voice in their head to be vented to, provide reassurance, and repeat the answers they devised on their own. His physical presence seems redundant. They never recognize him outside the office. He envies the doctors who confront professional ethical boundaries when acknowledged in public. Perhaps even some transference would be nice, to have one of his clients believe herself to love him.

"How would it have made you feel if she had kept the baby, at her age, without the desire or resources to care for it?"

What is transference, but a mere illusion of psychological confusion? Paul thinks. Or is it? Can there be emotion without a will? Incentive to engage that will? Perhaps it is an illusion of the desires. Not a physical desire, per say, but one psychological that attempts to stretch the boundaries we call reality. Since reality in itself is simply an illusion with rationale justification, then isn't it true that with enough justification, enough will, enough incentive, any illusion can be made reality? After all, it is all just perception, and perception does not require solidity of physical matter to exist.

"Do you feel you'd be able to successfully fill your void with a child whose maternal mother is not you?"

But what is enough rationale to justify illusion? How do actors adjust their reality to the identities and environments in the script? They must fully submerge themselves into the role through anonymity. And how does one achieve that? Transformation.

"Are you going to get that?" the physical present beckons to Paul. Feeling disassociation, something, something so powerful, so exciting and new, in recesses needing further exploration, Paul presses the button on his watch to shut off the alarm with fluid motion. He leans forward with his elbow on his knee and cradles his chin speculatively in his fingers. He looks her intently in the eyes.

"I apologize. You intrigue me, so much so that time is suspended for me." He is so connected to her in that moment, he can feel the heat of her blush crawling up her face. "Perhaps the origin of your difficulty does not rest with you."

She fumbles with her purse, clears her throat. She is reacting to him. To him! "Well, that's an interesting thought, Dr . . . Dr . . ."

"Paul."

She averts her eyes, not looking at anything in particular. "So you're saying that I should bring my husband next time?"

"If that is your desire."

She glances at him and quickly down casts her eyes.

"Well then, until Thursday, Doctor – um – Paul."

Paul follows Mrs. Lois to the front desk and slowly admires Nancy as she talks to the client about insurance and payment options. He'd found Nancy nearly five years ago when she'd begun undergrad studies. Her college didn't offer internship opportunities, so she had gone out seeking such an opportunity herself to gain experience. In five years, that is the *only* thing he knows about her. Also that she'd only missed one day of work in five years due to Pneumonia, and only once had she attempted to use her vacation time, but something had happened last minute and she'd shown up for work that week like nothing was out of the ordinary. He'd never questioned her about it. He doesn't even know if she has a boyfriend, a fiancée, a kid, or anything that might even minutely be of reference to her life outside his office.

She's attractive in that big-boned cushiony way, with big curves and their jiggling accessories. Her hair is a light blonde, layered and poofy in that 80's style. Blue eyes. Dark lashes with thick mascara. Lots of rouge and pink eye shadow. Arched brows. Pouty lips. As she moves about the office shutting things down, wiping things up, he wonders why only now he is noticing her strong aura and the almost raw sexuality that courses through her. Why hasn't he noticed before? Why has he been so long without a woman? But now in seeing Nancy like this for the first time, his interest is peaked. Not in specifically Nancy, but in any person that has those sexual origins that he does not and that man has spent centuries failing to be able to understand.

"So, you're closing up shop, hah?"

"Yep, 6:00. Just like I've been doing for the past five years," she smiles. "You didn't need me to stay late, because you didn't mention – ?"

"No, no, you put in a hard day's work, like you always do." Paul leans against the wall and crosses his arms. "I don't know what I would have done these many years if not for you."

"Are you okay? You look funny."

Losing his nerve, Paul straightens his trying-to-be-casual pose. "Listen, Nancy, it's been five years." He moves toward her slowly, but trips over himself. He clears his throat and wishes he could tear off the tie that suddenly seems to be cutting circulation to his throat. "I've been watching you and find you to be indispensable. I feel like if I don't make a move now, I'm going to lose you."

"Oh my God, is this – is this about a raise? Oh, Dr. Stevens –."

"Paul."

"Paul, you don't know how much that means to me. I didn't want to say anything to you, but – I mean, I love my job and stuff, but, I haven't been making ends meet, if you know what I mean." She giggles, then quickly wraps her arms around him in a hug. He's in his glory. Too much so. The feel of her. The warmth. The smell of her hair and perfume.

"You deserve it," he says awkwardly.

"I'm sorry. I didn't mean to – Was that unprofessional? It's just, I've had my heart set on this condo for rent. It's a beautiful two bedroom on the fourth floor. All hardwood floors. The view is outstanding. There's an enclosed patio." Paul listens like the respectable guy he is, though his mind is bent on trying to find a way to ask her out. "Look at me getting carried away, and you haven't even specified what the raise is," she flushes.

"What will make this dream condo of yours affordable?"

"Wow, this is awkward. Um . . . a dollar . . . fifty . . . an hour? Is that too much?"

"Can we afford it?" he says without thinking. Her head falls. Bad. Bad. Bad. "No, I didn't mean –."

"No, you're right. You know what? That condo isn't really that important. What – uh – whatever you want to - ."

"I didn't mean it like that. I just – You know our profit-margin. I was just –."

"No, it's okay. I'm not very good at – ."

"2 dollars. 2 dollars an hour," he says, and prepares himself for another glorious hug, but she doesn't hug him again. Instead, she thanks him numerous times without taking even one step closer to him or leaning toward him.

"Let's celebrate. I'll take you to dinner," he says with what he hopes is enough, but not too much, enthusiasm. He leans on the desk and scatters her papers. Clutz. The silence seems to last ages.

"I'm sorry, Dr – "

"Paul," his voice lilts into desperation.

"I can't. I'm supposed to be – I have other plans. But it's so nice of you to offer. Oh shoot, I – uh – I gotta go. Thank you." She offers her hand.

Paul walks home, feeling heavier than usual, each step pain-staking and exhausting. He unlocks the door and steps in. Pockets his keys and hangs his coat. Only once retracting his arm does he notice the silence and emptiness of the room.

"Missy? Missy," he calls. "Here Kitty, kitty, kitty." One hundred pounds of dread knock against his chest. He almost doesn't turn on the light. He almost turns and walks back out the door. His throat constricts. The wheezing of his breath and pounding of his heart sound like thunder amidst the silence.

"Missy?" he croaks.

He finds her in his bed. Dead.

XXX

Paul retrieves the last TV dinner – BBQ ribs and corn. He picks up Missy's dish, untouched from earlier, and empties it into the trash. She hadn't eaten well all week. She'd meowed a lot and was needy for attention. He'd blown off these odd behaviors. Could he have saved her if he had taken her to the vet?

Paul washes the dish and tosses it into the garbage. She'll never use it again. He pours himself a red glass of wine and robotically brings his food and beverage to the TV stand in the living room. He stares at the news without watching it, eats without tasting it, drinks without savoring it. In the shower he tells himself they had a long life together and, 7 years for his 1, she had lived longer than most cats. Death was inevitable. It always is.

Paul opens his mail and finds a rejection letter from the board regarding his research proposal. His shoulders droop. His head burrows itself into his hands. Sometimes the only thing that keeps moving forward without fail is time. Paul goes into his bedroom, curls into fetal beside his cat, and cries.

Sometime in the middle of the night he awakes to the loud annoying sounds of an infomercial. A type of enthusiasm that is unrealistic in real life. Another how to get rich quick scheme. The balding spokesman is in a large yacht with four beautiful women, the background revealing his private mansion. Before drifting back to sleep, Paul has a slight visionary recollection of his interactions with Nancy earlier, and how excited she'd gotten over the prospect of more money. So excited, in fact, that she'd trampled past the boundary of their professionalism to embrace him in a hug. Affection he hasn't known since Claire.

CHAPTER 3

Following a restless night, Paul arises Saturday morning to a distinguished smell, one unmistakable. Missy stinks. His heart lurches, *I'm not ready to let her go. If I just keep her in a cold place.* He visualizes opening the fridge morning and night and finding her dead glassy eyes staring up at him. Foolish thoughts, trying to hold on to false security, like a child and their blankie. Merely an illusion of security, just like his one-sided nightly conversations that provided him the illusion of companionship. Now he's all alone. The sooner he gets it over with and finds closure and acceptance, the more quickly he can get re-accustomed to a life without her.

Another cat? Replace her? It isn't right to her memory to have her so easily replaced. No other cat had been there for him 12 years of his life. Missy has his history and no other mammal can compete with that.

Paul spends half an hour drinking coffee, then grabs a shovel. *I don't want to do this alone*, he thinks. He stares at his phone and thinks about calling Nancy, but it's not Nancy he wants with him. He wants Claire, the salve to his wounds following his mother's death. For the first time in 14 years, his heart truly aches for Claire.

She was the prettiest girl to ever give him a 2nd glance. He had asked her about it once. Why him? She'd kissed him on the forehead and said, "Guess you got me all figured out now, Paul Stevens. I like dweebs." And she had given him the prettiest smile, her blue eyes gentle with nurture while her knock out body screamed fire. He called her his Barbie doll because she had long straight blonde hair, a meticulously sculpted face and chiseled body. And he'd let her go. By now she was probably married to a hot guy named Ken, living in her dream house with two or three miniature Claire's.

Thoughts of her occupy his mind while he digs a small hole in the middle of his pathetic garden bed. He pretends she is with him and it brings him peace. How much happier people could be if they didn't grow out of child's play of pretend, where kids have imaginary friends, tea parties, and even wars in their imaginary worlds.

Paul places the limp cat into a wooden crate and buries it. His eyes are dry. He'd done all his crying the night before. He plants tulip bulbs atop her grave. "Goodbye Missy," he says and returns to the house, half expecting to hear her meow. He takes a long shower, then right on time leaves for his Saturday morning run. Fortunately, the day is bright and beautiful.

He's hardly a block from home, preoccupied with his thoughts, when his shoe meets something squishy on the ground. Dog shit. Great!

"Ma'am. Ma'am," he calls to the woman he'd just passed, walking her three dogs. "One of your dogs just defecated on the sidewalk. I just stepped in it. It could be a hazard."

"Get a life!" she yells at him. Using a couple twigs, he scrapes it off the sidewalk and onto the grass, then scruffs his shoe on the grass. He continues his run and after five blocks takes a left. He finds another woman struggling to cart in a bunch of groceries.

"Ma'am, can I be of assistance?"

"Kids, go get your father. Back away from me, you bum," she says nastily.

"Bum? No, I'm a Doctor. I was just trying to – ."

"You have three seconds to get away from my wife and off my property," a large man comes out onto the porch.
'Wo, calm down. I was just trying to help her with the groceries, like a gentleman."
"Are you insulting me, you little shit?"

Paul takes off on a run, moving in the wrong direction and not following his usual course. *What is wrong with people, now-a-days*, he thinks, discouraged.

Once out of sight of the large man, he stops breathlessly, and looks at his watch. 10:10. He missed his morning bagel. Now what? He experiences the old anxiety of his routine being disrupted and the loss of how he can compensate. Breathing heavily from the rush of anxiety, he talks to himself as a Psychologist. Breathing exercises. Coping methods. Compensating behaviors. Illusive replacements. He spins in circles and his eyes focus on a library. He's got 50 minutes to kill before going to the store for bread, milk, eggs, sandwich meat, and a week's supply of dinners, before returning home at precisely noon for lunch.

Paul hasn't been to a library since college, before online library databases were introduced. He walks amongst the aisles until he finds the psychology section, still feeling bruised by his latest rejection from the research committee. These days it seems the story of his life, rejection after rejection, since the new psychotherapy became popular.

Unconditional positive regard. A good theory on paper, but in practice, highly ineffective. He'd wanted to help people and sometimes helping people means making changes to their disruptive patterns, but unconditional positive regard focuses on encouraging the person to feel accepted as they are, not to attempt to change them. This is based on the self-actualization process that everyone leans to bettering themselves in the right conditions or non-conditions. Give them freedom to fly and they will fly to the moon and change their stars. Beautiful in theory. In practice, Paul has found, most don't look beyond their reflection in the glass to see the stars. Most are a victim to their moods on a moment to moment basis. Most can't see past their conflicts and content in the present to see the much larger picture.

Paul wants to make a difference and to accomplish something significant, something extraordinary. He can't do anything about his miserable life, but if he can make other's happy, then he'd have enough purpose to get him out of bed in the morning and looking forward to a judgment day that promises eternal bliss if one does good things in life, as his parents had drilled in his head since the moment he began comprehending the English language.

To prove the current psychotherapy as ineffective is the first step to change, but the review committee won't promote his research study based on the principle that it would be unethical to provide some patients with unconditional positive regard and the control group none. This leaves Paul in dire need for a new project or he's just going to give up on the human race completely. Searching the stacks, he pulls out a book named, *Illusions and Subconscious Implantation.*

Or maybe it's not the whole entire race to be given up on. Perhaps it is the rules and the professional board of ethics committee who only want to support research that will bring more money into the dying field of psychology as psychiatry takes over. Psychiatry, which doesn't promote more significant to the human mental state, rather demotes the mental condition by manipulating biology and chemistry through psychotropic meds. Isn't that just another illusion, causing the patient to think they feel better, without touching the origin of their issues, making reliability on drugs permanent to maintain stable mental state?

Paul picks up another book on virtual reality. He's heard of the new Psych-tech, which incorporates modern technology into the field of psychology. Once a close-your-eyes-and-remember therapy, the new technology can actually place the person in the moment of their tragedy through virtual exposure.

Paul picks a third book on *The Psychiatrist's Handbook on Modern Meds.*

He checks out and starts heading toward the direction of his home, guided by his thoughts, but sharply jumps back when he sees six visions of himself in a store front window of an electronics store. People passing by pop-up momentarily on the screens. There are six small TV screens and a theatre-size screen stacked against the window. He moves in front of the window again and his form moves on screen. He moves side to side, forward and backward, searching for what must be a miniature camera.

What an amazing advertising antic. The door chimes as he steps in.

"Couldn't find it, could you?" a young salesman with bright red hair greets him.

"What?"

"We're having a promotion this week. Anyone who can figure out the mystery whereabouts of the camera gets it for free, in addition to one of those televisions. You a shrink or something?" the kid gestures to the books Paul has in his hand.

"Yes, a Doctor of Psychology."

"Well then, Doc, let me show you something that's gonna play games with your head. It was my girlfriend's idea. I'm the electronics tech guy, not very creative. My girlfriend, on the other hand, is real good with that kind of stuff. She's gothic, so she likes the dark and mysterious. You're gonna love this."

Paul immediately struggles with the great contrast between bright fluorescent lights and the darkness of the room he enters. A thin layer of smoky fog filtrates the room.

"You ready?"

Paul nods, wondering what his purpose is in being here.

The salesman begins pressing buttons on the remote. The sounds of thunder and torrential rain blast through the speakers. Paul sees himself surrounded by dozens of screens and monitors. The room fills with a smoky mist. On the screen is himself, but he's being splattered by rain and whipped by the wind.

"Behind you!" someone screams. He twists and sees a starved wolf sneaking up behind him. It growls and barks, bares its teeth.

"Run, run to the house. You'll be safe there," a woman's voice cries. Paul begins to run, the pouncing wolf so close behind him.

"Don't look back."

A house comes in sight. He runs faster, harder. A beautiful woman is displayed standing on her porch, beckoning him to hurry, her eyes full of fear. She reaches out her hand. Paul extends his.

"Nooo!" she screams, looking behind him.

He hears the unmistakable growl that comes before the pounce. "Nooo!" he yells and prepares himself for the pain of the wolf's bite.

Suddenly the lights flick on. Paul is crouched on the floor, shaking in real fear, sweat coursing his brow.

"Pretty cool, huh?"

Paul shakily stands. "That was unbelievable," he says breathlessly. "I knew. I knew none of it was real, but at the same time I could feel everything that was happening."

"I'm telling you, man, mind games."

Paul feels his hair, half-expecting it to be wet. "Do you deliver?" he asks.

"Yes, sir, we do. Free of charge."

"There are three cameras. Not one. They're embedded in the brick, no bigger than a needle head.

The kid looks genuinely impressed. "What're you an electronics junkie?"

"About to be," Paul says.

"Well then, my new pal, let me show you the things you might want to make the most out of your new flat screen and NanoXCam."

XXX

Paul returns home, and once there, remembers that he'd completely forgotten to stop at the store. It has been a long time since he's felt this kind of excitement, like when he first opened his practice with so much hope of the prospect of helping others and making a difference. Like Peter Parker turned Spiderman, he'd been given the gift of intelligence to use for the greater good, even if it means defying certain rules. Ignorance is bliss, they say, but knowledge is power. The most profound and memorable people in the world are the ones who deviated from the rules of the four walls keeping them contained under an illusion of freedom. They managed to escape the confines of the box.

Paul spends all afternoon researching. Just a small manipulation of reality can be the determining factor between one just existing day after day and one living to their fullest.

Paul's stomach growls and he looks at the clock. Only then does he notice the bothersome silence. He'd missed breakfast, lunch, and his 6:00 dinner, and thus the news. It's now 7:30. Paul ambles to the kitchen, feeling light-headed and drowsy from the hours spent reading and researching. He yawns and opens his freezer, an abrupt reminder that he hadn't gone to the store. He throws on his coat, auto-pilot expecting Missy to give him an affectionate goodbye, and leaves the apartment.

Paul intended on turning right toward the grocery store, but turns left instead, toward The Cave. The thought of eating in silence is not a pleasant one.

At The Cave he sits in the furthest corner away the bar. From the bar menu he orders a large antipasto and a glass of Riesling. The bar is emptying of the happy-hour drinkers, reluctance in their leave, perhaps not wanting to go home to silence, like him, or perhaps dreading the nagging they'd get for having missed dinner.

Gradually, they're replaced by a younger, more excited, crowd, wanting to enjoy their Saturday night. Mostly beer drinkers, except for a few girls carrying mixed drinks. He's the only one drinking wine. The happy-hour middle-aged bartender is replaced by two young females, blonde and brunette, smiles on their faces and an energetic sway to their revealing curves. No one pays Paul any mind, as they come in together or greet each one another as they walk in. All of them seem excited and happy to be there, the night young. What is the premise behind their smile? Relief? Hope? Expectations? The illusion that this is the place where people check their day and stressors at the door; where others drown it with sweet inebriated solace? Facial expressions, so universal and vague, barely scrape the surface of the truth.

So accustomed to sad faces, tense shoulders, and tears, it's as though he's stepped into a new world full of vibrant energy that is shared. Such an amazing difference he could make to manipulate the energy charges from negative to positive, which would inspire positive change. Positive energy, positive perceptions. One can live the same exact life they had before, but perceive it in a completely different way.

Paul finishes his drink. Checks his watch. Almost 9:30. Late night for him. He's readying to leave when a whirlpool of energy is released in the bar upon one kid's entrance. His step doesn't just bounce. He leaps as he walks with an air of confidence and charisma.

"Can I get you another Riesling?" Paul is asked by the brunette bartender whom has apparently made a special trip to his table and actually remembered what he's drinking.

"What is your name?" he asks happily.

"Kate."

"Kate. I'd like – I think I'll try a beer. Whatever that guy's drinking."

"Michael?"

"Is that his name?"

"Yea, he's in real estate for the richies. Aspires to be rich by his 26th birthday. He comes in here every night, bragging about his successes and his successes to come. He's usually one of the last to leave. Likes his alcohol, if you know what I'm saying. Me and Lilly don't mind too much, though. He brings in a lot of business and tips good. He's got a magnetic personality, like yin and yang. Love and hate. You'll see. Do you want me to put it on his tab?"

"No, no, he doesn't even know me."

"Don't matter. Everyone's Michael's friend, but Michael is no ones. You understand?"

Paul hands her a 50 and tells her to keep the change.

"Thanks," she says with real feeling. She returns with his beer and 2 chips. "Those are from me," she says and winks at him. He's made a friend.

"Kate, sweetheart, stop trying to get more money off of old men. Come over here and grace me with your beautiful presence. I got all the money you could possibly want. And I can still get it up, if you know what I'm saying." The bar fills with laughter.

Michael tilts his hand at Paul after having slighted him and says, "Get the guy a drink on me for being a good sport. I'm going to get old too, but not at least for another 50-70 years."

The crowd surrounding Michael laughs again, but Paul observes something in that laughter, like co-workers laughing at their boss's jokes, no matter how many times they've heard them or how lame they are. Not because they're really funny, but because it's expected.

"Katie, dearest, Katie. Come sit upon Santa's lap and tell me what you want for Christmas."

She gives that same laugh and scampers behind the bar. "Got a job to do, Michael, you know that."

"Lilly will sit on my lap, won't she? Got a jack-in-the-box special just for my little girl."

"You keep right on dreaming, Michael," the blonde bartender says playfully.

"I don't need to dream. I'm living it. There's people out there who dream to live, and they'll just keep on dreaming until life is gone and their ashes are spread out over the only small parcel of land they managed. Then there's men like me who go after what they want and get it. I'm a man who knows how to get what he wants. The secret is knowing how to make those people who have what you want, think that it's what they want. It's not that hard. People don't know it, but they all want the same thing. And it's what everyone else has and better.

"Was showing a $1.5 mil house today to some rich bitch. Hot, I'll tell you that much. She seemed bored out of her mind. The moment I told her that Nicole Kidman has a house just like it, except she paid double and it didn't have the second floor terrace, she was like putty in my hands. $1.5 mil on a house that's really only worth the commission I made from the sale. Most people work a year or more to make what I do in a day."

"So share the wealth, my friend. I'm dry," some young man from the bar shouts.

"You're absolutely right, my friend, because what I spend tonight I'll make 200 times tomorrow. Katie, get the bar a drink. Put it on my tab.

The hours pass while Paul sits there both completely enthralled and completely annoyed by Michael. Michael is everything he isn't and nothing he is. He throws money around like candy, attracting all those with a sweet tooth. How many of the other men around him wish they could carry so much confidence and be so sure of themselves?

By 11:00, Paul is seeing double. By 12, triple. As the bar thins out, Paul observes that each person who makes their leave is begged by Michael to stay, another drink on him. How about wings? Then he'll turn around and insult them, calling them old-timer, pussy-whipped, or don't know how to relax and have a good time. Only four people remain when Paul makes his discreet leave at 12:30. He whistles on his way home, looking very forward to the comforts of his bed, Missy or no. Nothing matters at the moment, except for the smile on his face, and the skip (and stagger) in his step.

XXX

Paul arises Sunday morning with a groan. The price to pay for altered conscious. The night prior seems all a dream to him, but the hangover is very very real. Nothing that coffee, a refreshing run, and cool shower can't cure, along with two aspirins for the road. He pores over the material, making additional notes as he gulps his coffee. He's running a little late this morning, a habit so recently formed. Donning his running clothes, Paul heads out, deciding to take a different route this morning and enjoy some different scenery. He returns to the house with 45 minutes to spare, and takes a quick shower before making his weekly penance, a monetary donation for every sin. Not that he's not already paying for it, as his head and body scream at him from his night's consumption.

He arrives at the church after a stop at the dry cleaners. A large crowd is gathered at the door, people he's never seen in his 12 years of Sunday mass. While awaiting single-file for the Parishioner's greeting, he picks up a pamphlet. Guest speaker today. 'The healing powers of faith.'

Only then does Paul notice that the majority of the person's attending have some form of disability. Wheelchair, tremors, or just plain ugliness.

"What're you here for?" a man in his late sixties asks him.

"I'm a regular," Paul says.

"I'm depressed and miserable. Been that way ever since chemo 15 years ago. Lost my job, my wife, my home. My kids don't speak to me. My daughter told me to give it to God. I can't imagine feeling any different than I've felt all these years. I don't know what joy is anymore, but my daughter – this is my daughter – said she'll accompany me and that makes me feel just fine, just fine indeed."

The congregation sits in quiet excited chatter. So much anticipation. The lights dim and percussion begins, booming through the speakers, silencing everyone. A large man walks onto the stage. Paul has seen this guy on TV. He's just short of claiming to rise the dead.

"You've all seen me. You know who I am. I am the medium between you and God, the all powerful. Through unconditional faith, I lend you God's healing touch. Those who desire to be healed must rid of all human science, speculation, skepticism, for God is not a hypothesis, a research experiment that is only believed once proving himself. No, God demands unadulterated trust in him and through this trust and eternal devotion, he will cure you of your human woes, so you may better serve him. Raise your hand if you don't believe."

No hands.

"Raise your hand if you have a single doubt that today, in this moment, God can heal you."

Several hands rise.

"Daddy, put your hand down," Paul hears the daughter of the depressed man.

"Now, raise your hand if you have not a doubt that you will walk forth from this room healed."

Many hands rise. Amen echoes throughout.

"What would you sacrifice to live a life free of your troubles? How much would you pay to be relieved of your pain, your suffering, your disabilities? Would you pay 50? 100? 300? What about 500?"

Less and less hands begin to rise.

"Look around you. The sins of man who falsify their belief. The greater the cost, the more diminished is his faith. And this, my friends, is where we find the true believers."

"I'll pay a thousand dollars!" a woman yells. Her face is strained and aged, a child in her lap.

She is beckoned toward the front.

"Please, my son. He is ill. The doctor's gave him four days. Please, I'll do anything to have his suffering end."

The Miracle Man lays the frail four year old child down, and the church becomes silent, but for harp-like tinkling. The child wheezes and coughs. "Son, do you believe there is heaven?"

"Yes," the boy whispers.

After an elaborate display of holy water, hand gestures, and chants, lights dimming and brightening, music ascending and descending, the Miracle Man places his hands on the child's chest and shouts, "You suffer no more!" The church goes dark. The silence is thick. In the dark is heard the mother's soft cries.

"He suffers no more. God has taken him to his kingdom where he will know eternal happiness. You will be with child again and this child will be born healthy. God has given you the gift of loss to enhance you appreciation of what's to come. There will be no greater and more devoted mother than you and you will raise him with God."

She thanks him profusely. Then is escorted away.

A thousand dollars became the ante. The woman in the wheelchair took one step and fell into the arms of her support system. "You will walk again, one step at a time, all the way up those stairs to the eternal gates."

Every one of them are escorted out afterward. After five alleged miracles, he falls in dramatic crouch, breathing heavily, as though all his energy gone. He staggers to the left, staggers to the right, until someone places a chair behind him.

"I can do no more. For those of you who hesitated in your belief, you shall carry the burden of human woes for another six months until my return. Perhaps then, you will believe. God bless everyone." The lights on the stage turn down and he exits.

"Why did you have to hesitate, Dad? Don't you want to get better? You make me ashamed. Mom was right. She said not to put anymore hope into you, but you seemed so serious. I trusted you."

While waiting in line to leave, Paul becomes annoyed at the sound of this man's daughter's continuous complaints. He approaches the older man and his nagging daughter and hands him his card. "I can help you"

"There's no help for him," the daughter says.

"Not when he's surrounded by so much negative energy. There is a reason for his misery and it is the misery of others." She storms off.

"She's just like my former wife," the older man says. "Can never do anything right."

Paul walks to the store, thinking of everything he just learned, and how ridiculously simple it all is. Once home, he makes his final decision and orders the equipment that makes virtual reality possible. The only thing he hasn't yet figured out is exactly what he is going to use all this knowledge and technology for.

XXX

By Tuesday, Paul is all set up and has Nancy's curiosity piqued, as he'd rescheduled all his Monday and Tuesday appointments and holed himself in his office, not even leaving for lunch. He needs a guinea pig and who better than himself.

A small manipulation of consciousness. He grunts from the needles pinch and sets the alarm. A few clicks of the remote and he's in a whole new reality, one beautiful and bright, incorporating moments of past, so real he can smell the lavender of his mother's nightly baths. All the magical memories of his life re-experienced, re-lived, happening now, in this moment, to be re-cherished.

A woman enters the room.

"Claire?" he whispers, afraid that anything louder will shatter this precious image. He glides over to her, grasps her hands, memorizes her from the roses in her hair down to her yellow-painted toenails. "You're beautiful," he says.

When the alarm beeps 15 minutes later, the images fade, and he's awoken. He has Nancy in an embrace, tilted over, his hand at the small of her back. Her lipstick is smeared, and she's looking at him with wide star-struck eyes.

Paul smiles and abruptly drops her on the matching sofa to the couch in his home. "My God, it worked. It worked!" he says excitedly, dancing around the room. "Nancy, I'm a genius. This is a start of a whole new life."

"Oh, Paul," she croons. But he's too preoccupied to notice.

"I'm leaving early today. So much I need to do." He leaves without grabbing his coat.

"Wait! Where are you going? You can't start something and not finish. For all your dull exterior, I never would have believed you so . . . passionate, like a whole different man."

But Paul is too busy talking to himself.

"How about dinner, then?" she nearly crawls after him.

"No, no dinner. Things to do. Lots to think about," he says distractedly.

"Paul, what just happened?"

He gives her an odd look. "It's Dr. Stevens," he says before closing the door.

CHAPTER 4

On his way to work Wednesday early morning, Paul notices something. He'd gotten the once-over by two different women. Not the turn-away looks but the head-to-toe-to-eye contact and smile looks. He's done nothing different with his appearance, except fail to shave the past three days, due to his obsession with this new project. Not to mention the vigor and bounce in his step and his whistling tune.

The greatest part about it, the girls were half his age.

As soon as he walks through the door, Nancy almost bulldozes him. "We've got a situation."

"Listen, Nancy. I'm sorry about yesterday. I didn't mean to lead you – ."

"Christ, not that. Remember the day I was late, the guy that called and hung up? He was sitting on the doorstep when I arrived, demanding to see you."

"Where is he?"

"He's in your office."

"Without me?"

"What was I supposed to do with him? He's not right right now. I didn't want him changing his mind and leaving. You've got another client coming in in 15 minutes. You might have to work through lunch. I don't know why you wanted so many appointments scheduled in one day. There's no way we're going to fit them all in."

Paul places his finger beneath her chin and looks her in the eye, instantly calming her.

"Let me do my job. Focus on yours. I foretell a paid vacation coming your way very soon. Keep up the good work."

"Yes, Dr. Stevens," she says with a glimmer in her eyes.

The man's name is Jerry, and he's wracked with nervous negative energy, refusing to sit, to calm, to do some breathing exercises that will relax him. The bags beneath his eyes are severe and he has not found reprieve from his anxious state since the accident. His throat tight, his voice comes out high-pitched, a tight wire about to snap.

"She was there one day, gone the next moment. The baby was due next month. I knew it was all too good to be true. A drunk. A fucking drunk. 11 in the morning driving drunk. He's in critical condition. I hope the bastard lives. I hope he lives, faces 25 years in prison, and he lives through that. Then on the day of his release, I'm gonna run him over. She was just taking a walk. She loved her walks."

"When is the funeral?"

"I had to identify her, what was left of her. Her skull was crushed. I couldn't even recognize the mess he made out of my beautiful wife. She'd never even had a pimple, she was so unflawed. Now she's going to be covered in dirt, left to rot in a fucking box, worms and bugs eating away at her. Whose idea was it to put dead people in the ground anyway? Is that all we're worth when we die?"

"You could have her cremated and put the ashes where you think they ought to be."

"You're sick. What's wrong with you? Throw her in an incinerator until her remains are nothing but ashes, like the ashes people carelessly flick on the ground at the end of their cigarette butts? So what can you do for me? How can you help me? I don't like people like you, you know that? I really don't. I think you're all full of shit. But morning comes and I don't want to get the fuck out of bed. What for? Got nothing to look forward to but the knowledge that my wife's dead and I'm not gonna be a father, because my child's dead too. Most days, I just don't want to live anymore, because every second I live I have to face the fact that they're dead. So what can you give me? What can you do that's going to make my life worth living again?"

"First, I need you to sit down and get yourself calm. Ever try giving someone a back massage to relax them while they're pacing back and forth?"

"Wo, you're going to give me a back massage?"

"No, I was just making an example. How did the two of you meet?"

He sits at the end of the seat, legs shaking, "Excuse me?"

"You and your wife. How did you meet?"

"Who fucking cares. She's dead."

"Friday night I came home to find my cat of 12 years dead. That morning she'd been fine. The loss was a shock. What do I have to come home to now after a long day of work? Who can I tell about my day? Who's going to keep me grounded when things happen? All negative devastating thoughts. These negative thoughts cause us to dwell on the loss and the hopelessness we feel instead of thinking about the good. Hopelessness will drown us. Cherished memories will carry us through until we're strong enough to stand on our own without them."

"Are you – are you comparing my dead wife and child to your fucking cat? Why did I come here? I knew this was a bad idea." He's back to pacing the floors. "Can we just skip the talking, you get out your prescription pad, and write me up for some serious meds that will *carry me through* as you put it."

"I'm not a Psychiatrist. I can't prescribe meds, but I can get you a referral to – ."

"You're fucking kidding me. This can't be happening. I have to go bury them in two hours and I can't do that without some serious meds, something to make me oblivious. So if you don't prescribe meds, what the fuck do you do?"

"Guide you through the grieving process. The grieving process is like building a home. If you don't do it right the first time, you can't just go back and fix it later. You'd have to tear down the walls you built in order to build new ones. Many people do not know how to grieve properly. They turn to other coping methods, destructive ones, such as drinking or drug-use. The only proper way to heal is to talk about it, talk about your feelings, allow yourself to feel, to cry, to yell, to crumble, mourn what is no longer, but treasure what once was in a positive light."

"I *am* feeling. I'm feeling so much that I'll do anything to stop feeling, anything, even if it means ending this now pointless existence of mine. My wife and child are dead!" he shouts. "That is something NOBODY wants to feel." He opens the door to exit. "You're a fucking joke. No wonder they call you quacks. Thank you so much for all your help, Doctor. I'm going to go plot a grave next to my wife's, skip all the details of living without her, and join her in death. In fact, I'll do it right here, right now!" He screams, pulling out a gun from his jacket and pushing it into his temple. His next client begins to scream.

"So help me God, I'll do it. I'll do it! I'm on my knees. I'm gonna pull the fucking trigger unless you think you can stop me."

In plain eyesight of the suicidal wreck, Paul returns to his office. Maintaining eye contact the entire time, he reaches into the desk drawer, and places a bottle of Blackberry brandy and a glass on the desk, also a recent habit he'd picked up. Jerry drops his head, then the hand holding the gun. Paul takes the gun and helps him to his feet. He shuts the office door behind him.

10 minutes later, Jerry emerges, a smiling glazed expression on his face.

"Would you like to schedule another appointment?" Nancy asks.

"What? What for? All just a bad dream, a nightmare. I need to get some wine, some chocolates, flowers, she loves flowers –." he leaves, mumbling to himself.

"What'd you do to him?" Nancy demands in a loud whisper. Paul has the same dazed smiling expression.

"I helped him."

XXX

The rest of the day flies by and Paul feels like a man who learned the secret to making a whole lot of money overnight. Before this day, he was a typical miserable man, living the honest path, working his tail off and caring about people that certainly never put him in their prayers. Work hard for very little reward. People didn't leave his office cured. They left with the condition of seeing him the following week where the only thing being productive and making progress was filling up the scheduling-book. At the end of the day, Paul went home exhausted, feeling used and abused and ultimately completely helpless.

The only real pleasure he ever really derived was when Nancy had a date after work, so therefore, looked especially nice and was especially sweet, being able to pay another month's bills, or splurge on a new black suit, and contribute to his growing retirement that daily he looked more and more forward to. Besides, if he wasn't going to get anywhere in life, he might as well be a retired man without a job, searching aimlessly for direction. He'd go to church twice a week, perhaps attend Wednesday bingo, join private clubs like the Elks or Moose, and contribute to some charities. He'd at least have the resemblance of something not too far from being a pathetic life, but with the excuse of retirement.

Now he's feeling alive again, with purpose, hardly working, yet reaping much larger rewards. 45 minute sessions completed successfully in 10, with a smile and laugh and profuse thanks, as they leave his office without any reason to return, because they're happy. They're happy to live the same life they've spent the past 20-30-40 years being miserable with. Paul was called amazing today, a true miracle-worker, a god-send, an angel. Four of his clients hugged him. Two kissed his cheek. Ms. Johnson now can't wait for her son to go off to college so she can have the house and her new-found exciting life to herself.

Mr. and Mrs. Lois could hardly wait to leave his office before attempting to procreate as much as possible, as Mrs. Lois had virtually shed 20 years and 75 pounds in 10 minutes.

Nancy had been afraid they wouldn't fit all their appointments in for the day? 3 o'clock, they're closing up shop early.

"Nobody scheduled another appointment, Dr. Stevens. Not one."

"That's great!" he says enthusiastically.

"Great for who? Certainly not you. All you've got next week are two appointments, for the entire week if tomorrow is like today."

"Reschedule them for tomorrow. Tell them we got a couple cancellations."

"What are you trying to achieve here, Dr. Stevens? I understand you want to cure people, but you cure them, then you don't have a job."

"Oh, Nancy," he pats her hand like she's a mere child. "There's a lot of screwed up people in the world. There will be more. I assure you. Next week they'll be piling in, looking for their miracle."

"I've never known you to be arrogant," Nancy says softly.

"Nancy, there is a big difference between being arrogant and shooting off at the mouth and being confident in one's abilities. I got a sure thing going. You saw it today. Be happy to know that you're a part of the miracle."

Paul sits back and relaxes, reveling in the past two days that he'd been capable of making so many happy. Will it last? How long? Will they return when the blinders wear off? Life is full of seasons, and not one season determines how the next season is going to go. Happiness is not self-sufficient, because it is mere emotion, and how many millions of years has man been trying to regulate emotion? Emotion isn't rational. It is a thing without physical presence. One can only make emotion rational by connecting it to something physical. "I am sad because . . .Happy because . . . This makes me sad. This makes me happy. I feel happiness when . . . Even though such emotion can be felt in the absence of the because, the what, the when, man's rational mind cannot tolerate it. He must make it up. Provide him the cause, the reason, the what, and emotion is created. There is a part in every person that wants to feel happiness, so he comes up with the conditions. There is also a part in every person that wants to feel sadness, so he finds a reason. After all, how can one truly appreciate beauty without the awareness of ugly?

Some people go too far, on the other hand, like Michael, who is presently raving about his week's successes. Some become obsessed with the physical matter, believing that emotion can only come in its presence. Michael believes happiness comes in riches and successes. He is the most unhappy of them all, because no amount of money or success will achieve his real happiness, so he will continue to try to get more money and gain more success until he finds himself at the top, alone and unhappy, because in his journey, he failed to create the foundation of what is meaningful. Elation may come with success and money, but elation is entirely too short-lived. If one spends their life constantly chasing their high, they'll need more and more to gain that high, until no amount of anything can achieve it. Then they crash!

XXX

Paul is exhausted by Wednesday. Nancy had carried such unnecessary concerns in losing their clients, as he has people lining up at the door, wanting their 10 minute cure. Paul feels like a locksmith, holding the only key to the door of happiness when that door isn't even locked. Everyone has access to it. Place conditions on happiness and happiness cannot exist. More money, a new mistress or spouse, a bigger house, children that are different than who they are, a different career, retirement, or for those retired, a new purpose. Youth. Society places standards on what should be required of happiness, but it is in the absence of such conditions where happiness, peace, and acceptance is obtained.

What may seem so important now will not be important in the future. What people think will make them happy and what actually does is usually completely different. Paul wants to scream at them all. He wants to reveal to them their ignorance, but who is he really to say such things as he's the same. Did he not base his happiness on helping others and making a difference? Time. Time is the only thing that holds the answer. Time, the only thing people can't control. If he could only give them the gift of time, the understanding. If a person was given the gift of a glimpse in the future, would they maintain such unhappiness in their present? Or would it calm them? Give them direction? Perhaps a degree of acceptance.

So many sit awkwardly on pins and needles, wondering what is going to happen next. Where is their life going? What do they have to look forward to or what do they need to prepare for? The unknown is the greatest agent of anxiety, worry, and fear. If one were to get a glimpse of the unknown, would they be satisfied?

By Friday, Paul comes to the conclusion that he doesn't want to do this anymore. He doesn't want to make a temporary insignificant difference in numerous lives. He wants to make a significant permanent difference in a few. And in those few, he will build a classic. His work will mean something. What expedites his decision to close his practice is the fulfillment of Nancy's other prediction. Unwanted attention. By Monday Paul is under investigation and by the following Friday, his license is revoked for not following the standards of the board of ethics. It was his very first trial patient to blow his cover - the man who had lost his wife and child. The fantasy had lasted two weeks, but he had needed someone to blame when he realized his wife and child were still dead. Paul won't get any credit for the fact that he kept the guy alive or that he gave the guy exactly what he thought he wanted. His life's work – gone – and Paul finds relief. He is now freed from all the chains he let bind him, and it is truly exhilarating.

"Nancy, don't cry. I'll give you a reference that no one in their right mind will turn down."

"No, please don't! That's very kind of you, but a reference from a doctor that just had his license revoked is not going to help me."

"But you didn't know anything about it. And it's not like I was really doing anything unethical. Morally, I think, it was appropriate. You saw their happiness, Nancy. That guy was going to kill himself. Sometimes, moral reasoning does not follow the code of ethics. Think of the man who has worked hard his entire life, supporting his family, and one day comes to work to find he no longer has a job, he's older and no one wants to give this man so close to retirement a future with their company. His family still has to eat. So he steals a loaf of bread and peanut butter. Ethically, it's wrong, but morally, he has a duty to his family to support them.

Ethics are black and white. There is a lot of gray matter that ethics can't touch."

"Doctor, I hear what you're saying. But it doesn't change the fact that I just put a down-payment on a condo that I now can't afford because I'm now unemployed."

"You think a nice condo is going to maintain your happiness? Another obligation?"

"No, but it's security and security is as close to happiness as you can get now-a-days."

"Security is nothing but an illusion. There's no such thing. Even animals who function purely on instinct don't have security that today they might be the predator, but tomorrow the prey."

"Not everyone thinks like you. Most of us just like simplicity, real or not."

"Four weeks of pay. How's that? Plus unemployment."

"Thank you," she says softly.

XXX

Paul starts writing his book by day. He performs observational research at night. His practice had been good and he'd managed to put away a decent amount of money, but he is so far from being rich and even further from being financially secure in the long-term. What will he do now for income? If there was a way he could commit to a project while making a sizable amount, his future would be both useful and meaningful. The future. How much is time worth?

He throws his pen down and grinds his eyes. He needs to get out for a bit. A leisurely stroll, a nice lunch. He heads out toward The Cave and is asked for spare change by a bum sitting outside the door. Paul offers him a meal. The man declines and mumbles that the money is not for him, so Paul gives him a five. He's halfway through his meal when, like a gust of wind, Michael bursts through the door, full of vibrance and energy.

"I'm telling you, Frankie. This is it. They're giving me a shot at the big bucks. I practically begged for this, told them that with my skills, I can get 15 mil for it. They kind of laughed, said if I could get 15 mil on it, they'd make me partner. With just the commission I could retire and live comfortably the rest of my life. Of course, just comfortable can't be part of my vocabulary. I set my sights on extravagance. I'll be eating for breakfast what mom and dad make in a day working 9 to 5. Ignorant. They're all ignorant. Go to college, Michael. All respectable young men who want success start at college. Screw that. What do they know? Look at me now."

Paul curbs a yawn. Always the same thing with this guy. What's he trying so hard to prove? That he can be better, do better, know better than anyone else? Paul feels his energy rapidly draining just being in this guy's presence. Kid's got a lot to learn about the important things in life.

Paul pays his bill and leaves. He's on the other side of the street when he hears Michael yelling.

"You're still here? I thought I told you to take your drunk scummy ass out of here. We don't need your kind around here. You ruin business. Is this what you make in a day's wages?" Michael kicks the tin coffee can holding the homeless man's living. Change scatters all over the sidewalk. The old man scurries to retrieve it all.

"Why don't you stop being such a drunk and get a real job like a real person, scrape your dignity off the sidewalk, and do something with your life." Michael spits on the sidewalk. "You're nothing but a waste of air. Do us a favor. Go crawl in a dumpster and kill yourself."

Paul approaches the old homeless man once Michael walks away. "I'll give you 50 bucks to wear this for a day." Paul pins it to the man's breast pocket. "I'll give you 100 tomorrow at noon when I get it back." Paul hands the man a crisp 50 dollar bill, and provides him instructions. The old man holds it like he hasn't held that much money in a decade. He cries, "Thank you. Tomorrow noon."

Paul finds the man's appreciation more sincere than all the people and clients he's attempted to help in the past 12 years. Enlightenment explodes in his chest. He knows now what he's going to do.

MICHAEL

CHAPTER 5

"If you like this, then you're going to be completely blown away by the surprise I have in store for you in the back yard. Liv's got a great one, you know Liv right? But not like this. There's nothing like this."

'Momma, I'm comin' home' begins playing on Michael's phone.

Perfect timing, he thinks. "Excuse me," he tells his client.

"Mom, oh mom, how great it is to hear from you. I worry. How's – how is dad?" He discreetly places his finger over the speaker, searches for a chair, and dramatically falls into it while his client eavesdrops. "Oh, no, mom, no, no," he buries his head in his hand. "Mom I'm at work now," he says more quietly. "I can't – How much more money is needed for him to get the surgery? Mom, you don't have to remind me he's going to die without it. I'm trying the best I can. I'm working three jobs, day and night. I don't know what more I can do . . . Mom, don't cry. Don't – ." Michael sniffs, wipes non-existent tears from his eye. "I gotta go, Mom. I'll call you as soon as I can. Give dad my love. Tell him – tell him I'll get the money. He's not going to die. I won't allow it. I love you. Bye."

Michael slowly closes his phone and makes a show of rising up to stand with an unbearable amount of weight on his shoulders. "I'm sorry. Please forgive me. Where were we? Yes, the rock garden. Do you see your parents often?"

"No, I – Not as much as I should," she says.

"Where do they live? Are they far?"

"Actually, they're only right down the road from here."

Of course Michael already knows this.

"Oh, that's wonderful. Priceless. I wish my parents were closer, but dad got sick and there weren't any jobs in Wisconsin, so I came down here with a promise that I won't let him down."

"Didn't you say Nashville when we spoke on the phone?"

"Yes, but we moved when I was in junior high," he says quickly. "My God! Forgive me if this is too forward, but you have very kind, very beautiful green eyes."

"Oh," she touches her hair. "Well, they're blue, but thank you."

"Yes, but with you standing against that picture window, the sun reflecting in it turns your eyes to green, like the ocean bottom reflecting on the surface."

"I'll tell you a secret," she giggles. "I always wished I had green eyes. They're more expressive."

"Well, in this house, they're green, because every room has a picture window."

"How soon can I move in?" she says smiling.

"We can discuss it over dinner, a bottle of wine, if you're free tonight. I'll bring the paperwork."

"6'oclock. I'll meet you here. Don't be late or I might change my mind, brown eyes."

"Wouldn't dream of it," Michael says with a wink. Then, on second thought, he takes her hand and kisses it. "Thank you," and walks away with a skip.

Time to celebrate his victory. He couldn't have closed out this appointment in better time. He's expected in half an hour. He walks two blocks to his hidden mustang convertible and flips open the top. He takes in the appreciative glances like a glass of water. Blaring K-rock, he rests his hand outside the window, lays his head back, and lets the car do the work.

"Hey Mick, have the paperwork ready in my office at 4. Got her on the hook. Now I'm just reeling her in."

Michael smiles and absorbs the praise, knowing full well it's his to own. He knows he's an amazing son-of-a-bitch, best thing to happen to the company. He started in the company kissing asses and now they're kissing his.

"Mick, I think I can get an extra ten grand out of her. I want 10%. That's non-negotiable, And I want bigger and better. I'm tired of fishing for bass. I want to start harpooning whales, you understand?"

Yes, he's an ambitious shit. Yes, he's moving up in the company faster than any other associate. Mick jokes about holding onto his own seat in the company before he finds Michael in it. Michael doesn't take it as a joke and knows that he will be in Mick's seat, whether shared, as a replacement, or in competition. Mick jokes, but Mick underestimates him. He didn't come here to just be someone. He came here to be THE one, and there's nothing in the world that can stop him.

Most of the associates sit there like pathetic little dogs waiting for someone to drop a dinner scrap, and they happily consume their tiny morsel. Michael jumps up on the table and takes the meat right from underneath their noses.

Michael squeals into the parking lot and spots the off-silver Taurus. Posers will never shine, posers like –

"Marcus," Michael approaches him with a faltering smile. Marcus knocks on the bar and tells Bill to make Michael a double Glenlivet on the rocks. Michael has been working with Marcus for the past year, as Marcus is a computer whiz, and just so happens to need extra cash. Formerly a police investigator prior to his being terminated, he has access to the most accurate history reports on people, as well as training in the most manipulative techniques to try to get people to crack. With his brown thinning shaggy hair, wrinkled suit, and bowed back, he's now just a wrinkle to his former self, to which Michael takes full advantage.

Michael shakes his hand, then steps in and gives him two quick slaps on the back. "Thank you so much for your help earlier. I thought for sure it would work."

"It didn't?" Marcus says with disappointment.

Michael shakes his head. "You know how those rising female stars go. Cold as ice. Frigid little bitches. Their compassion only goes as far as their reflection in the mirror. Come to find out, she hates her parents, which means she thinks everyone should hate their parents. She told me my father's death would probably be the best thing to happen to me."

"She actually said that?" Marcus says, downing his drink.

"It's become quite the world when bitches are more heartless and less nurturing than men. Fought for women's rights, saying they just want a slice of the pie. Some man pisses her off, so then she takes the whole damn pie with a gallon of icecream."

"Man, that's bull. I really needed that five grand. Marcy's threatening to leave me if we lose our home, but I just can't seem to make ends meet. Teddy's college is sucking up money faster than I can make it. You'd think she'd be more understanding. Bill, give me some of that 25 year old Grand Marnier and don't be stingy with it neither." Marcus throws a 50 on the bar.

Michael thinks that it's not just Teddy's college sucking up the money. Aside from Marcus's acquired top-shelf tastes, he also likes to gamble. He sucks at gambling. Michael is doing them both a favor by not following through with the five grand and lying about the sale. Marcus would have just taken the five grand to a poker tournament and lost ten grand instead.

"Well, love to shoot the shit some more, but I gotta get back to the office," Michel says, grabbing his jacket.

"All right, I'll think up some other scenario we might be able to pull off. Maybe a son with cancer or something. How can anyone not fall for that?"

"All right, you keep thinking. See what you can find out about Tina Swanson. Mick's her agent right now, but he hasn't been able to make the sale. I've a feeling I'll be taking over. You'll get the usual 1% if I make the sale. Here." Michael throws him a hundred dollar bill. "That's out-of-pocket for all your help. Soon. Soon we'll make a big sale and it'll all be worth your while."

"Hey thanks. Yea, the next one maybe."

"We got this. You and me."

Michael leaves and goes to The Cave, causing the usual excited commotion when he arrives.

"You're late," one of his groupies with a unibrow points out the obvious. Jim? James? Jason? Who gives a care? A lawyer whose only success is that, and useful only to that end. Pathetic like all the rest, just wanting a piece of Michael, hoping he'll rub off on them or something.

"So, how'd the house-showing go?"

"Got her in my pocket. By 8 tonight I'll have her in my pants."

The guys chuckle, high-five, order more drinks.

"What's that supposed to mean?" a beautiful, blonde-haired, blue eyed big-breasted woman exclaims. Shirley? Sherry?

"Hey, baby." Michael opens his arms to her. "Looking perky today. Didn't know you'd be here."

"We have a lunch date. You forget? Told me to meet you at Shooters. You didn't show, so I came here to find you." Hands on her gracious hips, why do they always take things so personally? Such a turn off.

"Listen, baby, I got work. This is business. I can't have you stalking me and interfering on my business appointments. Last night was great and lunch would have been nice, but I thought for sure by now you'd have your hands digging in someone else's pockets."

"What the hell is that supposed to mean?"

"Tony?" Michael snaps his fingers.

"It means you can find better," Tony clarifies.

"I can find better or Michael's found something else? Have her in your pocket, tonight in your pants?" Oh, God, not the screeching, not the dramatics.

Michael throws up his hands. "What can I say, baby, it's business. It's how I close the deal."

"Like you closed the deal with me last night?"

"You see that, Tony. Blonde's aren't always as dumb as they look."

"You bastard," she picks up her purse.

"Hey woman, I never made any promises."

"Except for your promise that you'd take care of me."

"And I did take care of you, didn't I? Three times, in fact. Had you howling at the moon."

She would have smacked him but for Michael's groupies surrounding him. They know the drill. She stomps out. Tony says dibs a hundredth of a second before the others.

"She's all yours, Tony." Nothing more vulnerable to a woman than a nice guy trying to calm her after she'd just been burned.

Tony chases after Michael's leftovers. Michael buys a round for the guys.

"Gotta get back to the office. See you guys tonight?"

"Can't, gotta be up early for work," unibrow guys says.

"Daughter's birthday," another says.

"Pool tournament. We'll play for money. 50 a game. Partners. Drinks on me," Michael says.

They all reconsider.

Michael walks away grinning. Money, the biggest evil, the greatest good. If you have money, you have it all. People just can't help themselves. The simplicity of it all. Where there's money, there's a will.

XXX

"You look absolutely ravishing," Michael holds the chair out for his date and takes his own. A retired actress, her divorce had made her more famous than her movies. Michael's had better, prettier that is, definitely younger, but no one of her fame, and for that, he admires her. Her doe brown hair with blonde highlights is braided around her head. Her eyes are most definitely not green, more like a dull blue, and the wrinkles defining middle-age are definitely present around her eyes and lips. She maintains the body of an actress, however, and looks divine in her long green dress with the slit leading up to her muscled thigh.

He immediately opens his briefcase. "For the sake of getting business out of the way quickly so that I may enjoy the pleasure of your company, I'll need your signature at the x's. I'll pull a few strings, have you in by next week. Place comes fully furnished, so if you're looking to make a fresh start, this is it."

"Boy, you do work quickly."

He winks. "You have no idea. A man doesn't go anywhere sitting on a bench, waiting for his ride."

Michael receives a check for the down-payment, signed by William Taylor.

"Daddy's helping me out 'till I get on my feet," she says.

Michael's research on her had revealed that she recently closed out on a nasty divorce. Both of them had long been cheating on one another, a marriage of convenience. With her completely unaware, her husband had gotten footage of her infidelity and filed for divorce with cause of adultery. She hadn't been able to prove his own and had lost a great deal of her material and monetary possessions. Michael had watched a clip of her testimony in which she had revealed that they had both mutually agreed to see other people, as long as it was kept discreet and they remained together for the public eye, but he had fallen in love with one of his affairs, a childhood friend, gone back on his word, by keeping his discreet, but not her own.

The whole shame in it all is that her husband had been a nobody, a nothing, when they married, connected only by the baby she had carried in her womb. The baby was stillborn, seven months after they married. He built himself on her successes, then stole them right out from under her, to live happily ever after with his nobody-no-money sweetheart.

Michael orders them a bottle of Vintage wine and begins working on closing the next deal. She's lucky she found him. He'll take real good care of her, make it a night she'll always remember.

She looks at him with a cocked head. "For someone struggling to make money for his dad's surgery, you certainly have some classy tastes. Vintage wines. Mercedes. And I've been around long enough to know that suit didn't cost you less than $300.00. "

"Would you trust a man who drives a beat-up Oldsmobile, wears thrift shop suits, and sticks you with the bill?" He'd nailed it. He sees the wince. Once upon a time she did, and look where it left her, dependent on Daddy's support.

"No, you're right. I've had enough of a life time of taking care of the man in distress. I think I'd very much like to be taken care of at this point in my life."

"As princesses deserve to be taken care of."

"Oh, and what are you, the charming prince?" She snorts indelicately.

"You've known me for a day and I've already gotten your dream house."

She laughs. "One in which you got handsomely paid for. What my question is. You sold the house, down payment in hand. Your obligation to me was over the moment you got those signatures, so what is this? Amusement? Entertainment? Your token of appreciation for buying a house that had already been chosen for me by Daddy?"

"I'm hurt," Michael says playfully. "I thought it was charm and my adorable dimple."

"It most certainly wasn't your sop story. For future reference, real tears and a sloppy sniff are more effective. You can't bullshit an actress."

"All right, all right, you got me," he throws up his hands. "My father and I can't stand each other. In fact, I can't stand either one of them and they don't like me much either."

"Why?" she asks, scooping a jumbo shrimp into the cocktail sauce.

"I don't think this makes for very good dinner conversation," Michael says, a bit awkwardly. "I like to lead the conversation, talk about the girl. Girls like talking about themselves."

"I'm not sure if you've noticed, Michael, but I'm no girl." She assists herself in ordering another bottle of wine.

"No, you most certainly aren't that."

"Will you answer my original question as to why you're still here?"

"Listen, baby, I don't lie. I'm here –."

She snorts laughter. "You're full of shit."

He grins, "Fine, I'm a 25 year old man, unattached. And you're a beautiful older woman, which to a 25 year old man means experienced. I thought I'd show you how we do it here in the city."

The second bottle of wine arrives, and she requests everything be placed in to go containers. She begins gathering her things.

"Wo, baby, where you going? You tell me you want honesty and then throw it back on my lap as you walk out the door?"

"First, don't call me, baby. I hate that. If you can't remember my name, don't waste my time. Second, I'm ready for the grand tour. I don't need to be romanced. That was for your amusement alone."

"Your place or mine?" he says with a happy grin.

"Your place. I want to see how many cartons of eggs you keep stacked in your fridge."

XXX

Michael lay in his bed, completely content, and places a kiss on her bare shoulder. "Now I'm famished. Get me a glass of wine?" he says as he lights a cigarette.

"You're a smoker?" she says in surprise.

"Only after sex."

She crinkles her nose. "I see you never empty your ashtray. Souvenirs?"

She starts getting dressed.

"That's fully unnecessary," he says. "Didn't you read the sign when you walked through the door? Please take off your clothes before you enter." Michael laughs at his own joke, finds himself laughing alone, while she continues getting dressed. Then she puts on her shoes.

"Wait, ba – uh - Susan."

Her coat.

"You're leaving? Just like that? But we haven't even eaten yet." He rushes to throw on his clothes.

"I'm taking mine to go," she says. "I like to eat while I'm in the bath, after sex, as you call it."

"All right, sounds good. I've got a Jacuzzi."

"Alone." She eyes him unfavorably.

"But I got us a movie. I thought we'd –."

"What, Michael, curl up together in bed, drink more wine, watch a movie and fall peacefully to sleep?" She laughs. He doesn't like the tone.

"I want you to stay, Susan." Even he is turned off by the whine in his voice.

"What, aren't you satisfied? You sold the house, provided a grand tour to the 200th broad, and showed me how you New York City men get it done, which is hysterical . . . when you're 21, trying to be a big man in a little boy's shoes. When I'm gone, you'll want to brag about your conquest, but you won't be able to, because it was my conquest, not yours, and this is how older, more experienced women do it. We learn from our mistakes, from boys just like you."

"You've got it all wrong. Don't get your panties all in a knot, baby."

"I warned you about that."

"I'm sorry. I didn't mean to – What do you want? What can I do or say to make you stay with me tonight?"

"Goodbye Michael."

CHAPTER 6

Michael drives to his retreat at The Cave, having nowhere else to go. Nights have always been most difficult for him when the excitement of the day wears down, and he has nothing but himself to occupy him. He should be happy. He closed on two houses today, came up with a potential buyer for another, and was absolutely right about the more experienced older woman. She was phenomenal, taking control, and leaving him feeling . . . almost inadequate.

Eleven o'clock on a Monday night the bar was fairly empty. He had come expecting his standing ovation, and instead was met by a few side-long glances from a couple of old hoots, and the ugly guy with glasses who always sat in the back of the room, never talking to anyone.

'Ol Betty works the bar Monday and Tuesday nights, and even full inebriation and desperate loneliness wouldn't make her an attractive prospect for the night. He thinks about giving the broad he'd been with the night before a call, and apologizing for having burned that bridge during lunch hour while he was still on a high from his day's successes. At 4 this afternoon, Mick had told him that if he sealed the deal on the house today, Mick's superior would give Michael one temporary opportunity in the big leagues. His cut would be a mil, which would place his earning at two million in the 1 ½ years he's been with the company.

Due to his date with Susan, he hasn't yet been able to meet up with the boys and tell all, so it sits in his gut like fizzling pop-rocks. He was going to tell Susan all about it, but didn't have the chance. They'd been in his condo no more than 15 minutes before she had him stripped down. He'd been feeling ahead of the game then, believing she wanted him so bad she couldn't wait another minute. Now he just feels used and more alone than ever.

Michael is on his 4th double scotch when he finds himself all alone in the bar. 'Ol Betty went into the kitchen a few minutes ago, grumbling about wanting to get home. The sudden sound of loud static alerts him. He throws up his head.

"Hey, 'Ol Betty, did you just turn on the –?"

A face appears on the TV screen, rolling with the static, seeming to struggle to find its position on the screen. The man on the screen, mysterious, wearing a black cloak, appears to tap on the screen. The picture instantly stabilizes.

"Hello." A creepy smile moves over the face on the screen, pausing as though waiting for Michael to answer back. He appears to be staring directly at Michael.

"If you could see yourself in 5 years, 10 years, 15, would you do it? A glimpse into the future at any moment of time of your choosing. Do you wake up every morning, go to bed every night with the insecurity of a future unknown? Where is life going to take you? Where will it lead? Would you pay a million dollars to see a glimpse into your future? 5400 Turnpike Street. That's 5400 Turnpike Street. The answers you seek you shall find."

At that moment, 'Ol Betty returns to the bar.

"Hey Betty, get a load of -," Michael points to the screen, which has now turned off.

"Shit. Are you messing with me, you old hag?" he says teasingly. "Where you got the remote hiding? I wouldn't think you'd have it in you. You're all right, Betty. You're all right."

"Michael, you've had one too many scotches. I don't know what in God's name you're carrying on about over there."

"The TV. You turned the TV on."

"Can't turn that TV on. Junk box. Thing hasn't worked in three years."

"All right, joke's over, Betty. I'm on to you." Michael climbs atop the bar and begins pressing buttons on the TV.

"You get down from there, Michael. Getting shoe prints all over my clean bar."

The TV won't turn on. Michael follows the cord and holds the tip in his hand. Not even plugged in. He thinks perhaps Betty had unplugged it, but knows that she hasn't even been on this end of the bar.

"Get out of here, Michael. Go to bed."

She returns to the kitchen. While still holding the cord in his hand, dumbfounded, the man's face reappears on the screen. "A million dollars. Cash. 7500 Turnpike Street. The future is in your hands." The vision gradually fades into static, then black.

"Betty?" Michael's voice pitches. "Hey Betty." He runs into the kitchen.

"Michael, you get out of this kitchen, now, you hear? You know you're not supposed to be back here. Get."

"Betty, come home with me tonight. Please, I don't want to be alone tonight. Please, Betty, no one has to know."

"Michael, you are making me very uncomfortable. I've asked you twice to leave. You're acting like a crazy man. If I have to ask you again –."

"Chill, Betty. I'm not a crazy man and I wasn't – You know what? Here," he throws her a 20. "I'm gone."

Michael walks backwards toward the door, not wanting to turn his back to the TV. He knows how ridiculous he's being, but Betty has never been one for practical jokes and he's never been one for hallucinations. He knows what he saw, what he heard. It rambles around his head like a broken record. "Would you pay a million dollars? 7500 Turnpike Street. A glimpse of your future. A chance to be revealed the unknown."

XXX

By the time Michael's alarm goes off at 8, he has convinced himself it was all just been a very vivid dream, and completely unrealistic. One too many scotches, as 'Ol Betty told him. Perhaps 'Ol Betty had all been part of the dream as well. In fact, it is completely possible that he'd never even left the house after Susan left. He isn't a wine drinker. Impacted so little by Susan's rapid retreat, he must have just rolled over and passed out to sleep.

Michael has a 9:30 appointment with Mick's superior. The big guy. Associates are lucky if they ever see him in a lifetime of working there. He's got the whole top floor as his own, restricted to all but those he personally invites up. Michael has definitely made an impression, against Mick's better interests.

Move over, Mick. I'm taking over.

As Michael faces the mirror, securing the knot on his tie, and looking great, as usual, a man with a face that no right-minded woman could pass over, the TV turns on. Michael peers at it through the mirror reflection, asking himself the questions he already knows answers to, but too unbelievable for them to be correct. After all, TV's don't just turn on by themselves, so a logical explanation is the only answer.

Logic is completely blown out of the water when the man's face from the night prior appears on the screen.

"To have the knowledge of your future, an awareness that no other has, would you pay a million dollars? This is a one-time exclusive offer. The future is priceless, but if given this power, what would you do with it? Can you handle the truth?"

Michael watches mesmerized and terrified, all the while trying to place it into rationale. Scrolling across the bottom of the screen is the address. 7500 Turnpike Street. Out of an act of sanity, Michael grabs the remote from the night stand and changes the channel. The creepy man's voice continues to drone on, promising something impossible, on every channel. Michael presses the power off button and flees the condo.

He rushes through the building of his work, eyes skating across television screens, expecting His face, His voice.

"Michael?"

"What?" he yells, and settles his gaze on Martha, who holds his coffee in her hand.

"Bit jumpy this morning, don't you think? Nervous about your meeting?" She straightens his tie, flattens creases in his suit.

"Nervous? No. You know I've been expecting this for quite some – Martha, do you watch TV?"

"This is the 21st century, Michael. TV is as much a part of our lives as –."

"Have you ever seen this infomercial declaring he can tell you your future?"

"You mean psychic hotlines?"

"No, it's a guy wearing a black cloak. His face is mostly hidden from the lights. He asks if you would pay a million dollars to get a glimpse of your future."

She shakes her head. "Sounds like someone trying to make a quick buck off of the gullible. Can you image someone paying that amount of money for something they won't even know is true or not until they've lived their life? I feel sorry for the sucker that falls into that ploy."

"But how would you know? What if it was real?"

"There's a lot of people who might give up an arm and a leg to have that knowledge. Then they'd look into the crystal ball and find themselves on disability with no hope of a productive future, because they gave up an arm and a leg. Now Michael, I am loving the fact that for the first time in all the time I've been a personal servant to you, you're actually striking up a real conversation, but you have a meeting and the man up top does not tolerate tardiness, or much of anything, but don't tell him I said that. Good luck."

Michael is pushed toward the elevator. He hits the button for the 8th floor and begins breathing exercises to get himself to focus on the upcoming meeting and his future success, and not the odd infomercial that seems unrealistically to be targeting him alone.

The door opens to a large hallway, a coffee table and plush white furniture set off to the side. The hallway leads to the office of the secretary/receptionist. She is gorgeous, mid-twenties, and gravity hasn't touched her. She flashes him a brilliant smile.

"Michael? Or do you prefer Mike?"

"Call me whatever you would like."

"Mr. Marx is expecting you. Step toward the door."

Double doors open to accept his entrance into an office the size of a presidential suite. His feet soak into the green carpet. The room is decorated with leather furniture, a huge cherry wood corner desk, a wet bar, and a number of surveillance TV's on the left wall. The man behind the desk is disappointing in proportion to the settings. He's frail and old. Not the face of a man owner of the top Fortune 500's most successful businesses. The desk seems to swallow him up.

Michael doesn't hesitate. He steps forward, offering his hand. "It is an honor to finally meet you, sir," said verbatim from what he'd been told. Michael is about to take a seat when the old man barks a command, and in that bark is all the authority he needs. It is deep, resonant, and powerful.

"Stand. I want to get a good look at the man who is climbing the ladder faster than any other associate in history." The old man puts on a pair of glasses that cause his eyes to be the size of oranges. "You're just a boy," the old man says. Is that a tinge of disappointment in his voice?

"My best asset," Michael says undeterred.

"Yes, yes, I see that. The young have an abundance of energy that acts as a magnet. People like energy when they don't have enough of their own. Hell, just looking at you, I want to be 20 years younger."

Michael thinks 40 years, and says, "Don't forget the good looks. I use my qualities to the best of my advantage."

"I see that. You charged 80 dollars to the business account lastnight, wining and dining our client."

Michael starts to make an excuse when the old man barks out a laugh-slash-cough attack and says, "So how much wine did it take for her to close on it? Tactics I never even dreamed of using."

Michael smiles, "None, sir. I had her signature and check before the first glass of wine. The rest was personal."

"Oh, to be young again. That is where we differ. I prefer pleasure before business, and as you see, that works for me. Can I get you a drink?"

"Whatever you're having," Michael relaxes in the leather swivel chair, and crosses his legs. This is cake. The old man probably sees in him what he thought he had when he was younger. Michael honestly can't see this ancient artifact as ever being young, but he'll entertain the old man until business is sealed. Michael can hear the future spoken words in his head, *Michael, I never had any children. Never got my boy. But you are the son I never had. I want you to take over the company and carry out my legend, as a son does for his father.*

Mr. Marx calls in his assistant to make two drinks of an unknown origin. Michael does not hide his wandering eyes until it is revealed she is the old man's niece. "Beautiful, isn't she? When I was your age, I had beautiful women all the time. One on each arm. Only for the night. The next night, they'd be different beautiful women. It was definitely the high life. If I could have known what it would lead to in the future, perhaps I would have done things differently, perhaps not. I wasn't a bad person, incapable of love. I just loved them all and thought it such a waste to have to choose only one."

Silence passes.

"But then there was none. Drink, relax, are you hungry? Of course you are. You have the metabolism of a kid. What would you like? Steak? Seafood? Clarmy's has excellent roasted duck. Here, I have a menu of every restaurant in the area. You pick." Michael is handed a thick manila folder.

"All due respect, but I do have a house-showing in about 45 minutes."

"No you don't. It's been rescheduled in consideration of our meeting. In fact, your whole day is free."

"Well I do have to finish the paperwork on –."

"All taken care of. Relax. Enjoy yourself."

Two things occur to Michael. First, it's going to be a very long day and second, here before him is a very lonely man. And it scares the hell out of Michael.

XXX

Following a drive in the stretch limo, a 5 course 150 dollar meal at Clarmey's, and a pit stop at the gentlemen's club for a game of cards and two more drinks, Michael attempts for the fifth time to talk about business, and is shot down.

"Persistent, fella, aren't you? A good trait. You still got your eye on the ball. Let me share something with you. When you're as successful and powerful man like myself, you are afforded no security of privacy, though I've spent hundreds of thousands of dollars trying to achieve just that. You trust no one. Never talk business in public. The only place I can relax is in the privacy of my office. I've got the security up there sealed more tightly than a banks vault."

Michael is feeling pretty buzzed and the old man had double what Michael did. Michael assists him up the stairs and into the elevator.

"Time for some coffee," Mr. Marx winks. "Go into my office. I'll be right in."

As soon as the door closes behind him, Michael looks at his watch and curses. He didn't expect this to be an all day excursion. He missed his lunch break with the guys. By the time he gets out, they will have all gone home to their wives.

All of a sudden the muted sounds of the television emerge with a sound of static. Michael looks up to find all ten screens rolling with the same picture. No other picture replaces the one on the screen, but he can hear His voice as if speaking from within his very head. "Powerful men aren't men with ambitious dreams and luxurious tastes. That power fades and turns to regret. The most powerful man already knows his future, sees it play out before him, and can then come to expect those things he may later regret, and act accordingly. Your chance is now."

"You're a fraud, a phony, a fake. You know less about my future than I do. I know where I'm going," Michael yells aloud.

"Do you, Michael?" The voice from the surround sound speakers respond to him.

"Shit!" Michael begins racing toward the door just as Marx enters.

"What's wrong, boy? Look like you've just caught sight of a ghost."

"Uh, not much of a drinker. Feeling a little nauseous."

"Can't bullshit a bullshitter, Michael." Marx hands him some coffee. "If you're not much of a drinker, then I'm not reaching upon my 82nd birthday. I know everything about the employees I have working here, especially those I've taken an interest in. I know you close out the bars almost every night, except the night you find a girl to take home. I know your conversations, your arrogance, your lust for life's most devious pleasures – money, women, status. No privacy, Michael, and you are a very public speaker. I know of the laid-off police officer that you have run checks on potential clients, the retired lawyer who will act the professional with suspicious clients smart enough to want a lawyer to look over the contract they're signing, not smart enough to know that he is paid well for his misrepresentation. I know you, Michael. I know your game. And that's why you're here. I like it. You will stop at nothing to make a sale. You are without conscience, without heart, you do and say what you have to to close the deal. You have a future in this company and we are here now to determine exactly what kind of future that's going to be."

"I'll settle for nothing but the best," Michael says proudly, though perturbed about this old man knowing so much about his personal business.

"And that you will have, my boy, in time. There have been many men come into my office, looking for the big leagues, and then they buckle under the pressure. The smaller real-estate you've been working with have a great margin more potential buyers. If you fall out on one opportunity, you will have another the following day. The larger real estate brings in a large dime, but they are only sought after by multimillionaires that can make such an investment without batting an eye. If you fall out on an opportunity, you may not have another for four to six months to show that house again. I have to see first if you can handle the pressure. Prove yourself to me, Michael, and you're looking at partner, the youngest yet."

"I will prove myself. No problem. I can handle it," Michael says enthusiastically. Michael is handed a large manila folder.

"All you need to know is in there, plus whatever additional research you perform. Do your work. We were lucky to have found a prospective buyer so quickly. Don't disappoint me." Michael thanks him profusely and begins walking out the door. He stops at the door upon seeing the TV screens with different surveillance images throughout the building.

"Would you pay a million dollars to see the future?" Michael asks.

"I'd pay a million dollars to go back in time. We spend our young lives believing we own time. Then we look in the mirror, feel our body ache with arthritis, and realize that time has the upper hand. I achieved the future I wanted. I wanted it more than anything. But getting what we want doesn't necessarily mean it will make us happy and feel satisfied. Oh, and one more thing. Call it experience. Keep it in your pants as far as our clients are concerned until payment has been made in full. Good day."

XXX

Michael should have felt elated, overjoyed. He is being given an opportunity of joining the big leagues should he succeed where many others have failed. Instead, he feels slightly depressed and alone. He admires Marx's power, status, and influence, like the image in one's head of a Greek God being so big and powerful, but then you see them face-to-face and see just a man. Marx is just a man, a very old man who wakes up every morning a stander-by to time's disintegration of the great man he must have been in his youth. Watching Marx consume one drink after another until he was drunk at three in the afternoon, using this meeting as a means to break himself out of the monotony of his days and loneliness, Michael almost pities him. Prior to today, Michael's life plan had never gone further than his making it big and being successful. It's all that mattered to him, a driving force so strong and so powerful to overcome his origins.

He was born an only child when his parents were middle-aged. Whatever ambitions they may have had when they were younger were gone by the time he came into the picture. They'd been good to him, taken care of him. There's really not much he can complain about, per say, as far as his childhood. No big tragedies. No traumas. No hardships. No excitement. Nothing really at all. Perhaps he would have liked to have a sibling to beat on, look up to, and protect.

There had never been drama, except the time Aunt Cindy came over carrying a gun, ready to shoot her cheating ex-husband if he tried to go after her. He didn't go after her, not that night, and so the anticipation of a potential uprising in their calm lives died down. His parents never even argued. They'd settled some sort of compromise prior to his birth that gave each of them their roles in the relationship. What dad says goes. There was never an, "Ask your mother." No amount of manipulation could deter her from taking his father's side. Everything always had a place and if it didn't fit into their comfortable box, it was disregarded – including Michael, especially Michael.

Before retirement, mom had been an RN, and dad a Postman for the government. They remained at the same place all of Michael's life, securing a decent pension and 401K. They didn't have goals or what Michael would consider hobbies. They had no ambition to being better, doing better, making life better. They were completely satisfied with their mediocre calm lives, having the same friends, going to the same places. Hell, he'd never even seen his father look at another woman.

Michael hadn't been satisfied. He hadn't been satisfied at all. He wanted change. He wanted more. He wanted better. He felt their lifestyle was stunting his growth. He had nothing to talk about as a child. They could never understand that. He didn't have any stories to tell when younger. So he'd make them up. He'd create this fantasy life for all his friends, even use sympathy to get women. When that wasn't good enough, he'd make experiences happen.

Michael was the disruption in his parents' calm lives. He was their drama.

"You've got a good life. Why aren't you happy?" his mother would say to him while picking him up from detention.

"Do you do these things because you're bored? If you're so bored, come work with me," his father would say while bailing him out of jail.

They'd try to set him up with stupid jobs paying minimum wage. Newspaper delivery boy. Dishwasher. Cashier. Fast food. They never lasted past his first paycheck. He wanted out. He wanted to be where the big boys were with a big boy job, making big boy bucks in the big bad city life. In his junior year, he found himself a free ticket. He forged an acceptance letter to college. Forged tuition bills for the money that he collected. He went off to his fake college in the big city and began living his dream. He even forged report cards.

In the third year, his parents made a surprise visit to the college and found they'd never heard of a Michael Scully. The checks stopped. The phone calls stopped, at least his answering them. They had made it clear to him he was their lives greatest disappointment. Michael did his research, lied a little on his resume, and got into real estate. A year and a half later, and about to be a millionaire.

He will not be speaking to his parents until he's on the cover of Fortune 500. He will deliver it to them personally and watch as they wallow in shame and remorse and regret for not believing in him. He will let them take their regret to their graves. They will never take credit for his successes.

Feeling that forceful drive, anticipation, and restlessness again, Michael calls Marcus to meet up with him to go over his new client.

"Marcus, its Michael. Got a big one this time. You want in? Give me a call and we'll meet up. I'll be over at Scooters. See you there."

Michael drives to Scooters and sits down at the bar for dinner and a drink. The only time he comes here is to meet up with Marcus. Purely business, though Marcus probably thinks they are the best of friends – which is why Michael has never introduced him to The Cave.

Michael checks his watch every ten minutes, spans the room. Not many people out on Tuesday night, at least ones he wants to associate with – except for that one.

"Hey there gorgeous. My name's Michael, but you can call me whatever you want." Wink. "May I offer you a cocktail?"

"Can I call you Hey-Jackoff-Get-Away-From-My-Girl?" a large man comes up behind her, carrying two drinks.

He puts his hands up. "Hey man, easy. I'm helping the bartender out and getting drinks."

She looks at Michael apologetically. He turns toward the bar, glances at his watch. Two minutes.

At 1 minute 45 seconds she's by his side, beckoning toward the bartender.

"Hey, Michael, I'm really sorry about that. Male ego, you know how it goes."

"No, I don't know how it goes. No ego of mine tells me to treat a woman like she's a piece of property. Where's Hulk Hogan now?"

She laughs. "You're funny. Cute too. He's in the man's room."

"Not the little boys? You know what they say about insecure men, right? Inferiority complex," Michael says, looking down.

She playfully slaps him. "Stop. It's not the size that matters. It's how it is used."

"Did he tell you that?" He nudges her and leans in to whisper. "Was he right?"

"I'm not having this conversation," she giggles. She receives her drinks. "Okay, it's been fun. Gotta go."

He slides a 20 toward her pinky clutching the glass. On it is written his phone number. "Just remember. Close your eyes and it'll all be over in a blink of an eye . . . literally." She takes it and walks away, her head thrown back in laughter.

Glimpses of her entertain him for the next hour, especially when he catches her glimpsing at him, which she does again as they walk out for the door for the night. He calls Marcus again. Voicemail. He decides to leave, but doesn't know where he's going. The things that have been happening have him all freaked out. He doesn't want to be anywhere alone with TV.

While sitting in his car, he calls Susan. She answers on the second ring.

"I'm so glad we're learning so much about each other. I learned that you like one night stands. I live day to day and today's a new day, a new night. How about a one-night stand?" Michael says.

She asks him how long it took him to come up with that.

"No seriously. Or we can go see a movie. It doesn't have to be about sex."

She laughs at him. He hates that. She asks him with a great deal of sarcasm if kid-player Michael is looking for a companion, someone to fill the dark void in his life. He wants to call her a bitch and hang up. He can't do that.

"Why are you being so mean?" he says with an emotional tone. "What did I do to make you hate me? I'm not a hater. I'm a lover."

She tells him she doesn't hate him. She just hates what his surface represents and if she chooses to be used, she'd prefer a much better and more experienced lover than a guy who keeps cigarette butts as souvenirs for his sexual endeavors.

"I just said that because you seemed so turned off by the prospect of me being a smoker. I am a smoker, okay. And as far as my being inexperienced, you didn't exactly give me a chance to show you how competent I am. I was saving it for the second round, getting warmed up."

She throws in his face the comment he made about the sign on his door.

"It was a joke. I was trying to lighten your Lorena Bobbitt mentality."

She tells him it was retarded.

"Then give me another chance. I like you. I want to show you who I am. I'll even tell you about my parents."

She declares that he doesn't like her. He's just infatuated with the dislike of rejection, so he's pursuing her to ease the disappointment and humiliation of being used and rejected. She tells him she did him a favor by showing him what it feels like for every woman he does it to.

"So you want to fix me? Like a doctor? You want to play doctor."

She tells him he's so into himself and the flaws he passes off as perfection that even God couldn't succeed in that miracle.

He wants to tell her no wonder her ex-husband fell in love with someone else, someone with a heart. He can't do that. She tells him she has to go. She has another prospective client waiting in bed for her.

He gets off the phone seething, while looking forward to the conversation he'll have with her tomorrow. She's getting under his skin and it's as uncomfortable as an army of red ants. On a whim, Michael decides to find 7500 Turnpike Street, all the while berating himself for having a million dollar folder in his hand, but not getting to work on it because he's afraid of possessed televisions and being alone.

Once in the 7000's, he slows down to two miles per hour. 7,444, 7446, 7448, 7502. He reverses and looks again. There isn't a 7500 Turnpike street. Just an empty space between 7448 and 7502, like something used to be there, but has been gone for quite some time. All that still stands is a small shed missing half the roof with a big gap in the side from rotted plywood.

Michael laughs at himself, his ridiculous behaviors and thoughts. It's an infomercial, perhaps a 7500 Turnpike Street in another place, TV transmissions crossing lines, breaking in to the wrong frequencies. He doesn't know anything about that stuff, but he knows well enough that there has to be an explanation. Michael has never been one to believe in ghosts, the paranormal, pseudo-science, psychics. All just playing on vulnerable minds like the teaching of religion. All a part of the money game.

He's sober when he returns home, which results in an alertness and sensitive awareness to the silence and his being all alone. Every sound magnified. He unplugs the TV and tells himself it's merely to avoid distraction. He opens the thick manila folder and gets to work on getting to know the potential buyers and developing his tactics accordingly.

CHAPTER 7

Two days later, Michal is on the phone with Susan.
"Please, Susan, please, I'm on my knees in a 500 dollar suit. I
can't tell you enough how important this is. We're talking a
million five dollars on the line. Please, please, just this once.
Besides, I miss you."

She snorts and tells him he got his own self into this
mess. She's not going to be a part of the deception.

"They're newlyweds looking to buy their first home
together. They're all kissy, touchy, lovey-dovey. It made me
think of you – not the kissy, touchy, lovey-dovey part, but,
you know, the sex. So when they asked if I was married, I
thought no harm to act like I myself am a newlywed, and if I
could afford it, I would have bought the house myself. I
didn't know they would invite us out. Come on. It'll be fun.
Dressing up. Pretending to be married."

She tells him she doesn't have to pretend to be
married to know that it is not fun.

"Well, that's the funnest part. Pretending. It's not
real. No pressure. I've got a chance to be partner. I could be a
very rich man. Don't you care?"

She tells him she doesn't care, and to stop whining.
It's annoying.

"They'll be a lot of rich men there. You said yourself you're looking for someone to take care of you. Someone very very rich."

She asks him if that's all he ever thinks about is money. A woman doesn't necessarily mean financially when she wants to be taken care of.

"What? You want to be pampered too. You want a back massage, flowers, a box of chocolates? You want me to sit there and hold your hand while you vent about all your ex-boyfriends, trials, and tribulations?" he teases her.

She tells him she's never had a boyfriend and never experienced the whole courting ritual. Just a husband that used her, a few one-night rebounds, and pity sex with Michael.

"So pity me again. Look, I'm pathetic. I'm whining. I'm so desperate I'm definitely to be pitied," he continues to tease her. He knows he's wearing down on her defenses. "Please, please, please. Then I'll owe you. I'll let you do anything you want to me. Please." 5, 4, 3, 2…

"All right, if I do this for you, will you promise to leave me alone thereafter?"

This crushes him. "But we're having so much fun," he says.

She tells him he's the one having fun, with the challenge of trying to get something, for once, that he can't have. She demands he promise her. That's the only way she'll do this with him.

"Okay, I promise."

She doesn't believe him.

"Hey, I gave you my word," he says with a grin.

XXX

Susan said she'd meet Michael at his place. He watches her through the window as she steps out of the only asset she'd been able to keep following the divorce. A simple, yet surprisingly fitting silver Kia with a moon roof. She is gorgeous in a long, dark blue shimmery dress, and black open-toed shoes.

Michael is surprisingly nervous, but then she's the first woman to ever reject him and make him feel self-conscious. Her now champagne-colored hair is simply done up in a high pony tail with Shirley Temple curls. His heart falters.

She doesn't bother to ring the doorbell, doesn't bother to knock – just walks right in and says, "Come on, let's get this over with."

"You look absolutely magical," he says, grinning ear-to-ear.

She pulls her hand away. "And you look quite the same you always do. Such a man's world. Throw on a suit and tie, shave, and slick back your hair, and it works wherever you go. Never have to change your style.

"No, but we change our smell." He grabs her waist and pulls her into him. "It's called Honeymoon. You like?"

She sneezes.

"You got green contacts. You're right. They are very expressive. But your reddening cheeks are the biggest give away as to how you really feel."

"It's called blush, you ass. You get some points for noticing the contacts, though. I see my training has been effective. Pretty soon I'll have you watching Chic Flicks and crying at love scenes."

"If that is the kind of man you want me to be."

"All right, Prince Charming. Let's go. Your car or mine."

"Hey, wait. What's the rush? I have something for you."

"A preliminary bottle of SoCo?"

"Better," Michael reaches into his pocket and pulls out the little box that every woman hopes to see at least once in her lifetime.

"You didn't spend money on that thing, did you?" she says, a grimace of distaste on her face, not exactly the reaction he expected.

"No, I asked the clerk over at Tiffany's if I could borrow it for the night, what do you think?"

"Why would you do that? That's so stupid, Michael," she stomps her foot, turns her back on him, crosses her arms.

"Hello, newlyweds? Couples dance? Girls like comparing rings."

"So you made sure I'd have the biggest ring."

"Exactly."

"You know. You really are an arrogant bastard. Spend $50,000 on a whim, on a false pretense of a marriage, just to sell a god damn house."

"I don't understand. I thought you'd be thrilled. Women love jewelry. Especially diamonds."

"I'm glad you're learning so much about women from radio advertisements, Michael."

"Is this another one of those it's not the size that matters, it's how it works things?"

"Pretty much. A guy can give a woman a ring the size of Everest, but it won't change the fact that he's a complete douche bag. Let me tell you something, Michael. If they did a study on women who had the biggest diamonds, the most jewelry, the most expensive clothes, wines, and accessories, you will find them to be the loneliest women out there, because the men they're married to are so self-centered and ignorant that the only way they know how to show their love is by having their secretary –slash –mistress go out and buy the wife the most expensive things when money has no means to the man when he has it, causing it to be a futile gesture. A man calls in sick to spend the day with his wife. A penniless man collects cans and bottles off the street to buy his wife a 14 karat gold necklace. *That* is meaningful."

"And for the fact that I just spent almost all the commission I made selling your house to you is meaningless?" Michael says discouraged.

"When you have an ulterior motive, yes."

He grips her waist, "And what's my ulterior motive?"

"The best way to sell to the upper class is to be a part of it. That stupid ring is just a way for you to weasel your way in."

Michael kisses her, puts the ring on her finger, and whispers, "Be a good pretend wife and get in the car. I'll drive."

She stomps off. Grinning, he watches her depart.

XXX

The party goes very well, Michael in his glory, finally being a part of something he can take pride in. Susan acts the perfect wife. They eat. They drink. They dance. Susan seems genuinely happy and to be enjoying herself.

Michael softly chuckles when he glimpses Susan holding out her hand as the others admire her ring. He watches her head tilt as she laughs and catches himself thinking that if he wanted to get married and share a life with someone, Susan fits the profile. She'd be a great asset toward his ambitions and business endeavors. She fits right in. More so than he. It is her presence that completes the picture. Marriage is a part of the social elite, whether love is involved or not.

Michael, as usual, is the life of the party. He has the men rip-roaring with laughter and slapping his back and the females giving him sidelong glances. When he catches Susan yawning, he takes her by the arm and they begin their goodbyes. "My little darling bird is getting sleepy," Michael says to the famous young newlywed couple, nuzzling Susan's nose.

"Oh, I'm sure you'll find a way to wake up once you make it to the bedroom," the fast-rising Eric Kutchner winks at him. "Good time tonight. Funny guy. Susan, a pleasure.

Keep Michael out of trouble. We'll be calling you on Monday. You've done very well in convincing us that Moonlight Manor will make the perfect home for us."

Michael thanks them and takes Susan's hand. As soon as they are in the car, she tears her hand away from his.

"You were beautiful ton -."

"Congratulations," she says dryly. "Looks like you made the sale and succeeded in becoming a millionaire. Only I know how much of a fake and phony you are."

"Hey, all that in there was all very real to me, whether you believe it or not. I enjoyed having you by my side."

"Flaunting me like a delicacy to make *you* feel good."

"You *are* a delicacy, a fine wine, the only one of its kind."

"Enough, Michael, you don't have to try and charm me anymore. You made your sale."

"Listen, Susan, I've been thinking tonight. I enjoy being around you, though, I could do without all the insults. You heard everyone. They called us a perfect couple, and I agree. We look good together, you and me."

She yawns.

"Why don't you keep that ring on for a while, see if it grows on you? Let's try this thing."

"You drank too much, Michael. You're talking crazy talk. All the excitement has short-circuited something in your brain."

"Is this about love? We'll grow to love each other."

"Now you sound like my ex-husband. It's not about love. You don't listen to me. I've made it as clear as I can make it, right there in your face and you're still refusing to see it."

"All right, I'm listening. Eyes are wide open. What am I missing?"

"I don't even like you, Michael. Not feeling it. You don't turn me on in that way. I did you a favor before, did you a favor tonight. Now it's your turn to follow through. You gave me your word."

Michael is silent for a long time, chewing through his disappointment and anger and hurt her words caused. Doesn't she know she's the only woman he has ever pursued more than once?

"So you really want this to be the end of the road for us?"

"There was never a beginning. You sold me a house. I was a client. You are my real estate agent. The association ends when all the paperwork is signed."

"I get it. You're bitter. What your ex-husband did to you was lousy. We can take it as slow as you would like.'

"Slow? My biological clock is ticking, Michael. I'm almost 40 years old. I want what other women want."

"And you don't think I can give you security?"

She punches the seat. "A child, Michael. I want a child with a full grown man I don't have to babysit. You're so young and ambitious. You've got your goals and dreams and I'm not about to sit around and wait for you to accomplish them. I want a man who is done dreaming, who is settled, who can happily spend the rest of his life as a family. No drama. Just peace."

Michael recovers a flashback of a similar experience, except it was his mom in the driver seat and he slouched inside the passenger seat-belt, being reprimanded, once again, for disturbing the peace. He grimaces at the memory and the implications in her words. Susan wants the very thing he has spent his life running from – normalcy, average, a nothing, a nobody.

"Do you see something really disgusting on the windshield or is that your reaction to my words?"

"You're right. I think I had too much to drink. Crazy talk. Feeling quite . . . sick, all of a sudden."

She does not say goodbye. What's the point? They both know they'll never see one another again.

XXX

Monday at 10 am, Michael is called back into Marx's office. He is provided a drink upon entering, a clap on the back.

"I have to tell you, Michael. I am amazed. Less than a week you held this property. Unbelievable. How's it feel to be a millionaire, son? I know, I know. I can see it in your eyes. I remember my first million. I wanted it so bad, so bad. Then when I had it in my hands, I could have been holding a 50 for all I cared. I wanted two million, five, ten million, and it never seems enough, because when you're playing in the big leagues, you're spending in the big leagues. A million dollars is nothing and I think you've already figured that out.

"Do you know how long Mick was holding that property? No, never mind, none of your business, but I'm going to tell you anyway. 13 months. He showed it four times. Nothing. Mr. and Mrs. Kutchner had nothing but good things to say about you. They loved the house, but hadn't intended on spending that much. That is, until they met my key player - a Mr. Michael Scully. The youngest associate yet to have this kind of success. I'm giving you two more properties we've had sitting around for a while. No potential buyers, as of yet, but with greater privileges come greater responsibility, and I want to see more. Previously we've given you the properties, given you the clientele. We're giving you more independence, and with more independence comes a bigger salary. How's that sound?"

Michael smiles and nods silently, asking the unspoken. How much?

"Three months probationary period. If in three months, I'm not happy with your work, you'll go back to where you are."

"And if you are happy."

"Then you keep climbing that ladder."

"Partner?"

"Something like that."

XXX

Michael reports his own version of Marx's words to his boys at The Cave. "You're the son I've always wanted that I never had," Michael says. "He says to me, 'You want this office? You want a floor all of your own? Your own personal secretary to do by your every bidding?' Course I'm thinking. I don't want just any personal secretary. I want the one he has. Calls her his niece. I'm telling you. She is grade A. 110 percent. She's got – ."

A man's power is his knowledge of the future. What is a million dollars? Is it worth the future? To know beyond a doubt where you're going and all that you have to look forward to? Or is the future your demise. Will all your dreams be torn – .

Michael whips his head around at the voice, so close he can feel breath on the tiny hairs of his earlobes, but there is no one behind him. There is only one he does not recognize. Michael tries to glimpse his face before he turns into the restroom. He turns to Tony, "Did you hear that?"

"Hear what?"

"Whispering. A glimpse of the future," but even to his own ears, he sounds ridiculous.

Michael moves toward the restroom, cautiously, as if expecting . . . what exactly? He enters. The bathroom and stalls appear empty. One went in, but didn't come out. How?

He opens the stall doors just to be sure. The window is small, barely able to fit a child through. "I've got to stop drinking," he murmurs, turning on the cold water and splashing it on his face.

"Michael," the walls echo.

His eyes shoot open.

"Reality is just an illusion, so then are illusions reality? Seeing isn't always believing. Now you see me. Now you don't. But I'm still here. Do you believe in fate? Destiny? Or that our life becomes what we make of it? But then how can I hold your future in my hand if the future is always one step beyond your reach?"

His vision appears in the mirror, but he, it, seems not to otherwise exist outside the reflection. "Why me? Why can't you play games with some other poor bastard? You've got the wrong man. I don't believe in people who can tell the future, in things that don't exist. You are not real. Everything real makes sense and this, this does not."

"Calm down, Michael. I don't mean to upset you. You need not fear me. I mean only good. You ask, why you? There are those who base their present decisions on their past, those who make present decisions on a present day impulse, and those, like you, who base their present decisions on their future, always striving for the future. This leaves us to wonder – how can we base a decision on a future we're completely unaware? How many people find themselves with a future they never planned for? How many times have you heard other people issue regrets that they should have done something differently? You are being offered a gift, Michael. Do you want this gift? Do you want to know your future five, ten years from now?"

"But how can I know if it's real?"

"The future awaits and will be yours to own. Bring the money to the address you drove to the other night. I will be waiting, but not for long. I can give someone else the gift, and you will always be left to question a future even you cannot predict. It is not like anything you've so far imagined. You will be quite –."

Todd enters the bathroom at that moment and the vision is gone and silenced.

"Quite what? It will be quite what?" Michael yells into the mirror.

Todd raises a brown in the mirror's reflection, "You all right there, man?"

Michael wipes the chill from his arms, though his forehead is perspiring.

"Wonderful, never been better. I'll – uh – I'll catch ya later."

Michael exits quickly and leaves the bartender yelling after him about his tab. Without seeing anyone or anything, he goes to the bank with a briefcase, then to another bank, then to the safe in his home until the briefcase becomes weighted down with a million dollars cash. He does not think. He speaks to no one as they call his name. He does not drive. He walks, seeing only a whisper of His black cloak, like a mirage, shimmering. Somehow he knows no one else can see what he is seeing.

He follows him to 7500 Turnpike, the abandoned lot with only the remains of a broken shed. He begins to enter where the man had disappeared, then feels a sharp pain in his neck, as though bitten by a spider. He slaps at the spot, then rubs it to soothe the sting.

It is dark in the shed, but he keeps walking the long narrow hallway. Somewhere tucked deep away in his awareness he knows that the small shed he entered is not the place he is walking now.

Small candle flames flicker along the hall, producing dancing shadows. He recalls the words, 'If reality is just an illusion, then are illusions just another reality.'

The halls open to a magnificent parlor with a large-crystal chandelier spiraling blinding lights. Black cherry floors lead to a spiral staircase, whereupon a woman that could definitely be voted in as most beautiful super model in the world beckons him to follow.

"My name's Michael," he says with a toothy grin. She turns and continues walking. "Hey, wait up. What's your name?"

He follows her up the spiral staircase, down another lit hall. Her perfume lingers in her trail. He feels dizzy.

She opens a door for him, the entryway enclosed by a black curtain, and gestures him inside. He moves through the curtains and turns expectantly, but she is gone. As well as the door. There are only four walls. Only one candle burns. He is not alone, but he cannot see the other's presence.

"Place your briefcase on the table behind you," he hears His voice. A table appears.

"Face the wall. You will pick any day in the future, no matter how close or far. You will be shown your future beginning on that day. The image will last as long as you continue to look. What you do with the information you're shown is entirely up to you. You will not see me again. Begin."

Michael faces the wall, wiping sweaty palms against his jacket. He thinks of his dreams, his goals, the successes that are going to be his. He thinks of Susan and her want for a modest life. He thinks of Mr. Marx, wealthy and powerful. Old and alone. He wonders what the hell happiness is really supposed to mean?

"10 years. I want to see me in 10 years."

The wall suddenly lights up, a white contrast to its black. The picture shimmers like water, slowly focusing into clarity. He does not see himself. Instead, the image reveals a large park with grand houses lining the circular private road. He knows this place as it is a goal of his to live here. Only the wealthiest people can afford to live here. A private community with one interest in common –money. Passer-byers look directly at the image and Michael realizes that the vision is from his own eyes, which is why he can't see himself. He walks to a bench and sits down, peering out at the rich folk, couples out for a stroll, well-dressed children being pushed on the swings. Two hands holding what appears to be some kind of sandwich that had seen better days come into view. Oh god, is he eating that? He looks at the fingers, grimy, nails long, broken. A disgrace to a man who spends 50 a week to keep his nails groomed and hands soft.

A pretty woman walking her dog sees him. Michael watches as her face distorts in disgust. She turns and walks quickly away. *I like having you come, but I love watching you go,* he thinks.

A hand grasps his shoulder. The image follows the hand to the young face of a police officer. "Pack it up. You know you're not supposed to be here. If I catch you here one more time, I'm going to lock you up. These people around here pay lots of money to be here. They don't need bums and beggars littering their streets."

Bum? Beggar? The image points toward worn scruffy shoes, the big toes peeking out with dirt encrusted in the toe nail. Michael steps back, "No, this can't be right."

He doesn't get a response. The disgusting hands raise to take another bite of the unrecognizable sandwich. Michael turns. "Is this some kind of – ?"

The image disappears.

"No, no, no." He hits the wall with his fist, but it has become a door again. It opens with a loud creak. The briefcase is gone, the table replaced by a wooden bench with only three legs. Light pours in through the open door. Something rank permeates his senses, like something had died and decomposed there. He exits the door and is blinded by sun light. Michael turns and looks at the small half-fallen shed he'd just exited. Just a shed.

"Hey you. What are you doing in there?" A Police Officer yells from his open window. "Get outta there."

"No, wait, Officer, there's been a horrible mistake. My name's Michael Scully. I work over at Marx's Realty. I've just been ripped off a million dollars. I had a briefcase with a mil – a million dollars," Michael suddenly feels sick. "I was asked to meet a man here, at this address."

"Are you armed?"

"No, I'm not – ."

"Put your palms against the car."

"What?"

"Do as I say?"

"Okay, okay, but you need to listen." Michael finds himself being patted down. "Are you searching me?"

"Where's the drugs? Where are you keeping them? Are they in there?"

"Drugs? No, no drugs. It wasn't a drug deal. Jesus, will you listen to me?"

Michael is hand-cuffed and shoved in the backseat of the patrol car as the officer searches the shed and surrounding premises.

"You're lucky I can't cite you for being drugged."

"But I'm not –."

"No, you're completely sober and you just have a rare disorder that makes your pupils dilated and act like an idiot, right? I've heard them all so you can save it."

"I was drugged. Oh my God, it all makes sense. The prick on my neck. I thought it was a spider. Someone drugged me and stole a million dollars. Said he could predict my future. The shed wasn't really a shed. It was this big – And there was the girl. So beautiful. Why are you looking at me like that? It's true. You have to believe me."

"Can't arrest you for being crazy either," the Officer unlocks the cuffs.

"I'm not crazy. It's true. Look, look at my neck."

"Looks like a spider bite. So what did your future foretell? Riches, happiness, love?"

"I was a scumbag beggar. A homeless friggin' bum."

"Hmmm, millionaire turned bum. That's original. Lay off the drugs. If I catch you here again, I will arrest you."

Michael starts with the uncanny resemblance to the image.

But that wasn't for 10 years.

He'd been jipped, completely jipped. One man smart enough to never let someone pull one over on him, because how can one be a victim to their own scams of deceit? Michael begins walking back, hands in his pockets. He's okay.

I'm okay. I closed that deal. Got another mil five coming on Friday and there's more where that comes. There will always be more. Because I'm Michael Scully, about to be the youngest associate turned partner the business has ever seen. A million dollars gone. No sweat. All just a learning experience, he thinks. *And kudos to the man that beat me at my own game. Hopes he enjoys the mil.*

Michael does not return to work. Nor does he return to The Cave. He drives right home. Showers until there is no hot water left. Finds that he has no food in his fridge or cupboards. He calls Susan to listen to it ring and ring with the telltale beep she's on the other line. He can't leave a message. Finding stale crackers and peanut butter, he snacks in his bed while searching the TV channels for Him.

CHAPTER 8

It's Wednesday lunch hour. Michael is at Scooters with Marcus. Marcus looks forlorn and carries the expression of a man who ate something that isn't sitting well in his stomach.   "This time is a little different. I don't have a name. I need names. Names of very wealthy people who are selling their home, thinking of selling their home, separating, divorcing, marrying, or looking to buy a home, whether year-long or seasonal. I'm talking movie stars, CEO's, fortune 500's, stock brokers, the Bill Gates of the world. People who can spend multi-million dollars on a home with a mere shrug. Can you do that for me, man?"

"No, Michael, I'm sorry. I came here today to tell you that this little business arrangement we have is no longer. I'm not doing your dirty work anymore. I got into it thinking it would be profitable, and to help you out, but . . . You've been screwing me over, man. Lying to me so that you don't have to close on your end of the bargain and pay me my fair percentage."

"Lying to you. You think I've been lying to you. It's me, Michael. You're my pal, like an older brother to me, watching out for me. Come on, man, don't do this. Don't quit now. We're just cracking the surface. We're finally getting our foot in the door. I'll up you to 2 percent. Do you know what 2 percent is on a 30 million dollar home? Do the math."

Marcus pulls a rolled newspaper out of his jacket pocket. He opens it to an article on the 3rd page headlining Michael and his recent sales to the once famous Susan Taylor, then the rising star newlywed Kutchner's. The purpose of the article, however, was not to highlight his successes, rather to put two and two together. Susan Taylor client? Susan Taylor wife? A picture captures Michael and Susan at the couples' dance, a distinctively marked circle emphasizing the ring on her finger.

"Son-of-a –where'd you get this?" Michael yells, flipping to the cover. It's the Times. "Shit. Shit!" He searches for the reporter's name, the jerk off that exploited him, but it is not listed.

"Listen, Marcus, it's not what it looks like. I ran into some financial problems, had a million dollars stolen from me. You're the first person I've told about it. I didn't want the news to go public. Anyway, it left me almost completely dry. As has been made pretty obvious now, yes, I did close the deal on the house with Susan Taylor, and for the record, she didn't buy the story one bit about my sick dad. I needed the money, that's why I didn't tell you. I was just waiting for this one big sale. Then I was going to come clean and pay you your due. Hey, Stacey, do you think for one second you can move your fat ass and get me a drink?"

The place falls into silence. Michael tries to crack a smile, like it was a big joke, but his smile falls short of its target. She slams a water down in front of him and glowers at him, daring him to comment. "Ha ha, very funny, Stacey. Are you forgetting who pays your bills – so you can flaunt those acrylic nails and get your hair done up nice and pretty? Double-scotch. Hold the ice."

"Your money's no good to me, Michael. Not when I got my dignity. Treat me like some serving wench like God put me on this planet to cater to you. Drink your water and leave."

"My money's no good, no good to you now? You haven't had a problem taking it for years, just like you haven't had a problem ripping your boss off by pocketing the money and not ringing it in the register. You hear that, Bill?"

She gasps and begins to cry. "Just because you're a liar, a fake, and a cheat doesn't make everyone else that way. He's lying, Bill. He's had too much to drink so I cut him off. So he's acting like an asshole."

Bill is a man everyone knows not to mess with. 6'4", 300 lbs of muscle, and a short fuse. "Is it true? Have you witnessed this occurring?"

"Not just me. Everyone knows it. It's like an inside joke, right guys?" Michael looks around the bar, looking for nods of agreement. He meets no one's eyes as they've all suddenly found something very interesting in their drinks, their hands, their laps. "Marcus?" Michael pleads with his former friend. "I've only had one drink. You've seen it too."

"I don't know what you're talking about," he says coldly.

"I don't appreciate you coming in here making false accusations against my staff."

"All right," Michael holds up his hands. "I'm leaving. This is bullshit."

"Pay her for your drink. Give her a nice big tip."

"She gave me a water. I'm not – ." Bill's face reddens. "All right, fine," Michael shuffles through his pockets, his wallet, all he has are five ones. "Here," he throws it on the bar and walks backward out the door. He hardly has one foot out the door when his phone starts going off.

"Marx wants to see you in his office immediately!" The phone clicks dead.

Michael buys a paper and searches the masthead for a directory. He calls the paper to inquire into who wrote the article. He's told it's an anonymous freelancer who wishes to keep his information in confidence.

"The facts are there, can you deny the facts?" he is questioned.

Michael goes to his office. Everyone greets him with nervous silence. He steps into the elevator. How has all this happened? Who wrote the article? Someone's out to destroy him, to exploit him. Who? Why? What did he ever do wrong to them?

"Should I have worn a vest?" he jests with Marx's niece.

"He's been waiting. Go on in," she says somberly.

The doors open. Marx has his back facing the door. The newspaper is open on his desk. As soon as the door clicks shut, Marx turns. "When I say I want you in my office immediately, I mean IMMEDIETELY. Not when you feel like gracing me with your presence."

"Sir, I apologize. I was out to lunch. I was not in the building. I was doing some research."

"Sit down."

"Would you like a drink, sir. I can get you a –."

"Sit DOWN!" Michael sits. "I received a surprising phone call from the Kutchners pulling out of the deal. He was furious, questioning the integrity of our company, saying he didn't appreciate being played for a fool. He had liked you, thought you legit. Then read this article and was left with the same question as everyone else who reads this article. Did you really go so far as to pretend you and Susan were newlyweds in order to get in his good graces and sell him this property?"

"Sir, it's so much more than that. It was a way in. What rich bastard is going to trust a nobody, someone not of their own class? I needed a way in – get on their level. It wasn't just selling the house to them. I didn't tell you this before, but I also got a list of names and numbers of other big wigs, super rich, who may be looking for real estate in the future and wanted me to represent them. Look." Michael pulls cards out of his wallet, tosses them on the desk. "I was thinking of prospective clients while simultaneously closing on the current."

"You messed up, Michael."

"No, I messed up because I got caught. Do you know who wrote this? Who's out to get me? Do you have any idea? If we can find them, we can silence them. Bribe them to take back the article. Keep them close. Is it Mick? That bastards been getting green since you gave me his property."

"You got caught because your plan wasn't foul-proof. It's not like you chose a nobody to flaunt as your pretend wife. It's Susan Taylor – the Susan Taylor. Once-upon-a-big name falling into the shadows until you opened her back up to the public. You are or at least were a nobody. No publicity is good publicity. Susan Taylor is not a nobody. She's news. Now you're news, which means this company, specifically ME, is news. I've had reporters calling all morning, looking for answers. Did I know one of my employees was doing this? Do I think this is going to impact the integrity of this company? What am I going to do about it? And you know what the public will want to hear? That I had no idea. This has impacted the company's integrity, so to compensate, a Mr. Michael Scully has been discharged and I will never let something like this happen again, because the integrity of a service-oriented business rests on the integrity of those it has employed."

"No, please, sir. Don't do that. Hold off on the interviews. I'm going to fix this. I will fix this."

"How? How can you possibly fix this?"

"This article questions the implications in the facts. Susan Taylor, recent client. Susan Taylor, wife. I just need to make it legit."

"Stop with the riddles. What are you trying to say?"

"I'm going to get married."

"You can't just – ." Marx stops, seeing the expression of determination on Michael's face. "Well I'll be. You like this job that much?"

"Job? No, it's the money I'm after."

"Now how are you going to get someone like Susan Taylor to marry you?"

"Her biological clock is ticking. She wants a baby before it's too late. And it's almost too late. I'm going to give it to her."

XXX

Michael drives directly to her house, his tank on E, no money in his wallet. He makes a pit stop at Central Park and pulls out a fistful of flowers, running like a madman toward his car. His car sputters and stalls two blocks from her home.

He runs the rest of the way and stops in his tracks upon seeing the eight vehicles and 15 people with cameras, notebooks, and microphones out in her yard. It's too late. They've already spotted him. They start running toward him.

"Michael, is it true you and Susan are married?"

"Is it true you scammed Eric and Ashley Kutchner into buying a house by pretending you and Susan to be married?"

"Is it true you and Susan fell deeply in love when you were selling her this house?"

"Yes," Michael yells, giving them something to ponder as he skirts around them through the back yard, and down through the basement hatch. He runs up the stairs and confronts a locked door.

"Susan!" He knocks on it loudly.

"Do you people have no boundaries? Get out of my house."

"It's me, Susan, Michael."

"Michael, what the hell are you doing in my basement? Did they see you?"

"Let me in, Susan. I have something for you."

"I hope it's a bottle of valium and a shotgun I can shoot you with."

As soon as she opens the door, he grabs her flailing body and embraces her.

"Get off of me, Michael."

"Here," he pushes the flowers into her face.

She takes them, throws them on the floor. "That's the best you can do? Stupid store-bought flowers. I hate you, Michael!"

"They're not store-bought. I picked them."

"Yea, and I'm 23 years old and a hopeless romantic," she spits fire.

In the moment's silence that follows, he notices her. She's a wreck. Eyes puffy and red from crying, mascara stains on her cheek, raw red nose from blowing it too many times. Bathrobe and hair completely astray as though she'd been trying to tear it out of her skull.

"You're beautiful," is all he can think to say.

In flash-fury, she picks up the flowers from the floor and starts swatting him with them. "Why you lying, arrogant, conceited, deceitful, manipulative little man. And when I say little, I'm not making a reference to your immaturity, though that's next."

He can't help but laugh. "Susan, stop, stop it, Susan." He manages to grab one wrist, then the hand with the flowers, but she belts him with a knee and he collapses to the floor, just as a camera flash lights the room.

She laughs in victory. "Gotta love those picture windows, right, Michael? And there's one in every room, just like you said. At least there are some things you don't lie about, you, you ugly, squirmy, slimy little snake."

"Snakes aren't slimy, Susan."

"If they fall into a mud puddle, they are," she snaps, swatting him one last time with the poor mangled flowers.

"Why don't we start with a drink, Susan? Talk about this. Then if you're still upset, I will let you beat me into a bloody pulp if that will make you feel better."

"Have you any idea what you've done?" she shouts.

"I'm sure I'm about to find out." Michael picks himself up off the floor and wipes himself off. He heads for the kitchen to get a drink. What is it about this woman? He had all the words. He knew what he'd say. Sweep her right off her feet, until she's clinging to the chandelier begging for more, but every time he's in her presence, he finds him struggling more to contain his own emotions than to sway hers.

"Did it ever occur to you to wonder why I moved to basically the other side of the country? Do you have any idea what it's like to wake up every morning and turn on the television and watch your hardships, your personal life exploited for the world's entertainment? I moved here to get away from it all, and now, because of you, I can't step out onto my front porch without being hounded by a bunch of cameras and reporters. Susan Taylor – another scandal. I wanted to put that life behind me, Michael. I just want to live out the rest of my days without scandal, without drama. I just want peace. I just want to be able to live a normal life without every single wrinkle, sag, and cellulose being magnified for the world's viewing pleasure."

"Well, that's what I came here to talk about. It doesn't necessarily have to be a scandal."

"What are you talking about?"

"Well, we already got the ring and the newspaper announcement. Let's follow through with this," he takes her hand.

"Are you out of your mind? I already made that mistake once, remember? Shotgun wedding. Avoid scandal. And look what I got out of it. A childless, loveless marriage that ended in a nasty bitter divorce that cleaned me out of all my life's work."

"It's not the same. In fact, it's the complete opposite. I know you're broke, so I'm not after your money. You're not pregnant, but you want to be before your clock stops ticking."

"And what's in it for you, Michael? You looking for a mommy figure to iron your clothes and wipe your ass. Or is your ass on the line at your job and the only way they'll keep you on is if you fix this scandal of yours by marrying me?" She looks at him and gasps. "It's true, isn't it? This is so you can keep your job. You're low. You're . . . you're dirty. You're unbelievable."

"Susan, honey, do you hear yourself. I'm 25 years old. Young and fun. In your eyes, a womanizer. Why in God's name would I get married, settle into a life-long commitment for the mere sake of keeping a job that I can get anywhere?"

"Because I know you, Michael, more than you know yourself. The Michaels of the world don't get married for love. The Michaels of the word are incapable of loving anyone but themselves. Always a means to an end. And your word, Michael, even in the form of vows, is as useless as your appendix."

Smile. Get down on your knees. Tell her you do love her and that you've never had to deal with these feelings before. Tell her you don't know much about love and how those things are supposed to work, but you do know one thing for sure. You don't want to lose her. You want to be able to see her every day, wake up to her in the morning. You want to be her man and give her all the things she wants in life, and if that means giving her a child and being a daddy, then by all means he'll be a Daddy, Michael thinks. He now wishes he'd watched more Chic Flicks so he'd have the right words to say.

Instead his face flames red and he feels an anger he's not accustomed to. "All right, Susan, all right. I've known you, what, 2 weeks? I've been nothing but cordial to you, treated you well, and I've sat her for two weeks allowing you to degrade me, insult me, disrespect me, and I've taken it. I've taken it like the man you don't think I am. I'm not perfect, Susan, but you're not perfect either. You want to judge me, throw all my deceitful, manipulative means to an end in my face when you're no different than I. You married a man not for love – but to make a pregnancy legit. The child never happened, yet you held onto a loveless marriage, held onto him, wouldn't let him go, though knowing you didn't love him and he loved someone else, all to avoid the scandal of a divorce, because you care more about what other people think than the lives of two people. Now you're so bitter, you have to make every man pay for your own choices in life. It's so wrong of me to want to get married to keep my dreams, to progress in life, but it's not wrong for you to want to be with a man purely for the sake of having a child? How messed up is that, Susan? Means to an end. But I thank you for showing me the kind of life and treatment I can expect if I were to marry you. I'd be an idiot to marry a cold, heartless –."

"Don't you say it, Michael! Don't you dare!"

"Bitch."

She smacks him. She smacks him so hard his teeth clatter, stunning him. He wants to strike her back, wrestle her to the couch, shout at her to never to hit him again. Kiss her. A knock sounds at the door.

"Police. Open up," The door is opened. "Michael Scully."

"Yes."

"Got you on two counts. You're parked in a no parking area."

"My car ran out of gas."

"And we got information that you took flowers from Central Park, which, as you know, we don't take lightly. Gotta make an example. We're booking you for the night."

Michael glares at Susan, rubbing the red spot on his face as he's hand-cuffed.

"I told you they weren't store-bought."

XXX

Michael has three hours to reminisce over the past 24. Where did everything go wrong? 24 hours ago he didn't believe what the one million dollar image revealed to him. Being a bum, a beggar seemed so far from a possible reality. He had the world in his hands. 24 hours later, it's no longer an impossible reality. He's broke. About to lose his job. And he's sitting in a god damn jail cell for stealing flowers he didn't have the money to buy. Right now his lawyer friend would come in handy. Put up some argument that Central Park is a public park, those flowers paid for out of residential taxes; therefore, technically, the flowers belong to the residents who reside in that county. Granted, Michael does not own his condo, and doesn't directly pay those taxes, but he pays a landlord a significant amount of money each month to pay those taxes. A significant amount of money due tomorrow that he does not have.

Marx gave him two weeks. Suspended for two weeks, no pay, to give him enough time to fix this, let publicity die down a bit. But it's that simple, isn't it? To lose everything. Landlords don't care how many months, years, you've paid rent on time. It's that month you can't pay. That moment you just don't have it. You lose your home. Welcome to homelessness. It can happen to anyone. Anyone who allows it. Anyone who throws their hands up in resignation. There's always a way, an alternative course. Michael has always believed in this.

Michael was given a gift. A gift of forewarning, a glimpse of a future that could be his own if he doesn't make some rash changes. Security is like walking on a floor with a bunch of broken boards. You're secure, as long as you don't take the wrong step. He has to marry Susan. His future depends on it. Marriage is but a piece of paper, a stupid little document bound by meaningless words of commitment. Hence divorce. He's committed to the idea that after all this blows over and he's back in the game again, he doesn't have to stay married.

"How's jail life treating you? You a hardened criminal yet?"

"Susan," Michael jumps up. "Please, tell me you came to bail me out. I have to go to the bathroom so bad my eyes are starting to cross, but there's no way I'm using that thing."

"I came to apologize. You're right. You were right about everything. I've been a rotten, cold-hearted –."

"Don't say it, Susan. Don't you dare say it!"

She chuckles. "I've been thinking of your god-awful proposal – my clocks almost done ticking, as you put it. And I realized, as offensive as it sounds, it's true. You were offering me the very thing I want, no more and no less. And I still shoved it down your throat. We both want something and neither one of us has the time to wait around for it. Besides, my reputation has been so soiled, any smart man would keep his distance."

"So you're saying I'm not a smart man?"

"No, you're a desperate man, as I'm a desperate woman. You want to keep your job and become the next Marx and make millions. I want to give birth to and raise the next President of the United States."

"So what are you saying, Susan. We getting married or not?"

"Yes," she exhales sharply.

"Living arrangements?"

"You'll live with me. Daddy's already taken care of the mortgage, as you know."

"Oh, thank God, cause I don't have rent this month. Something about a 50,000 dollar ring and a million dollar deal fallen through. Wonderful talk, Susan. Don't mean to cut you off, but I really need to go."

XXX

Michael stares at his reflection as he readies for his meeting with Marx. Even though Michael and Susan eloped within two days, and they spent the rest of the day sitting for interviews, hand in hand, discussing that the implications of the article were false, as they are, in fact, newlyweds and deeply in love, Marx kept Michael suspended without pay the full two weeks. In the meantime, he'd been getting by on half the money made for the interviews and a few sold items from his former condo.

"Happy to be going back to work?" Susan asks him, straightening his tie.

He grunts a reply, when, in fact, he has mixed emotions. Does marriage really change a man or was his ego just that sorely bruised?

Upon entering the building, he is greeted with enthusiasm, "Nice to have you back," and, "Congrats on your marriage. Never knew you were the settling type of guy."

He feels the urge to scream at them, two-faced colleagues. He hasn't even gone back to The Cave these two weeks, feeling a brutal sense of betrayal. For years he's always had people surrounding him, greeting him enthusiastically as he entered the doors. Taking, taking, taking the drinks he bought. But when he's in need, when he needs money, when he'd like a drink bought for him, there's not one volunteering. Susan was the only one to buy his drinks when they went to The Cave to celebrate their wedding night. A woman buying *him* drinks. How did he fall so far and so fast?

Marx's niece no longer looks so beautiful to him, though she greets him with a big smile. He enters the doors. Marx is standing beside the bar, smile on his face, holding a drink up to Michael.

"Michael, when I think that you can't amaze me any more than you already have, you blow me out of the water, and prove to me that I don't have to doubt you. I can't believe you pulled this off. So how's married life treating you?"

"Why did you keep me suspended for the full two weeks without pay even though I closed my end of the deal?"

"Why, to let the publicity die down, of course. It's all in the past now. We can start fresh."

"I read that the Kutchners decided to buy the place after all."

"You did, huh? Yea, I cleared it up with them, told them it was all a big misunderstanding. Dropped the price down a little bit. They wanted to extend their apologies to you."

"And the commission?"

There's an awkward silence.

"It was closed on Monday, Michael, by me. You'll find it in the employee handbook. Suspension no pay means no commission either. Your mistake could have cost this company quite a bit of money. No sweat, Michael. You keep proving yourself, you'll have another opportunity in no time. Lesson learned."

Michael stands up abruptly. "You're right. Lesson learned. I'm putting in my two week notice. You'll have the written statement tomorrow."

"You see, Michael, this is what got you into trouble the first time. You're a great associate, but you're impulsive. You don't think before you act."

"And that's where you're wrong. I had two weeks to think about why your associates never advance into anything more. A man can only go as far as the man above him allows. You want the big sales, but you don't want to share the proceeds. Your wealth and power came, not in your successes, but in using the successes of others. Tell me, how many suckers have you made promises of partnership, then taken the credit for all their hard work? I was just another stupid ambitious schmuck that fell for it."

"No one comes into my office and talks to me like that. Are you forgetting who I am? I could have made you rich beyond your wildest dreams."

His niece runs into the room as something begins beeping rapidly. "Uncle Marx, your blood pressure. Now the doctor warned you about this. Hurry up, swallow these. You may leave now," she tells Michael, barely glancing at him as she tries to calm her Uncle. Just a man. An old one. We all have our downfall at one time or another. Money will never make him young again, nor will it save him a golden path to the beyond.

XXX

"No, Michael, this wasn't part of the bargain. We got married so you could keep your job and make millions, not quit and be unemployed."

"So you did marry me for the money?"

"That is not what I said. I've had millions, Michael. It doesn't make you happier. But I do want to live comfortably and be married to a man who can pull his own weight."

"Coming from the woman who wants to be a stay-at-home Mom when you're not even a mom yet. Daddy's not always going to support you and who do you think is?"

"That's low, Michael. Real friggin' low."

"Right back at you, baby. Yours was just as low. You have no faith in me. I'm not a bum and I'm nothing like your former husband."

"I just can't believe you didn't talk to me about this first. We're supposed to be in this together."

"Yeah, and what would you have told me, Susan? The same thing you just told me now. The man screwed me out of my million dollar commission, suspended me no pay for two weeks. No security. I'm a man, Susan. I got my pride. You should understand that."

"I do understand it. Been there, done that, Michael. The more pride you have, the harsher lesson you have to learn. Pride has nothing to do with survival and supporting a family. You're about to have a child. It's not about you anymore. It's about him . . . or her."

"Oh my God, I hate being married. Aren't wives supposed to be supportive or something?"

"I told you I'm so far past supporting a man while he pursues his dreams."

"No, but you're so much for having a man support you while you pursue yours, right? What do you want from me, Susan?"

"I want you to think about the baby."

"There is no baby, you got that? Not yet. And maybe there won't be if this is how it's going to be. I've got what it takes to run my own business without having to kiss ass to some greedy lonely old man. I'm doing it regardless of what you have to say about it. I never once agreed to give up my dreams, my pride, my dignity to *you.*"

CHAPTER 9
2 YEARS LATER

"Do you like nature? The stars, the moon, sunrises and sunsets? Look at this. Skylight. You're not going to find one of these in this area. Isn't it great?"

"It's nice. This place is great, but the asking price just seems so high. I mean, all the other houses in the area average about 50,000 less." God damn he hated people that did their research.

"That's because all the other houses in the area aren't this house. Do you want mediocre, or do you want to excel? You don't have to have what the Jones have. You can have better. I mean, look at this terrace. Wrap around porch. Cathedral ceilings. Tell ya what? I see you in this place and it fits you. It belongs to you. I'll knock off two grand from the asking price and throw in the furnishings and blinds. How's that sound?"

"I'll think about it."

Michael's cell phone goes off while he's at The Cave, half-way to oblivion. He goes into the restroom for some quiet.

"Yea?"

"Did you forget? It's William's first birthday."

"Why are you whispering?"

"He shouldn't have to hear this? Why aren't you home? I can't wait much longer. He's getting tired. Where are you?"

"I'm – uh - finishing up a closing on a house."

"At 8 at night? Michael, you promised you'd be here. There's only one first birthday. Daddy's here. And Terry."

"This is how the business goes, baby. You want William to have his little toys and cake, then Daddy's gotta make the money."

"Michael. Michael, where are you? I'm counting to three, and then I'm coming in!" a girl's voice carries through the bathroom walls. He tries to cover up the speaker, but it's too late.

"You're drinking again, aren't you? You're not closing on a house. You're out – ."

"3, I'm coming innnn," she sings.

Thinking quickly, Michael grabs a handful of bathroom towels and crinkles them. "Susan . . . phone cutting . . . home . . . soon. Love . . ." Click.

Michael shoves the phone in the same pocket as his wedding ring.

XXX

"I sold the house, Michael," Susan says to him. She looks more like 50 than 39.

"What?"

"I'm going to stay with Daddy for a while. Me and William."

"And me?"

"I want a divorce or a legal separation. I don't care."

"The money for the house?"

"It's gone, Michael. All gone. To pay off your debts, your *business* investments. Maybe one of your whores will let you stay with them."

"I'm sorry, Susan. I'm trying. I'm trying. I just need a little more time, then we'll have millions."

"It's been two years, Michael. You've sold only four houses. Whatever you've made is spent at the bar. You're a drunk . . . and a cheater."

"I promised that would never happen again. I meant it."

"Just like you meant it the past five times, Michael. You don't care about me. You don't care about your son. All you care about is making money, then spending it more quickly than you're making it. And that's why you can't sell these houses. You've got greed written all over you. We have two weeks before the new owners move in."

"Susan, don't do this. Where am I supposed to go?"

"Call your parents, Michael. If they're even still alive. It's over."

XXX

6 MONTHS LATER

Michael feels it's just another ordinary day until he finds the quarter. Bright and shiny. Heads up. He races toward it and laughs when he has it in his hands. His hands – cold, raw, bleeding. His back arched, weighted down by the belongings on his back. A small worn blanket. A wrinkled suit and tie, a few books he never returned to the library, and a couple cans of food he'd gotten at a food drive before winter set in.

"A quarter a cart. A quarter a cart," he mumbles to himself.

"Hey, you found my quarter," a gruff voice connected to a scruffy face calls to him.

"Finders keepers. A quarter a cart," Michael says, clenching the quarter tightly to his torso.

A moment of recognition passes between them, seeming so long ago, another place, another life. A flicker of rivalry passes quickly through the other mans' eyes.

"Life has a funny way about it." The man laughs.

Michael follows suit. "Yes, I suppose it does."

"Nothing you can really do about it but laugh. If you don't laugh, you want to cry. You're not going to make it through winter dressed like that. I'll get you fixed up. I know all the right places. You hungry? You got food on you?"

"Little bit."

He grins a toothless grin. "Got any hard stuff on you."

"I wish," Michael says.

"Yea, me too. Hard stuff warms you up all nice and fuzzy, even on the coldest of nights. Got a hole in my pouch, see? Lost a bunch of change. Followed the trail back."

Michael fingers the quarter possessively. "I was going to get a cart with it. My back hurts."

"Carts no good this time of year. Snow and slush. Can't push the cart. Gets stuck. Those luggage bags you can drag behind you. Those are nice. Been looking for one of them for a while. Maybe find one in the spring. Get lots of things in the spring. People just throw things out. Take it all for granted. Haven't had a friend in a long time, though. Some die. Some get off the streets, return to the places and lifestyles they were runnin' from to begin with. Some move on to warmer places. Let's do inventory. See what we got. Better to work as a team. Like family. Hard bein' out here alone. People of the world hate us. Fear. Like we're contagious or something. Like we gonna bite their necks and make them homeless like us."

Michael laughs. It's the most he's laughed, genuinely laughed in – Oh, hell, what's the point in remembering. Sometimes he laughed with Susan. He laughed the first time William peed on her when she turned to retrieve a diaper. He used to laugh those times she threw her ridiculous fits. Kiss her until she shut up. They laughed a lot in the bedroom.

"So do we stick a thermometer in there to know when it's well-done?" he'd said as she progressed through her pregnancy. Those rare moments in life when he'd felt true joy. He feels it now and it warms him up.

"Ohhh, look at your spiffy suit and tie. Could get good money for this. 20 bucks maybe."

"It's not for sale. It's for when I get a job," Michael says.

"Looks like you haven't wore it for awhile."

"Not since I've been out here. I just can't seem to – I'm mad."

"I get it. I'm good and mad too. People hustling and bustling, going into cardiac arrest over being late for work just to hold on to the little bit of security they have, always worrying over what if . . . what if . . . never smile. Never laugh. Never sleep. Never rest. Never look at time and treasure it. Bad as this is, I don't want to go back."

"I was a millionaire once," Michael says.

"Now if that ain't bullshit, I don't know what bullshit is."

"It's true."

"I had a family once. Wife. Two kids. Worked as a Delivery boy for my one job, worked grave shift in a factory the other, trying to make ends meet. Wife kept telling me, something's wrong with the furnace. Something's wrong. Everyone's tired all the time. Kept telling her when I found the time, I'd look into it. Carbon monoxide. Took both the kids one night when I was away at work. Big crack in the exhaust pipe. Leaking all those fumes. Cold night that night. Record cold. Furnace had been running all night. My wife didn't die that night, but there wasn't much left to her. Tried to help her. Tried to fix her. Tried to get the medicine and the treatment. A desperate man loses all pride and dignity and inhibitions. Did everything I could. Wound up on the streets. She died. Maybe her heart could have kept pumping even though her head weren't right, but her heart was broken too."

Somber silence passes as both men reminisce a life that no longer belongs to them.

"Hey, my shoes. You're wearing my shoes! In the vision, those shoes were on my feet," Michael says excitedly.

"Vision hah? So in this vision, what did you trade me for these shoes? Been with me for a long time." The man stares enviously at Michael's worn un-polished business shoes.

Within minutes, without speaking, they make their transaction. Michael stares happily at his feet with the brown broken loafers, big toe sticking out at the end. He only had to feel the desperate fear of the vision coming true for two years. Now he feels content that he hadn't had to wait 10 years to live the destiny he never imagined would be his, just as he'd been told.

PAUL

CHAPTER 10

Dr. Paul Stevens closes the notebook on Michael's case-study, wrought with a sudden restlessness. Almost three years have passed since he first began his experimentation. He did well, but feels neither pride in his accomplishments, nor relief in its completion. Michael wasn't the only one confined in his self-created box.

The black briefcase lay on the floor next to his sofa, untouched. He hasn't even opened it to see what a million dollars in cash looks like. Up to this point, he's held no interest in the money. Money is one of the most powerful means to one's self destruction. A material object whose temptation has broken many with its conditions.

Paul looks around his small home of 15 years, the only change made in these many years was the lost presence of his cat. Everything else remains the same. Once his place of comfort, his safe and secure home, once bringing him an abundance of relief after a long day, he suddenly feels stifled, suffocated. This is his box, his place of confinement, his illusion of protection and safety when it has only kept him bound. Filled with a type of gnawing nagging frustration, he throws on his black cloak and leaves this place of unrest.

It is pouring outside and he buckles his coat more tightly around him. Why hadn't even ever gotten a car? Because he'd never traveled anywhere that his legs could not take him. A car would have been an unnecessary expense, but now he wishes he had one he could get behind the wheel and drive. And maybe just keep driving. And never look back.

He walks in the rain for a long time, feeling downcast and miserable, as somber as the sky. He doesn't know how long he's been walking or even the destination he's walked to, but he stops at a place featuring a blinking neon light that reads "Stop-on-by". So he does. It is a little bar, completely vacant except for the middle-aged bored bartender reading a magazine. She reminds him of a librarian as she peaks up at him from her reading spectacles. Her look almost tells she resents his coming.

"You're not closing, are you?"

"Not for another five hours." She goes back to reading.

"Can I have a drink?"

She snaps the magazine shut. "What do you want?"

"Your sign seemed so inviting." *The company is not,* he thinks. "Do you serve food here?"

"Popcorn," she gestures her head to the left end of the bar.

He doesn't bother asking her how fresh it is. "A beer then. Whatever you have on tap." He thinks that a steak and a bottle of expensive red wine would be nice, and then wonders where such a thought had come from. The only steak he knows is the Salisbury steak that is microwaved, and his experience with wine comes from a box. He never did have expensive tastes, which is probably why money never had much means to him other than the barest of living expenses. Hell, he doesn't even have cable.

Paul grabs himself a bowl of stale popcorn and sits in silence, sipping his beer, and munching on popcorn. She ignores him completely.

"Would you mind so much turning on the TV for the six o'clock news?"

She tosses him the remote without even looking up at him. His mood is falling swiftly from frustration to misery to plain depression. He puts on the news and stares toward the TV without looking at it.

"We are here live to confirm suspicions of Mr. Whitman's affair with his secretary, Miss Claire Dellafar."

Paul's internal inspection is disrupted and he focuses abruptly on the screen. A news anchor woman is standing outside a Starbucks. The door opens and the screen fills with a close-up of Claire Dellafar, *his* Claire. She is carrying a tray of coffees. "Miss Dellafar. Miss Dellafar. May we speak with you?" She keeps walking and the anchor woman chases after her. "Miss Dellafar. Just one moment of your time. You have been doing a lot of personal favors for Mr. Whitman and rumor has it –."

"I am Mr. Whitman's secretary. I get paid to do a lot of personal favors."

"You've been seen frequenting his home in the middle of the night in a secretive manner. Do you deny this?"

"Not very secretive if I've been seen going through the gate and walking through the front door."

"You have a key. You let yourself in. That seems a little too personal."

"Which makes it none of your business."

"It is my job to make it my business."

"So who am I supposed to be sleeping with? Bill or John Whitman?" Claire asks.

"So you're confirming that you're having an affair with one of them?"

"Maybe both of them," she smirks.

"So you're not denying this affair, Miss Dellafar. It is Miss, correct?"

"Nor am I confirming it. Good day," and she walks briskly away.

"I know her! I know her!" Paul yells, the silence magnifying his excited outburst. "Once upon a time I was the love of her life. She wanted to get married. She wanted to marry me!"

"Ha, in your dreams," the bartender says while glancing at the screen.

His exhilaration cruelly stolen from him, he reaches across the bar and steals her book, so that she finally looks at him. "What is your problem? You've got an attitude the size of Mount Everest and that's probably why I'm the only poor ignorant soul that's here. And I won't be coming back. Then you can sit here all alone actually wondering why no one is very nice to you and why you're alone to begin with."

"Well that was very rude."

"Welcome to the club. Have a good life." He tosses the book back to her and walks out the door.

6:00 am the next morning, like a regular day of work, Paul heads out the door. This time, instead of turning right, he turns left toward his driveway where his brand new registered and insured Buick awaits him. He feels like Christmas. In the trunk is Michael's engraved black briefcase, and in the back seat only one box containing his books and files. In the passenger seat are the printed directions to his next destination. Texas. Paul had humbled Michael and shown him a different type of existence, but it was Michael who taught Paul to go after what you want, less you want to remain the inconspicuous old man sitting in the back of the bar room that no one ever pays any attention to.

XXX

Parked in the Starbucks parking lot 27 hours later, Paul feels the old set of nerves that has served to hinder him from having any meaningful conversation with the opposite sex. He gets out of the car, straightens his two-day worn suit and tie, and rubs the scruff that grew on his face during the long drive. His bones creak and crack. He's exhausted, but he couldn't waste any time, so he drove straight-through, only stopping for gas, a snack, and a bathroom break.

On second thought, he probably should have reserved a room at a hotel, gotten cleaned up, a good night's sleep, and come back here the following morning. Only now are the doubts creeping in, whereas he'd been so sure when he'd originally set out. Perhaps he should have planned this better and not set out on such an impulse. He could have booked an apartment or a room online, but that would have taken probably three days for all payments to clear.

Actually, what the heck is he thinking? Moving half-way across the country on a whim, because of a picture he'd seen on TV? What is he expecting? To just walk up to her and –.

Claire exits the Starbucks and he is struck silent by her beauty, so very close to him, yet so many years had gone by. She looks so different from the 19 year old Claire he'd known, but even more beautiful, if that's possible. Age had only matured her. Her once long blonde straight hair is now layered around her face to mid-back. She was model-thin when younger, but now both her face and body have more substance, more curve, declaring to all that she is now a woman, no longer a girl experiencing her first time away from home.

"May I help you carry your coffee?" he says, attempting a deep resonant sound, but coming out a little on the squeaky side.

"Are you talking to me?" she says. He nods, gulps. She frowns, "I only have one coffee." They are standing at a distance of no less than 25 feet and are almost yelling toward one another. He steps closer, a few feet from his car. "Claire? Claire Dellafar?"

"Yes?"

He inches closer, trying to appear casual, and not the jumbled mess of nerves he actually is. He suddenly realizes what an ass he's going to feel like if she doesn't recognize him. If she keeps looking at him with confusion and a tense, "Do I know you?"

"Oh my God, Paul Stevens, can it be true? Is that my Paul Stevens all growed up?"

"It is I," he grins. "Claire, what a pleasant surprise. I never thought you could become so pretty."

"What?"

"I mean, I meant, you were so beautiful before, I – uh – didn't think it possible for you to grow any more beautiful. I'm afraid I haven't grown into my good looks yet."

"Oh, Paul, you were never a good looking guy." She smiles at him. "What are you doing here? Let me get a good look at you."

"Well, I –uh – I guess I just moved here. Yea, I'm a new resident of the state of Texas."

"You're not kidding," she says, gesturing toward the box of files in his car.

"I saw you on TV," Paul says proudly, though instantly regrets his words.

"But that was only a couple -." She gasps. "Paul Stevens, did you move all the way out here just to see me?" she says laughingly.

"What? No – I –."

She laughs, "Oh my God, you did. You still got your boxes in the car. Your clothes are worn. Your face." She touches his cheek. "I don't think I've ever seen you with anything more than a 5 o'clock shadow, and this looks to be about three days old."

He looks properly embarrassed times one hundred. What was he thinking? That she wouldn't notice? That she would think he just happened to be at that particular Starbucks at that particular time and run into her?

"Claire, do you want to grab a cup of coffee?"

She looks at the coffee in her hand.

"What I mean is, can I grab a cup of coffee and you and I can sit down and drink it together and catch up?"

"Well, 9:30 in the morning, I'm not exactly on my lunch break. But it's not every day I run into a man who moves all the way to Texas in order to have a cup of coffee with me."

"Claire, it's not like that. I –."

"Oh come now, Paul, don't ruin it for me. It's probably the most romantic gesture I've ever seen."

"So you want to go inside?"

"Actually, I've got a lot of attention around here as of late, what with me having an affair with the former and present Mr. Whitman and all. Let's go somewhere a little more discreet."

They find a small coffee shop, run by a couple kids.

"So, where's Mr. Dellafar?" Paul says, leaning back as casually as he can manage.

She giggles at him. "You still suck at this, Paul. Normal people say, 'So, are you married? Got boyfriend? Kids? Where you working now? Are you happy?' Dellafar, as you know, Mr. Stevens, is my maiden name. If I were married, it wouldn't be Dellafar anymore, now would it?"

"It's possible. There are men that take the woman's last name, especially if that woman wears the pants."

"I'm wearing a skirt, Paul."

"I noticed," he says instantly without thought, punctuated by a grin.

"Well, there you go. You see what happens when you let your body do the talking and not your brain?"

"It must be the liquor talking that I snuck into our coffee."

"Is that a joke, Paul?" she laughs. "Paul with a sense of humor. I don't know this Paul. What happened to my little dweeby Paul that was so serious about the world and had to have every moment of his day carefully planned out to the minute?"

"He grew bored with himself. Decided to try something else out for size."

"So what about you? Any marriage or kids or serious relationships in your life, recent, or past?"

"You first?"

"Never got married. No kids. Lots of boys that are friends, but no man."

"Why not?"

"Oh, I don't know. I once had this fairy tale of meeting my fairy tale prince charming and getting married and having kids and living happily ever after."

"Dare I ask what happened?"

"That, I think, is something you can figure out yourself." He notes a tinge of sadness in her deep blue eyes before she looks away.

"Me? We were so young, Claire." He laughs.

"What?"

"I don't know. I always imagined you getting married to a Ken, living in your dream house, with a bunch of little blonde hair blue eyed babies pitter-pattering across the marble floors. I never imagined that you would actually be happy with me. I mean, I'd make ugly babies."

"Sometimes I think you are your own worst critic."

"I had Missy for almost 12 years. She was my companion. I miss her so much sometimes," Paul says somberly.

"What happened to her?"

"She died. Don't know how it happened. She stopped eating and then within days I come home from work and find her dead on the bed. I buried her in the back yard."

Claire chokes on her coffee. "You buried your wife in your back yard?"

"No, Missy was my cat. Did I not say that?"

"Your cat? You're telling me the most serious relationship you've had after me in all these years was with a cat?"

"Missy was the greatest companion a man could find. I lost her three years ago. I've thought numerous times of getting another cat, but I can't do it. I'm just still so loyal to her. I can't fathom replacing her."

"I'm jealous," she says.

"Why?"

"Because after me you didn't hesitate to replace me with another pussy."

"Well, she didn't have your blonde hair or blue eyes, but she purred when I touched her."

"Paul Stevens!" she chastises. "Now this is definitely not the Paul I remember. Looks like you're growing into your charm after all. Always knew you had it in you." she winks.

He clears his throat, becoming serious. "I do owe you an apology, Claire. I've thought a hundred times about wishing I could have said I was sorry, but then I'd think a hundred more times that I was probably just a passing fancy and you'd laugh at me. I guess I became quite the jerk, hah?"

"It's not your fault, Paul. I could be so selfish at times, wanting your attention when you were so distraught over what had happened. I just didn't give you enough time, thinking that you'd just bounce back quickly from something like that with the right kind of person around. Guess I wasn't the right kind of person and I didn't have the patients. Besides, it was me who walked away."

"But I didn't go after you."

She smiles a sad smile. "No, you didn't. Better late than never, I suppose. Listen, Paul, I gotta get back to work. Do you have a place to stay? I'd hate to have you spending all your money on a hotel room when I've got a decent-sized apartment, and I'm not even home most nights, so I think you could be comfortable. At least give you some time to get acquainted with the area and get set up with a place you like."

"I wouldn't want to impose –."

"Not at all. You're an old friend."

"Well, not *that* old." He chuckles, while feeling slightly affronted at her obvious implication of their only being friends.

CHAPTER 11

Paul likes the place. It is definitely Claire, her personal touch down to the sunflower theme in the kitchen, the flower portraits hanging on the walls, the lavender curtains, and the porcelain trinkets strewn throughout the house. In fact, he feels right at home, even her familiar scent bringing him back 17 years ago when she decorated his dorm room. He used to complain about her trinkets lining his bookshelves, but he'd missed them once they were gone. The only area he hasn't seen is her bedroom, feeling he'd be intruding on her little sanctuary. He still feels pretty baffled at these smooth turn of events. He'd purposely made this trip without any expectations except for a great hope that he'd just be able to see her one more time and apologize. Within 45 minutes of her company, she'd handed him her only key to her apartment and told him to make himself at home, and she'd be back between 5 and 6.

He doesn't want to make himself too much at home, so decides to leave his clothes in the travel bag, books in the car, and hang his suits in the backseat of the car. Despite what she said about his not being an imposition, he can't help but feel that her invitation was more out of kindness and generosity, but temporary all the same. The last thing he wants to do is wear out his welcome.

He takes a quick shower and trims his face, trying to analyze her comments on whether she liked the scruffy look better or not. He takes a quick peak in her kitchen cupboards and refrigerator and then heads out. A nap probably would have been good for him, but he's got other plans at the moment. He talks to a passer-byer about the closest dry-cleaner, a grocery store, and a liquor store, and still has two hours to spare before she comes home. He puts away the grocery items and then sits down to the paper, grudgingly circling rooms and places for rent. Something modest for now. Even though he has the money to buy a really nice place, cash, he'd hate to buy a place and have Claire not like it.

When Claire arrives at 5:22, almost 5:23, he stops pacing the floors and meets her at the door with two glasses of red wine.

"Oh, wow, what a . . . nice surprise. You're so sweet." She pecks him on the cheek.

"I didn't know if you drank wine, and if you did drink wine, what kind you liked, so I just got a bunch of different kinds. Unless you still like beer. I got some of that too. Or I know a lot of women like mixed drinks, so I picked up some vodka and orange juice. But I can also –."

"Paul, you're stuttering and sweating profusely. If I didn't know any better, I'd think you were a virgin school boy taking a girl out on their first date."

"No, I'm not – this isn't – I just wanted to show you how grateful I am for you being so kind."

"You're welcome. And yes, red wine is fine."

"I didn't know where you wanted me to put the rest of the stuff, so I just put them on the kitchen counter."

She follows him into the kitchen as he frets over doing right or doing wrong and how inept he feels at this whole thing.

"Oh," she says, stopping upon seeing the steak, garden vegetables, and baked potato servings on the table.

"You made dinner." Her enthusiasm is gone, however, and there's a note of . . . something in her voice. Disappointment? Discomfort? He didn't think she might be a vegetarian. Stupid, stupid, stu –."

"I'm sorry, Paul. I should have told you sooner. I just didn't expect – I can't stay. I have other business that I need to take care of."

"Of course you do. I'm so sorry I didn't think of it. How thoughtless of me."

"This is far from thoughtless of you, Paul. I really appreciate your doing this and it's really sweet, but I just have other engagements I need to attend to that I can't cancel. I need to get ready. Please, sit down. Eat. Don't let me keep you from enjoying your meal. You worked hard on this."

But Paul has suddenly lost his appetite. He's embarrassed and feels like a fool. Why didn't he think that she possibly had another life, being that she'd been living her life without him in it for 17 years?

He pretends to eat so as not to make her feel worse while she moves throughout the house, the bedroom, the bathroom, getting ready. The music he'd turned on low is now depressing and he turns it off. She returns to the kitchen, dressed up in a fitting black dress, her hair done, and makeup on. She looks amazing, but he doesn't know if he should comment on it. After all, it's someone else she's looking amazing for. He is just an old friend.

XXX

She returns at 9:00 at night. Happy and tipsy. He noticed that no one had walked her to the door or given her a good night kiss. But then again, she drove herself. He's lounging on the plush flower-print pink and crème sofa, flipping through the cable channels, pretending to be interested in whatever he's watching. He's on his fourth glass of wine, but she doesn't know that.

"Hey," she says as she walks through the door.

"Hey, how'd it go?"

"Good, really good. Watcha drinking?"

"Oh, I'm watching the Discovery Channel. Sometimes they have really good things on here. You learn a lot."

She looks at him funny. "I'm going to have a beer. Do you want one?"

He looks at his wine glass, ¾'s full. "Yes, let me get it for you." He starts to get up.

"No, no. You keep relaxing. I'll get it. How was dinner?" she calls from the kitchen.

"Oh, it was good." He'd hardly eaten it. "I wrapped up your plate for you to eat, whenever." His stomach rumbles in hunger.

"I'm sorry to have missed it. It looked and smelled really good. It's been a long time since a guy has cooked for me."

"What did you have?"

"Oh, it was some Italian restaurant. Spaghetti and cheap wine. It was okay." She returns with the beer.

"And the company?"

She gives him another odd look that he can't decipher.

"I'm sorry. That's probably none of my business."

"This is just all so sudden, so unexpected. If I had known you were coming, I'd be a better host, but – I can't break plans I already made."

"No, of course not. You don't owe me anything, Claire."

"But you came all the way down here to see me and – ."

"No, no, no, that was just a benefit. I've got business here."

"And what kind of business is that?"

"Oh, you know, treating people, research, stuff like that."

"So you succeeded in becoming a doctor?"

He nods his head rigidly. "I had my own practice for 12 years. I decided I'm better fit for research than clinical stuff, so I closed my clinic and started my research."

"And what research led you here?" She lights a cigarette. He hates cigarettes.

"Oh, a client. Hey, can I have one of those?"

"You smoke?"

"No, it's more social, recreational. When I'm drinking beer." She hands him her lit cigarette. He inhales and coughs up a storm.

"Paul, Paul, Paul, you're not trying to impress me, are you?"

"What do you mean?"

"Guys will go through great lengths to impress a woman. I prefer honesty."

"Me too. I just got a tickle in there or something." He coughs again for affect. "It's winter in New York, you know. Lot different down here. Perhaps the change in environment is affecting me."

"Hmmm," she says, smirking. "My beer's almost gone. You ready for another?"

His is 2/3rd's full. "Yea. They go fast when you're having fun."

As she retrieves more beer, he swallows his as fast as he can.

"So how did you become the Whitman's personal secretary? You didn't continue to pursue Psychology?"

"I dropped out, Paul. I left you, dropped out of school, and moved half-way across the world."

"Claire, I didn't – it was a big campus. I just thought –."

"Oh, come on. You can't take all the credit. Yes, I was heart-broken, but you were brilliant in Psychology and I was having a hard time with it, grasping the material, the friggin' Master's thesis? I was born and bred in Texas. Went to New York for a change of scenery. Mom got sick."

"I didn't know. Why didn't you ever tell me?"

"You were grieving over your mom's death and I was trying to get you through it. Bringing up my mom would have, you know, triggered more of your grief."

Sympathy or the alcohol or something else causes him to reach out for her, to put his arms around her. "I was so selfish then. I could only focus on my own agony. Oh Claire, what happened? Is she okay?"

"Mom died. The cancer took her. There was nothing I could do but encourage her that there's another life out there and she doesn't have to be afraid. She was in so much pain. She was suffering." A tear departs from her eye and runs down her cheek. That's the end for him. He begins to kiss her. Absorbs her tears through his lips. "Claire, I'm so sorry. I'm so so sorry. You loved her. I remember you speaking of her. And you loved her so much."

"I did. I did," she cries. And then she starts returning his kisses with fervor. "I loved her so much."

"And I wasn't there for you. You had to grieve alone," he keeps kissing her.

"It was so hard, Paul. It was so hard. I can't tell you how many times I picked up the phone to call you. You were my best friend, my only friend."

"I'm sorry I wasn't there for you."

"No, you weren't. You weren't. And I resented you for that for a long time."

"I'm so sorry, Claire. I'm so sorry I've been such a disappointment. I'm so sorry I've been so selfish."

"Make love to me, Paul. Make love to me. Just like it used to be."

"When I was your first?"

"When you were my first."

"And I'll be your last?"

"You'll be my last."

He begins kissing her neck and attempting to clumsily unbutton her shirt. As he struggles, he says, "It's been a long time for me, Claire."

And then her phone rings.

"I'm sorry, Paul, I have to – Hello? . . . Yes, I'll be right over. Bye."

She slowly closes the phone. "I have to go," she says.

"Now?"

"Yes, he needs me. I'm so sorry. There's blankets in the closet. You can sleep on the couch, or take my bed. I probably won't be back until early morning or so. I don't know. It's hard to say. Goodnight, Paul." Paul watches as she grabs her coat and scurries out the door 11 at night. Then the alcohol he consumed turns his stomach.

XXX

Paul doesn't see her again until 5:17 the following evening. He did make dinner, but he doesn't have it displayed on the table, just in case. Which is a good thing, because at 5:10 her landline phone rang and a message was left. "Hey babe. It's John. Can't get ahold of you on your cell-phone. I'm assuming it died. I don't know how many times I have to remind you to charge that thing. Chuckle. Little change in plans. I need you to meet me at the B B Que at 6:00. Hope it's not too short notice."

Claire returns, looking exhausted. She listens to the message and groans. She murmurs, "They're killing me. They're god damn killing me. The B B Que is 40 minutes away. Like I'm the fairy godmother and can just wave a wand and change my clothes into a beautiful ball gown and ride a magic carpet." Her head droops momentarily into her hands.

Paul chuckles awkwardly. "You don't have to go, Claire. You're a free woman and can say no."

"Yes, I do have to go. There's a lot you don't know, Paul."

"Then why don't you tell me."

"I can't."

"Why?"

"Because I can't, Paul. Jesus, you're acting like we're married. You've been here two days."

"You're right, Claire. You're absolutely right. I don't know why I'm acting this way. Being way out of my element, maybe. This has all been such a big change, and I'm so grateful for your generosity, and I'm just screwing it up. I'll be checking out some places this evening. I'll get out of your hair as soon as I can," he says awkwardly.

"I'm sorry, Paul, I'm sorry. You're not acting that way. I'm just . . . tired. He's been keeping me up all night. Then to work all day. Then this. Don't go. Not yet. We've hardly had time to catch up on anything. And to be honest with you, I like the idea of you being here and me coming home. If I could just *stay* home for once."

Paul watches as she opens the cupboard and drinks a shot of 5-hour energy. In 10 minutes, she exits the bedroom wearing a cow-girl get-up. She looks sexy as all get-out, down to the high-heeled cow-girl boots. He wants to grab hold of her. He wants to resume where they'd left off last night, even if he had been quite drunk. He can't get the smell of her out of his head. Perhaps she had been a little drunk too and now has regrets. The vulnerable moment combined with alcohol and convenient company. Perhaps he should be more careful not to pressure her during those vulnerable moments. Take a step back. Give her space. Let her live her life without being an additional burden. Paul is thinking of these things as she walks out the door.

An hour later he hears the ringing of her cellphone. It keeps ringing, only stopping to pause for voicemail. After the fourth call, he begins his search for the phone, which leads him to her bedroom. He opens the bedroom door and looks in, feeling like an intruder, even though the night prior she had offered him her bed. The ringing is coming from the closet. He opens the closet and takes a shocked step back.

She's got a full-wardrobe that can't cost less than 10,000 dollars, if not 50,000 dollars, not being a good judge on designer female clothes. It is the only place in the house that doesn't say Claire. Claire was never one to care about designer clothes or fashion statements. At least she hadn't been.

The phone keeps ringing. Fifth call. Sixth call. Hesitantly he presses the button to listen to the voicemail, telling himself if the person keeps calling it must be something very important. "Claire. Cough. This is Bill. I need – cough, cough, cough – you to stay with me tonight. Please, Claire, please answer your phone."

Paul gets on the internet on the phone. Leave it to Claire to not password-protect anything. She always had an issue with locking things. She'd say, "If I have to protect my stuff or lock my doors, then I'm not living in the right place, am I?" He looks up the B B Que and 45 minutes later he arrives.

The place is packed with loud music playing. His research revealed that Whitman owns the B B Que, or at least the majority of the stocks of the franchise. He walks up to one of the staff members. "I'm looking for Claire Dellafar. Or John Whitman."

"And your business?"

"An important message from Bill Whitman. I need to see them right away."

"He's in the VIP suite. That door over there to the left."

Paul doesn't think to knock. It is a public place after all, but instantly regrets not doing so, when he opens the door and finds John Whitman sprawled out on the couch, Claire's cow-girl boots kicked up in the air on top of him. He hurriedly closes the door. So it wasn't just a rumor. Claire had called it business. That did look far too personal, as the anchor woman had speculated. None of his business, though he can't help but feel hurt over it. Not to mention he'd never foreseen sweet love-and-family-and-happily-ever-after Claire becoming some rich man's mistress . . . or two? He leaves the restaurant and decides to just leave her phone and a message in her vehicle.

As he opens her driver's side door, Claire almost tumbles out.

"Claire, I just saw you – What're you doing in here? Are you okay?"

"What? Yeah, just taking a little snooze. Paul? Paul, what in God's name are you doing here? Are you following me? What were you going to do in my car?"

"No, no, not like that. You left your cellphone at the house. It kept ringing and ringing, so I thought it must be important, so I was just going to leave a note and your phone in the car so that you could get your message."

She listens to the message, then hurriedly calls John. "John, it's your dad. I gotta go. The keys are in the vehicle. I've got another ride. Bye."

She grabs some luggage from her trunk. "I always bring a change of clothes with me, just in case. You don't mind giving me a ride, right?"

"No, not at all."

She shoves one of her bags in the back seat and catches sight of some of his reading material in the box. "What exactly are you researching?"

"Oh, nothing too exciting," he says quickly.

"Is this all you brought with you from New York? I don't even see a computer. I know you must have had a computer."

"No, I just packed up and left. I might send for the rest of my stuff once I find a place."

"It just sounds so unlike you, Paul. To just pack up and leave. Were their problems?"

"No, I just got bored. Needed a change of scenery. Not the same Paul I once was."

"And your business down here too, right? Your secret client?"

"You know that's confidential information, Claire. Unless you're willing to share with me the predicament you're in."

"It's not a predicament. It's just work and it's confidential. And I get paid very well for keeping it that way."

"Doesn't seem too confidential with the media all over you."

"You can hardly ever believe anything you see on TV," she says tightly.

"And if I saw you with my own eyes?" he says, and knows instantly he shouldn't have said it.

"You are following me, spying on me. Oh my God, I'm not your secret client am I? Is that what this is about? Am I your case study?" she says nastily.

He sighs. "No, you're not. I'm sorry I said that. I went inside the restaurant, the VIP lounge, to give you your message, and saw that you were otherwise engaged, so then decided to go to your car and leave you the note."

"I don't like secrets, Paul."

"And I don't like being lied to. I know this isn't supposed to be any of my business, but you're sending me a lot of mixed messages, Claire. Last night you were practically begging me to make love to you, and maybe it was the alcohol, I don't know, but then tonight you're all over some other man."

She looks ready to smack him, but then she starts to cry, her head dropping in her hands. He pulls over to the side of the road and puts his arm around her, feeling always and ever the idiot.

"I wish I could tell you, Paul. I wish I could. It sounded so simple when I got into it and the money? How could I turn down that amount of money to do something that seemed so simple? It's just a temporary thing, but the money could support me for many many years. It seemed the right thing to do. Now that I'm in, there's no way out. I have to follow through."

"Claire, I want to show you something. Come here. Come with me." Paul gets out of the car and opens the trunk. Then he opens the briefcase with the million dollars cash for the first time. "You don't have to do whatever you're doing for the money. I have money. And there's going to be more, so much more. You won't have to worry about money. I'll- I'll take care of you. That is – uh – if you want me to."

But instead of the reaction he expected, Claire takes a step back from him, and stares at him as though she's seeing a monster. "I don't know who you are. I don't know who you are anymore? Why are you carrying that much money in your – Is that why you had to flee from New York so quickly?"

He takes a step toward her and she steps back. Another step and she backs up more. "It's not what you're thinking," he says quietly. "I just wanted to show you that I have the means to take care of you and that you don't have to do what you're doing if you don't want to."

"What's in there? Like a million dollars? Psychologists don't make that kind of money, especially in cash."

"Unless they're very rich clients that want to keep the nature of their business in complete confidence," he says.

She slowly nods her head, taking in this information, but still flinches from him when he tries to touch her. "Claire," he says quietly.

"Just drop me off at the gates of the Whitman's," she says coldly.

CHAPTER 12

Claire returns the following morning, a Saturday, strained, mascara smeared. She's been crying. "Is there coffee?"

"Of course," Paul says, concern in his voice. "Do you like it the same? Sit down. I'll get it for you." He leads her to the couch. She nods her head.

"Throw some alcohol in it?" she says.

He returns with a cup of coffee for both of them, Irish style, and sits down beside her on the couch.

"I'm so sorry about last night. I said some things I shouldn't have. Ever since coming here, I haven't been acting like myself."

"S'not that, Paul." She flicks on the TV. Bill Whitman's face appears. The reporter talks somberly about Bill Whitman's death around 2:30 in the morning, a peaceful and painless death.

Claire snorts. "Far from peaceful and painless. He fought it tooth and nail, cried, because he didn't want to go until he saw his first grandchild born. His breathing stopped before his heart did. They could not resuscitate him."

A shot shows Claire and John at his bedside, head down, shoulders shaking.

"Not my best shot," she says.

"So this is what you've been doing at night? Caring for him while he was dying?"

"Trying to keep him alive. He refused to sleep at night, too afraid it would take him in his sleep. So he'd have me sit up with him all night, keep him company, talk to him, and wake him up every time he dozed off. He knew he was going to die at night. He'd known it all along and did everything he could to keep that from happening. He did not die in his sleep. He died while awake."

"Here I didn't want to be an imposition and I feel like I've been nothing but. Just making things more difficult for you when I should be a friend for you, supporting you, and trusting that you knew what you were doing and that you were doing something out of the kindness of your heart, because that's Claire. Kind, selfless Claire. "

"There's still more I have to do, Paul. The funeral is going to be postponed for a week. In the meantime, I have to travel out for a week and take care of more business. Will you be here when I get back? The burial will take place on Sunday, and then there's to be a huge reception afterward at the Whitman's. It's going to be very difficult for me and I'd like it very much if you could come with me and be my diversion."

"Of course. Where are you going?"

"I can't tell you that, Paul," she says with regret in her voice. She looks at him, stares into his eyes for a time. "Paul, can you do me a favor?"

"Anything."

"Can you make love to me before I go?"

"Are you sure that's what you want?"

She nods, and wipes her nose with the back of her hand. "I know I'm a mess right now," she laughs sadly.

"Aren't we all?" Gently, he lays her down on the couch.

XXX

For the week Claire is gone, Paul follows the news updates. At first it was speculated that John could not handle his father's death, so took off somewhere to grieve. Three days into it, footage shows a flash shot of John and Claire getting on a private jet together. By Thursday there's unconfirmed information that John Whitman and Claire Dellafar eloped. Friday it is confirmed by the photographer that John Whitman did get married in a cathedral in Las Vegas. Now Paul understands why Claire had so badly wanted him to make love to her, knowing she was getting married. But if she really loved John, then why would she have another man make love to her before her wedding? She would have been faithful. John Whitman, now one of the richest men in the country. And he couldn't even give her a real wedding.

Paul's money doesn't even compare to the billions that are John's. Is this the fairy tale Claire had in mind? Money. It leaves a bitter taste in his mouth. Money, not love. She made her choice. Paul no longer wants to be the guy on the sidelines.

XXX

The following Sunday, Paul is pacing the floors of his new first-floor one bedroom apartment. His equipment will be arriving Monday so that he can get back to work. He's still so irate and bitter over the going-ons with Claire, but it is definitely not escaping his conscious that she specifically requested he be there for her during the funeral reception. As a diversion, she said. Would John, her new husband, not be there to console her, or would he be so caught up in his own grief that he would not be able to be there for precious Claire, just like Paul had been so caught up in his grief over his mother's suicide that he wasn't there for Claire while she endured her own mother's death. He does owe her that, no matter how upset he is with her right now.

Taken over by guilt and duty, Paul showers and shaves and puts on his freshly laundered suit and tie. For all he knows, Claire could have revoked his invitation as soon as she returned to her home and found him gone, without even a note. He still had to try, for Claire, just today. Then they would move on with their separate lives. Besides, there is one thing really nagging at him, non-stop, and he can't get his closure until he has his answer. He needs to know if she really loves John.

He arrives at the gate, behind 30 other cars. He provides his name at the box. A long hesitation follows. "Ah yes, there you are, Dr. Stevens. Enjoy the reception."

"Thank you."

Aside from New Year's Eve at Time Square in New York City, Paul has never seen so many people in one place at one time. Bill Whitman was very well-known man, or at least his riches were. Paul feels the bitterness creeping in the pit of his stomach again. He scans the room for her. It is she to find him.

"Paul. Paul?" she shouts from across the room. "You came. Thank God you came," she gives him an enthusiastic hug. "I didn't think you were coming. I mean, I came home and you were gone. No note. No nothing. You could have returned to New York for all I knew."

"I didn't think I was coming either. How are you?"

"I've had better days. I can't believe how many people showed up."

She looks stunning, her face aglow, wearing a fantastic black-fitting skirt and blouse outfit, but he has more important things in mind.

"Where's your husband? Why? Why didn't you tell me?"

Her head falls. "Not now, Paul. Please, I can't talk about this right now. There's too many people. It's complicated."

"You're right, Claire. I'm sorry. I owe you this. You don't owe me anything. I've been out of your life for 17 years. I don't know what I was –." His shoulders sag, a lifetime of insecurity.

"Jim! Dammit Jim! How long does it take to get me a drink?" a woman's loud ugly voice pierces the room and everyone looks to see where Jim is. He's a small-boned man with a balding head and pale complexion. His shoulders stoop as though he has the weight of the world on them. "What is this? You call this a drink? I told you a double. What'd you get me generic vodka? It's disgusting. I specifically told you Greygoose. Tastes like water with a bad aftertaste. Just give me your wallet. I'll get my own. You can't do anything right. You can never do anything right. I have to do everything. I should have listened to Daddy when he said you'd never be good enough for me. But you had so much potential, I thought. Now this guy is really gonna go somewhere and he's gonna take me with him."

"Quiet your voice, Shelly. Everyone can hear you."

"What? Be quiet like you? A manless voice. A coward's voice. Straighten your shoulders, Jim. Carry some pride on them. Do you have no dignity whatsoever? Guess that's the problem with being raised by a whore mother. Never taught you how to be a man. Oh my God, is this all you brought with you? Walking around with only a hundred dollars in your wallet. And I'm supposed to feel so secure?"

"I just bought you that 500 dollar dress," he says quietly. "I don't get paid again until next week. How much money do you need at a funeral reception?"

"Oh, yea, my great big executive. How many years have you been saying you're going to get that promotion? And here I am growing older every year scraping for money, barely surviving, while waiting for you to get your big break. You're pathetic, Jim. What boss is going to give you a promotion when you can't even talk like a man?"

He shuffles through his pocket. "Here. If you run out of money, use the business card. I'll make an advance against my pay."

"What, and I'm supposed to be grateful? I'll be grateful when you get that promotion. If I don't leave you before that."

Claire and Paul exchange a look. "Do you know him?"

"Yeah, that's Jim Peirsall. Assistant executive at one of the largest banks in Texas. That's Shelly Peirsall. Gold digger. Daddy, Shane Brickman, owns the bank. Jim's never going to get that promotion. Shane hates him, thinks he's not good enough for Shelly, which, as you heard, is the type of attitude Shelly picked up as well. But Shelly's a brute, so it works out for Daddy, because Jim gets the maintenance and Daddy gets the love. While Shelly's degrading Jim, she's not embarrassing Daddy."

"Does Jim have all the responsibility of an executive, like access to the vaults?"

"Oh yeah, Jim carries all the responsibilities of an executive. He just doesn't get the name and doesn't get the pay." Claire looks at him funny. "Paul, why would you ask me that question?"

"Claire. Claire, there you are. I've been looking all over for you." John kisses her on the cheek.

"John, this is Dr. Paul Stevens. Paul, this is John Whitman."

"Pleasure to meet you. So, this is the guy, is it?" John says with a tease in his voice.

"Stop that," Claire blushes, playfully smacking John.

"If you two want some private time together, I can –."

They both look at him and laugh and he feels like he's on the outside of some kind of inside joke.

"Come on, Paul, let's go have a drink and get some food," she takes his arm.

"You kids don't have too much fun," John winks at Claire and she blushes again. Perhaps Paul misjudged the situation. They look very much like a couple in love. He swallows the lump of regret that causes. Just friends, always and forever. Nothing more. And he can be happy with that. Just having her in his life is good enough.

XXX

Claire giggles and stumbles drunkenly, then giggles some more. It is late. The reception went on for hours and it's now beginning to thin out with more people leaving drunk than sober. The ways of the rich, though. They have their chauffeurs and their designated drivers. No DWI's for the rich.

"I want to go to your place, Paul. I want to see it."

"What? Why?"

"So that I know where you live and you can't just disappear on me again," she says seriously. "Come on," she tugs at his arm. "Take me to your home."

"But, what about John? Shouldn't you be with –?"

"John has other things going on. He doesn't care what I do in my personal time. Go to the car. I'll be right there."

Paul watches as she approaches John. They bid goodnight to those remaining and then walk arm in arm into a room before shutting the door. He goes to the car, wondering how long he is going to have to wait. She's hopping into the passenger seat less than five minutes later.

"Well, that was quick," he says. "No foreplay?"

She punches him in the arm with a laugh and tells him to drive, while resting her head on his shoulder.

Claire runs into the house, does a speed-through tour, then jumps on the couch before plopping down on her butt comfortably. "Get me a drink, Paul?"

He does and sits what he thinks is an appropriate distance away from her.

"Oh, don't be such a prude." She curls into his lap. They sit there for a while, Paul a little bit more tense than she as she is quite jittery on his lap and cannot quite sit still, making it very difficult for him not to react.

"I want in, Paul. I've thought about it ever since that night. I want in."

"You want in what?"

"I want to help you rob the bank. I know Jim well. He has access."

"Rob a bank? Are you – I told you I wasn't robbing banks."

"Then how else would you get that money. I didn't buy what you told me one second. Then the question you asked me about Jim having access. I put it together. It's okay. Your secret is safe with me. I'm going to be your accomplice. It'll be an adventure."

"Claire, I'm not robbing banks."

"Then what's your secret? Are you doing something illegal?"

"Well, I wouldn't say illegal, per say, but it's not something the board approves of."

"Well, whatever it is, I want in. You and me together, Paul. You can trust me with your secret. And I will trust you with mine."

JIM

CHAPTER 13

Jim tip-toes out of the room as quietly as he can and shuts the door, leaving it open just a little bit for the hall light to shine through. He moves to the den, removes some books on the bookshelf, and grabs the bottle of Jack Daniels. Not even bothering with a glass, he drinks it right out of the bottle. He loves the burn down his throat, the burn in his chest, the burn in his stomach. And the silence – oh, sweet silence.

Jim is what you would call a silent drunk. He never accepts a drink or drinks around others. On the surface, he appears to be completely abstinent. Guys who have met his wife will joke with him about how, if they were in his position, they'd wake up drunk every morning and go to bed drunk every night until the blessed day they developed liver cirrhosis and died. Jim chuckles somberly. What they don't know.

He waits until he's in the peace and quiet of his home, Shelly dead to the world, and probably ¾'s of the rest of the population too, then he pulls out his bottle of Jack and does not stop drinking it until it is gone. He drives two hours away and buys four cases, containing 12 bottles apiece, then hides them in the den. After a month or so, he drives two hours away to return the empties and get four more cases. 10 years. 10 years of his life with Shelly. 10 brutal years that have aged him 30 years. And 26 years with his mother before that. He married his mother and had never seen it coming 10 years ago. His mother was brutal, very emotionally abusive, and sometimes physically too, if she was drunk enough. He had 15 dad's growing up, all of them gone after his mother cleaned them out. None of them ever gave him a Christmas card or Birthday card thereafter. He doesn't know who his real father is. His mother never felt it necessary to give him those types of details.

He didn't know another life, didn't know another way, didn't know it to be any different on the other side of the fence, so he stayed with his mother until he met Shelly 10 years ago. Shelly, so beautiful. Shelly, so sweet. Way back when he felt like the luckiest man in the world to have Shelly love him. In the beginning, he'd sang to her, "Ooooh, Sheelly, ooooh Sheelly." He's a genius with numbers, so Shane, her father, had offered him more money to transfer to his company, do some training as an assistant executive, and be promoted to executive. At least those had been the terms. But they'd never been put on paper.

The day he met Shelly, she had walked into her father's office while they were shaking hands. "And who is this strapping man, Daddy?"

"This is Jim. Our new soon-to-be executive. He's just come over from Chase Bank."

"So nice to meet you, Jim. Welcome to the team. I'm sure you'll be a very very big asset for the company." She'd shaken his hand and left him with a crumpled piece of paper. It had her number on it. Three weeks later she talked him into a diamond ring that cost more than the one year lease on his townhouse. She tried to get him to just elope with her, but this is the one and only time he ever stood his ground with her and actually won the battle. He wanted her father's permission. He wanted a wedding.

That was the first Jim had seen of her infamous fits, though she would later say that she wasn't prone to such fits and must just love him that much. When her father had not given his permission, she had thrown herself on the floor like a child and screamed, "But Daddy, I want him. I love him. You can't keep him from me. You can't. I will go off and marry him and never see you again, Daddy. I will. I will. I want him Daddy. I want him. Please let me have him. Please, please, please. I'll scream Daddy. I'll scream at the top of my lungs so that people will think you're beating me. I'll do it Daddy. I will do it."

And grudgingly her father relented. Once the wedding was over, Daddy took Jim aside at the reception, and told him that if Jim ever hurt his daughter or left her, Jim could kiss any job that worked with numbers goodbye, because he would make sure Jim never got another job again.

Disturbed by this conversation, Jim decided that it was just the protective nature of a father to ensure that the man she loves doesn't hurt her. The turn of events came that very night when Jim attempted to make love to her and she said, "Ew, God, gross, don't touch me."

Once so sweet, she became the very image of his mother. 10 years of making an assistant executive wages, and Jim knew he'd never get that promotion. Daddy liked seeing him squirm and was making him pay every single day of the work week for marrying his daughter, but Jim couldn't leave. Return to Chase. Because Daddy had told him if he ever left the company, he'd cut off Shelly's significant allowance she received and all the loans he'd given Jim to help finance her.

Jim hates Sundays. Hates them. They are the worst day of the week. They are so bad that he spends all week dreading them. Sundays are the only days he has off of work, the days he has to spend all day with her until he can get her drunk enough to pass out. After 10 years of getting her drunk, it takes her longer and longer to pass out. Every Sunday he feels completely hopeless and helpless. Every Sunday he contemplates just ending this pathetic existence of his. Every Sunday he thinks of a new way he could kill himself if he actually had the guts to do so. If he was man enough, as Shelly always tells him. Maybe one Sunday he'll have enough Daniels in him to actually do it. Maybe tonight. He could hang himself from the beams in the den. He could shoot himself with the gun that is in the desk drawer. He could suffocate himself or drown himself or swallow a bunch of pills all at once. He could – .

Jim finishes the last of the Daniels and puts it in the box with all the rest of the empties. He stumbles upstairs to the bedroom, making sure not to touch her at all, and passes out. Just another normal ending to Sunday.

XXX

Jim returns home from work at 6:30. He barely has his shoes off when he hears her. Hell, the entire neighborhood could probably hear her. "It's about fucking time, Jim. I'm starving. I want lobster tail. That's what I want and you're going to give it to me, because you owe me. I can't believe you forgot our anniversary, Jim. I can't believe it. I'll never forgive you. I'll never forgive you for that."

"Shelly, it's not our anniversary, yet. That's not until three months away. See, I have it marked on the calendar."

"I'm talking about three years ago!" she screams. "Did you forget? Did you forget how hard it made me cry that the man I vowed my life to can't even remember our anniversary? You stayed late at work and never bought me anything. What kind of man does that? What kind of man does that to the woman he loves?"

He sighs. This conversation comes up at least twice a week. "If its Lobster Tail you want, it's Lobster Tail you'll get. Let me get you a drink and then we'll head right out. Where do you want to go?"

"I don't want to go out to eat, Jim. Look. I'm in my pajamas. I'm wearing my robe. Maybe if you'd gotten home sooner, we could have gone out, but you didn't. I want you to cook them for me. I want you to cook me a Lobster Tail meal. Is that so much to ask for?!" she shrills.

"Shelly, you're getting yourself all worked up. Sit down. Come on, darling. Sit down. I'll bring you a drink and you'll get your lobster tail."

She sits and he moves into the kitchen. "You're never there for me, Jim. You're never there for me. You're always working. That's all you ever do is work. You don't care about me. You've never cared about me."

He hurriedly pours her a drink with about 3 or 4 shots of vodka, then grabs a pill bottle from a hidden drawer. He begins crushing the valium into powder.

"Are you listening to me, Jim? Or are you just ignoring me as usual."

"Honey, you know I care about you. I care about you very much."

He pours the powder into her drink and brings the glass to her.

"If you want Lobster Tail, I'm going to have to run to the store, because we don't have any here. Can I take a quick shower first?"

"While I'm wasting away to nothing? Is that all you ever think about is yourself?" He thinks that she's got quite a few pounds to shed before wasting away to nothing.

"No, you're right. I apologize. I'll go to the store now."

Jim arrives at the grocery store and walks idly through the aisles. He picks up a couple magazines and flips through them. Searches through the DVD's and the new bestsellers. He glances at his watch and brings a soda to the counter.

The boy eyes him suspiciously and Jim doesn't blame him. After all, he does this almost every night and the only thing he ever buys is a soda. "Avoiding my wife," Jim says with a smile.

"Oh man, I get that. That's why I work second shift."

"You're too young to be married."

"Yeah, I figured that out the hard way. But as long as I'm at the store working, then I don't get no shit over being at the bar with the boys. Then she gives me Friday nights to be with the boys as long as I take her out Saturday, which isn't so bad, because then she's happy and I get some, you know what I'm saying? Comes at a cost, though, cause then Sunday I gotta go to church. There's nothing worse than going to church with a hangover. Everybody keeps shouting Amen and you just want to shout at everyone to shut the hell up, you know what I mean?"

"Have a good night," Jim says.

"Yea, you too, man. I'll see you tomorrow?"

"It's a date," Jim says, and then drives home whistling.

For the second time that night he opens the door quietly, but this time finds her sprawled out on the couch, passed out, mouth open, and snoring.

He picks up her glass and carries her into bed. She is completely oblivious to it all. He lifts her robe and approves of all these nights without dinner. She's lost about 15 pounds. He satisfies himself, and wishes he'd thought of this eight years earlier. Then he tip-toes out of the room, and makes sure to leave the door open a crack. He moves into his hidden den and retrieves his bottle. If Shelly only knew. He throws darts at their wedding picture he secured to the dart board. Bullseye!

XXX

Jim's bleary-eyes open, blink, blink, as his vision focuses. He's not in a place he's familiar with. He's not in his bedroom or in the den. He's not at work. Suddenly he turns and wretches, and once he starts, he can't stop. His stomach is on fire and he's never felt so bad in his entire life.

"There you go. There you go. Get it out of your system. You'll be all right." A woman in white tells him. She's smiling. He's wondering how she can be smiling when his gut feels like all the acid from his stomach leaked into it. She gives him some water, tells him to sip it slowly, but he gulps it down, trying to rid of the disgusting taste in his mouth. He hates vomiting. It's his greatest weakness. It makes him want to cry. He feels it like a tidal wave and turns again to throw up.

Her laughter is like the tinkling of chimes. "I told you to sip it, silly," she says to him. He likes her voice, her laughter. He grins up at her. Thinks about asking her name, asking for her number, but he's hardly finished the thought before he's throwing up again. Only then does he become aware that he's puking in front of this woman and she must think him pretty disgusting. She probably wouldn't want to kiss him right now.

"If you give me a breath mint, then I can kiss you and it won't be disgusting."

Her laughter comes again and he feels so happy that he can make her laugh. But then he thinks that perhaps she's laughing at him. That she wouldn't in her wildest dreams want to kiss *him.*

"I'm not always like this," he says.

"Well that's good," she says. "So why'd you do it?"

"Do what? Try to kiss you?"

"No, try to kill yourself."

"I finally had the guts?" he says in wonder.

"You didn't succeed."

"I can never succeed at anything. I can never do anything right."

"Is that why you tried to kill yourself?"

"I tried to kill myself?" he says.

"You don't remember?"

"Remember what?"

"Everything's going to be fine," she pats his hand.

"Where you going?" he asks.

"I've got to make my rounds." She leaves him with the echo of her beautiful laughter and that's what he takes with him toward unconsciousness.

It is by far not the music he hears when he next wakes up.

"How could you do it, Jim? How could you? What kind of man tries to kill himself? What kind of man is that? Daddy's so pissed at you right now. He says you'll be lucky to even have a job after all of this. You're so selfish. You're so selfish, Jim. Don't you ever think of me?" He opens his eyes only momentarily. Then her ugly face begins to fade from his vision, gratefully. "Don't you fall asleep on me. Don't you dare."

He remembers now. He remembers everything.

XXX

The week had been especially hard. Shane needed him working overtime with it being tax-time, and had, as usual, disapproved of everything Jim did. He wasn't working fast enough, wasn't working hard enough. He worked through breakfast, lunches, and dinners, just to get home 9:00 at night to Shelly's raging. Each night of the week, he brought her home something. Food, flowers, chocolates, jewelry, anything, everything, something to get her off his case.

Not having enough time to lose himself into oblivion at night, he began sneaking Jack into his office and sipping on that throughout the work day, so he'd almost be completely wrecked by the time he returned. Then Sunday came, dreadful, awful Sunday.

She got after him as soon as he woke up in the morning. He wasn't even given the chance to have his coffee. "Why don't you ever take me on vacations, Jim? I'm so bored. I want to go on a vacation. I want to go somewhere. All you do is work, work, work, six days a week, and then Sundays come along and you're useless, completely useless.

I want to go to Hawaii. Tell Daddy you need some vacation time."

"This is not a good time of the year to be taking a vacation. It's tax season, Shelly, you know that. That's why I've been working so much."

"Which means you owe me. You need to make it up to me, Jim, all the time I'm sitting at home, all alone, while you're off doing nothing. We're going on a vacation, Jim, because if you don't take me, I will make your life a living nightmare."

"I'll talk to him."

"You'll talk to him? You'll talk to him?" she screamed at him. "That's all you got to say. And what if he says no, Jim? What if he says no? You just going to stoop your shoulders because you're not a man, and say, 'Yes Sir,' and not take me on a vacation?"

"Go sit down in the living room. You need some coffee. I'll get you some coffee. Okay? Go sit down and I'll bring you some coffee." He led her to the couch and sat her down. The blood was pounding in his ears and he knew he just couldn't take it, not another Sunday of hell, so he grabbed for the prescription of Valium and began crushing the pills to put them in her coffee.

"You know, you're always telling me to sit down, relax, like you're trying to get rid of me. Are you trying to get rid of – ." She walked into the room just then. "Jim, what is that? What do you have there?"

"Go sit down, Shelly. I will bring you your coffee," he said fiercely.

She grabbed the pill bottle. "Valium? Is this what you've been putting in my drinks? Is this why I can't remember – Oh my god, Jim. How could you? I'm going to call your mother."

"Don't do that," he cried. "It's to help you with your nerves, that's all. You remember how the Doctor warned you about your nerves."

"Hello, Jim's Mom, Mrs. Piersall. I need you to come over right away. Your son has been doing things that are completely irresponsible. I just think you ought to know. He needs help." She hung up the phone and turned to him, a wicked smile on her face. "Your mother's on her way over. I will never forgive you for this, Jim. Never."

He grabbed the pill bottle and walked to the den in some kind of fog. He grabbed the Jack Daniels from behind the books, swallowed the bottle of pills, and remembers nothing thereafter.

XXX

"I can help you." Jim hears a low unfamiliar voice. He tries to open his eyes, but the lights are so bright. He can only see black. A black cloak. A black hood covering the head and face. He can't glimpse the face.

"I can help you."

"What can you possibly do for me? Who are you?" Jim says hoarsely.

"I'm the man who is going to get you out of your situation. I'm the man who is going to help you. Bring me a million dollars. Cash. 45 Pleasant Ave. Tomorrow 6:00 pm."

"Where am I going to find a million dollars?"

"You know where. Tomorrow at 6:00. I'm offering you a gift, but you have one chance only to redeem it."

"Who are you?"

But the figure in black is gone and Jim wonders if he'd dreamed the whole thing.

XXX

Jim is discharged at 2:00 the following afternoon. He's told how lucky he is to have survived. He's approached by some Doctor that tells him he doesn't feel good about releasing Jim at this time, and believes Jim to still be a danger to himself, but his wife had threatened legal problems. He instructs Jim on the conditions of his release. He is to follow up with a Psychiatrist, Dr. Whitemore, Tuesday afternoon. Jim doesn't even know what day it is. He says thank you, and confirms that yes, he will definitely be following up with Dr. Whitemore on Tuesday afternoon.

"Mr. Piersall, your clothes," a nurse yells after him as he exits the hospital, still wearing his gown.

He grabs a taxi. The taxi driver looks at him suspiciously. "You an escapee from one of those psychiatric hospitals. You a schizo?"

"The voices in my head tell me I'm just fine," Jim says.

"You got a gun?"

"I don't even have underwear. Where am I going to put a gun?"

The driver grimaces. "Man, why do I always get the lunatics?"

Jim is dropped off at his place of employment.

"That'll be 10 dollars plus tip."

"No pockets, no wallet. Give me a minute to take care of business at this bank here, and I'll take care of you."

He exits the cab. Jim laughs. He feels great. Wonderfully great. Extraordinarily wonderfully great. He dismisses the draft of cold on his bottom and enters the bank.

"Mr. Piersall?" the secretary stands.

"Morning, Ruby. Shawn. Elaine. Got a few files I have to pick up." He keeps walking as though nothing at all is out of the ordinary. It takes him 15 minutes to collect what he needs. He throws a post-it note inside the vault that says IOU.

"Evening Elaine, Shawn, Ruby." He exits.

Seeing the bags of money in Jim's hands, the cab driver screams a bunch of curse words, then squeals his tires as he rips out of there.

Not bothering with another cab as he has some time to kill, Jim walks the entire way to 45 Pleasant Ave, which, he finds, is an abandoned lot with an old well. He feels a sharp, but temporary prick in his neck, and then he's told to "Follow me." Jim follows the wavering vision in black as he lifts the boards covering the well and disappears inside. Jim follows him without thought or question, descending the slippery rungs into deeper pitches of black. And only when he's in the darkest of dark does he see the light impossibly far down, but his next step down meets concrete and an inch or so of water.

His now soaked loafers squeak as he walks the steep slope toward the small shaft of light. He bumps into a door where the light is coming from. It is opened for him, then instantly closed. His eyes try to resist the shock of such a huge lighting contrast. Where he'd just come from had been impossibly dark, where he is now is impossibly light to an almost white. Mirrors and glass are abundant along the walls, reflecting this impossibly white light and cascading his reflection in an ethereal glow, a reflection that shows him tall and broad with a self-assured face, and the smile of a deeply contented man. He hears giggles and sees other reflections of various beautiful women around him. "Oooh, he's cute.", "Manly," "I want to take him home," echoes all around him.

"Are we playing hide n seek, ladies. Come out, come out, wherever you are," Jim sings as he jumps behind several mirrors to find them. He finds himself embraced by their giggles. He feels a peck on his cheek and swerves. Then an arm on his shoulder. A tickle on his neck.

"The bible says heaven has streets paved with gold. It never said anything about having an abundance of beautiful women who want to play." Even his voice sounds deeper, more resonant.

He sees the reflection of their running, a creamy leg here, long red hair being blown back by her flight, a perky little button nose and shocking red lips as one of their reflections turn and beckon him to follow.

"Now we're playing cat and mouse?" he says with a chuckle as he starts running toward them. He turns a corner and enters another room. There they all are, splayed out on a pearl white couch, 5 of them all together, each uniquely different from the other, every one of them extraordinary. The one with the shocking red hair pulls him to the couch and they all wonderfully crowd him, oohing and aahing, their hands working his tight muscles, fingers through his hair, palms on his cheek, silky hair tickling his arms. He laughs in ecstatic bliss and now knows for the first time in his life what it is to love and be loved, and that love is not meant to be a prison. It is meant to be free. To spread one's wings and soar to unimaginable heights as impossible is a can't and a never, which can't ever apply, because everything is possible should one just open themselves and have the courage to embellish on that journey.

He curls his hand around the back of the blonde's neck who he calls Angel, and pulls her toward his lips that have never truly known a kiss of a woman. He kisses her with such ardent passion and it is returned in kind. The most spectacular moment in his 36 years. And then they are gone and the room is dark.

"Thank you," he says with a rawness in his throat, he says to the man in black, knowing he is there, though not seeing him. "You have given me a gift that is priceless. I bow to your mercy and worship your holiness." Jim kneels on his knees. "I do not feel that I and the miserable and disappointing life that I've led are worth such favor."

Jim hears a deep chuckle barely containing a bout of laughter, and is confused by this, though also pleased that he has made his master laugh.

"Get up off of your knees, Jim. I'm not God and you're not in Heaven. You're still very much alive."

Jim feels the overwhelming pressure of vast disappointment. Does this mean that he will have to return to his miserable existence? He can't bear the thought of it. Not after knowing what he now knows.

"You will return to your life as you know it only briefly, for all is about to change for you, Jim, and it is up to you to decide if it is for the good or for the worse. Face the wall and declare how many years you want to see in the future. An image will appear and it will continue playing until you look away. Begin."

Jim hears seven echo in his brain, so he repeats it aloud. "Seven years." Suddenly the wall lights up. At first, the image is dark, though he can hear the sounds of footsteps and clinking. Then it turns to a lighter shade of gray.

"He's been paroled."

"The lucky shit is getting out." He hears around him.

"Hey, Jim, fuck my wife for me, will ya? Don't want her straying on me."

"I'll take care of your mother too. How's that sound?" the man walking responds, Jim assumes to be himself.

There's laughter and then a loud clank against the cell bar as they're told to quiet down. He's brought into another room, a stern square-faced woman behind a desk. He hears rattling of keys and handcuffs and two hands display themselves in the image, rubbing away the indentations of the cuffs.

"Sign here saying you've received everything we confiscated from you seven years ago."

A single solitary gold wedding band is placed on the counter.

"Keep it."

"Pawn it. It'll buy you a pack of smokes or a beer or a decent meal." Fingers pick up the ring and place it in a pocket.

He is escorted outside and on the other side of the gates. "Maxwell's Federal Penitentiary", the sign on the brick building reads.

The gates are quickly closed and locked behind him.

"Jim," one of the guards call. "We don't want to see you back here again. Good luck. Lucky bastard. They never did find that money," he hears their conversation as he walks away.

Jim drops his head and the image disappears. *It is up to you to decide if it is for the better or the worst.*

Jim turns and finds his feet in an inch or so of water. He is at the bottom of a well shaft. Nothing more. And he is freezing. Dazed and not knowing what to think or feel, he climbs out of the well and replaces the boards. He walks the hour and a half to his home. A police car pulls over and he thinks, *This is it. The end of my life. I was set up.* The police officer does not arrest him, but almost gives him a ticket for indecent exposure in his hospital gown walking down a main route.

"You don't look so well. Perhaps I should take you back to the hospital."

"A lift home would be fine," Jim says, feeling a sort of deliriousness and bubbling laughter at the Officer's obliviousness. He contains it.

Jim unlocks the door quietly and steps into the house. He ducks as a vase comes flying toward his head and smashes against the door. "Where have you been, Jim? I called the hospital. They said you were discharged at 2 in the afternoon. It is now 10 o'clock at night and I never got my dinner. You out whoring it with some slut, huh? Huh?"

A lamp comes flying at him next. "What in God's name are you wearing, Jim? People don't want to see that. That's nasty. At least in a suit you can somewhat resemble the man that you're not. You, you have become quite the disappointment, Jim. Even your mother agrees that her only child, her only son, is an idiot."

In flash fury, he has her by the throat, pressed up against the wall. "Stop bullying me. I will not tolerate it anymore from this moment and on."

"Help! Help!" she shrills. "He's going to kill me! He's trying to kill me!"

A loud knock hits the door. "Police."

They barge down the door, mostly for theatrics, he thinks, as he'd left it unlocked. And he finds this superbly funny and can contain the bubbling, rumbling laughter of hysteria no more.

"Oh, thank God you arrived. Arrest this man, he tried to –."

"You are under arrest for the theft of one million dollars from the Bank of America. You have the right to remain silent."

But Jim just keeps right on laughing, even splaying his hands out for them to make the placement of the handcuffs more convenient. "Take me away, Officers. I am guilty as charged. Oh God, please take me away from her."

"This one's a quack job."

"Theft?! Jim, what'd you do? You stole money from Daddy? Oh, Daddy is going to be so pissed. There goes your job. Now you're never going to be executive. Dammit, Jim, look at me when I'm talking to you. It's over, you hear, O V E –."

The door slams shut.

Years later, neighbors from six blocks down would still talk about hearing the maniac, Jim Piersall, screaming, "I'm free! I'm free! Oh God, I'm finally free!" before being locked up for seven years for robbing the bank. Had he been an executive, it would have been a white collar crime, and they would have called it embezzlement. But Jim remained blue collar with his Administrative title, and only Grand Theft and all its harsher consequences could be applied to him.

CLAIRE

CHAPTER 14

Claire stares at the photo of her long-lost family. They were only kids then. Thomas 5, Loretta 3, and Claire, at 1 ½ being held in her father's arms. It was the only thing she had that said at one point in her life she had a full family. Her mother, so very young in the photo, looked tired, but happy. But seeing the lost expression on her father's face, his dazed eyes, anyone could have predicted their future. Not a happy one.

The mother's future was one of being left to care for three young children by herself.

Thomas's future was one of never being taught how to ride a bike without training wheels, never being taught how to grow into a proper man, and learning how to run when the going got tough, just like his old man.

Loretta's future was to learn how to cook and clean and take care of Claire while the mother was working, trying to make ends meet. Then attempting to marry the first guy that proposed, and being left at the altar with a baby in her womb.

Claire's was one of never knowing what it's like to have a father, so it never bothered her as much as it did her older siblings. Claire's trials evolved around poverty.

Bounced around from one sitter to another, some of them nice, most of them awful, until she was nine years old. Then she became the responsibility of her eleven year old sister, who very much resented that responsibility. She was the hand-me-down child. Clothes, toys, and even meals. When she attended prom, everyone laughed at her, because they recognized Loretta's dress from only the year before.

When Claire tried to work, her mother refused, no matter how much Claire begged, because her mother relied so heavily on Loretta, sure that prom queen, beauty pageant winner Loretta would find a fine well-off man to support her, leaving only Claire left for the mother to support. While Loretta focused on using her looks and sweet personality to attract Prince Charming for their happily-ever-after, Claire had different plans in mind. She excelled in school. When Loretta was planning her wedding with the hugely attractive football pro with the wealthy family, Claire was applying for colleges and scholarships, having never had a boyfriend.

It was only when the wedding fell through with the promise of another mouth to feed when her mother finally took her up on the offer to work a job, but it was too late, at that point, as Claire had gotten a full scholarship at Drexel University in Pennsylvania.

Claire changed her major a dozen times, going for the highest-paying professions. First she tried criminal justice, then nursing, changed to business, then economics, and finally she settled on Psychology.

It was her freshman year in graduate studies when she met Paul. He was in a few of her classes and he was so very different from all the rest. No one paid attention to him, which is what caught her attention. He was the dweebiest of dweebs. The nerdiest of nerds. The clutziest of clutzes. But not the ugliest. Far from good-looking, but he had this thing about running his hand through his hair when he was concentrating on something, so his hair would stick out in every angle, and it made him look cute. At least to Claire. No one else seemed to notice, which was just fine by her, because he was going to be hers and hers alone.

So while Thomas had taken off and no one had heard from him in years, and Loretta continued living at home, raising her child, and the Mother continued trying to support them, Claire was pursuing Paul.

It was surprisingly difficult to get his attention. First she waved to him in class, and he looked behind him. Then she said hello to him in the hall, and after looking behind him again, he raised his brow and said, "Hi?" before walking off like he was on some kind of mission. Then she sat next to him at their next class and extended her hand, "Hi, I'm Claire." Again he looked behind him before quickly taking her hand and dropping it. She giggled, "Well are you going to tell me your name?"

"Oh, I'm – my name is – uh – I'm Paul. Nice to meet you." And that was the end of that conversation. He was obviously a genius, and she was struggling, so after a full week of sitting next to him, she sighed in exasperation and said, "I just don't get it. I need help." And it was like a light bulb went off. He instantly turned to her and said, "What do you need help with? Maybe I can help you?"

So he started off as her tutor. First they'd meet in-between classes, then they'd find an hour in the library a few days a week, and finally she got him to agree to her coming to his room to help her study.

That's when she kissed him. He was right in the midst of explaining to her the similarities and differences between Adler and Erikson, personality theorists, when she just leaned in and kissed him smack on the lips.

He was adorably confused and suddenly speechless, having lost track of what he was saying. So she took that opportunity to say to him, "I like you, Paul, and I would like it very much if you were my boyfriend."

"Me? You want me to be – but you're so – and I'm - ." And she kissed him again, and it was sealed.

She'd been mistaken, though. She'd gone after him precisely on the basis that a guy like him would worship a girl like her. She walked all over him, 100 percent secure in that belief. He'd never leave her. He'd never walk away. Because he would look at her like a Goddess and feel like the luckiest man in the world to have her. She'd been wrong. Because there was one thing more important in his life than having her. His studies. Due to the unfortunate suicide of his Mom, he was obsessed, and there was nothing more important than he becoming a Doctor of Psychology.

She reacted badly to it. She thought there was no way in hell a guy like that would let go of a girl like her. Even when she walked away, she fully believed he'd come after her. He didn't. Then she received the call from Loretta that Mom had cancer and didn't have much time, because after all the years of working, she still didn't have medical insurance. And here Claire was racking up college expenses while struggling to barely pass.

She dropped out and returned home to Texas, a failure, like all the rest.

She watched her mother die, but the debts didn't die with her. They took the house, a small 150 year old single family home their mother had inherited, and with it, the rest of their childhood memories.

Thomas went back to never settling down or sticking around, and this time it was Claire left with Loretta and the baby, instead of the other way around. Loretta knew their mother's personal life better than the rest of them, so was the most adamant against working and leaving the child in a sitter's care. Claire, feeling so much responsible for Loretta's lost youth, picked up any job she could find. Waitressing, retail, delivery, cleaning services, childcare, and got Loretta set up in a run-down one bedroom apartment for her to stay home and care for her child. Loretta got pregnant again, and this time the father stuck around until she was eight months along, then he, too, was gone.

While searching the paper one day for additional work, even though she was already maintaining three jobs, Claire came across the advertisement for a full-time, live-in Nanny. Struggling to pay both her and her sister's and nieces bills at the same time, she called the number and arranged an interview.

They met up at AppleBee's, which she'd thought was the strangest thing, but she was in for something far stranger. That's when she met Bill Whitman, in his late fifties, at the time. She did not recognize him to be the Whitman of Whitman Enterprises and Son. She'd hardly finished shaking his hand when he said, "Perfect, just perfect. Right age, right look."

He then pulled out his wallet and showed her a picture of a seeming much-younger him, a toddler boy, and his beautiful young wife who had a great deal of resemblance to Claire herself. "My wife passed. This is my boy, John. He's never been quite right, and I think it has to do with losing his mother. She was a beautiful woman, inside and out. Generous, loving, nurturing. If I could have that time back, I would gladly give up everything."

"I am so sorry to hear about her passing, Mr. Whitman. I imagine it's been difficult for both you and your child."

"Yes, well, I've got my business to run, and it keeps me quite occupied. My son, on the other hand, is a loose cannon, and his only true passion seems to be doing everything he can to ruin his own life and to hurt our company. He needs a mother figure. Do you have any children, Miss? Ms? Dellafar?"

"No, no children. Not married. I have two nieces. And I provide childcare for one of my jobs." She handed him her resume. "I can cook, you see, right there, I worked as a cook for a little while in a restaurant before I became a waitress there. Here are my childcare references. I also work part-time for a Cleaning business, where we go in and clean people's homes and businesses, or whatever they need cleaned."

"Ah, I see you got an undergrad degree in Economics."

"One of my many majors. I also studied criminal justice, business, nursing, and clinical Psychology. My own mother passed when I was working toward my Masters, so I wound up leaving. Ever since I've been helping to support my sister and her two children."

"Can you type and be professional on the phone?"

"Ah, yes, see, right there I worked as a receptionist for a law firm for a while, while the legal secretary was out on maternity leave."

"You've had a lot of jobs, Miss Dellafar."

"I know. I'm sorry. Struggling to make ends meet, and sometimes I can't get a higher paying job to work around the schedule of a lower paying job, so I just keep trying to find my match."

"You said you're not married. What about a boyfriend?"

"Um, no, between working all the time I just don't have the time to – uh – go out and pursue such things."

"Perfect. Simply perfect. We'll try you out for a couple weeks, see how it works. You can move in this weekend, all expenses paid, and I'll cover the cost of your current lodgings until it's been determined if you'll be staying with us on a more permanent basis. Your transportation, food, clothing, everything will be provided for. Apologize on my behalf to your current employers for you not being able to give proper notice. You are a hard worker, Miss Dellafar, and that's exactly what I'm looking for."

"Excellent, thank you so much, sir, but if I may? In the event that you determine you do not wish to keep me, if I quit all my jobs now I'll be left completely unemployed."

"You really don't know who I am, do you, Miss Dellafar?"

Claire shook her head.

"I'm the owner of the multi-billion dollar corporation Whitman Enterprises and Son. A reference from me will guarantee you employment in whatever job of your choosing, but I strongly doubt that is going to be the case. After all, I didn't get where I'm at by not being a good judge of character. From here on out, you work for one person and one person alone, me, and I will ensure you are very well taken care of."

Claire couldn't believe her luck. Not exactly the future she had planned, but a future that was far more promising than her current present. She shook his hand with all the gratitude she could place in a simple handshake. "So, where is your son now?"

"Oh, he's sulking in the car. He doesn't exactly agree with this decision."

Claire choked on her drink. "You left your son in the car this entire time?"

"Come, meet him, Miss Dellafar. I think he'll stop pouting once he sees you."

So she walked with him to the stretch limo parked at the curb. The door was opened and Mr. Whitman had some words with the person inside before he turned to her and said, "Just as I thought. One look at you and he's changed his mind. He wants to offer you a drink. I'll have the Chauffeur bring you to your residence so you may gather your things."

"Oh, okay, I live –."

He chuckled. "I know where you live, Miss Dellafar. I don't meet with people without doing the proper background check first. Nor do I buy them dinner if I don't plan on hiring them."

Claire maneuvered into the limousine to meet the child she'd be nannying, and instead found a full-grown highly-attractive male who was half-way to being inebriated.

He placed a glass of champagne in her hand and grinned at her lop-sided. "So, you're my new Nanny. Cheers!"

JOHN

CHAPTER 15

Before his father's passing, John Whitman had known, cherished, and definitely taken advantage of a freedom very few ever get. His father would rail on him constantly, and John was always left feeling inadequate and with the feeling that his father wished he'd had a different son after all their numerous talks. Or rather his dad's lectures about John needing to settle down and start learning the business and stop with this childishness. He's had 28 years for that. But whereas some son's look up to their father, idolize them, and dream of being able to walk in their footsteps and be just like them, John loathed his father's lifestyle, and the great negligence that it resulted in.

The loneliness he'd acquired in all those days and nights sitting outside his father's office, just waiting for his dad to take a five minute break so that he could show him what he did in school that day or what he built with his legos, or the new fort that he made that had two floors, 4 bedrooms, and even plumbing (a bucket with a hose connected to the bottom that emptied into one of the house's eight bathrooms).

Even more, John loathed the money and all the fake friends and girlfriends it brought to his home to entertain him. Like his father, John learned one after the other, that they didn't really care about him; they just cared about the money. And once learned, he would shut himself in his room and cry in such great feelings of betrayal and loneliness.

He remembers snippets of his toddler years when it was completely different. His mom and dad in the livingroom, laughing, as he did something funny. His dad crawling around on the floor, neighing, while giving John a horsey-back ride. All of them sitting on the couch, watching a movie, telling him to either sit still and watch the movie or go to bed, but he couldn't possibly sit still or sleep because of the candy and soda that he'd gotten with his popcorn.

That was when mom was alive. If she'd lived longer, perhaps John would have more family moments to share, and life, as he knows it, would be very very different. It's amazing that the smallest moments in life can shape the rest of others' lives. It took her only 20 minutes to die of a brain aneurysm, yet it impacted and shaped the rest of John's life. Dad threw himself into his work and never stopped until the night that he died. John was left alone to make and create his own way, without the nurture and affection of a mother, without the kinship, pride, and teaching moments of a father.

By age 10 his lonely vulnerable heart had transformed into a type of sarcastic hardness completely untrusting of anyone, completely unwilling to let anyone in and believe that they genuinely cared. Every smile, every pat on the head, every good grade and compliment turned sour in believing that none of it was genuine. Even the students in high school knew, for John never studied, and John never did his homework, but John passed with flying colors in the high honor roll. He wonders how much that cost his father in contributions every year.

And every smile and every compliment and every nice thing he said and did was, in turn, never genuine, and he'd congratulate himself over and over again throughout the years for how skillful a role he could play. Most popular guy in school, most sought after, most adored. He never had less than 10 people with him while walking to and from school. When younger, his house could have been a park for all the kids running around, and as he got older, park turned to party. But still when all the chaos died down and everyone left, he could not combat his fierce loneliness.

He stopped waiting around his father's office door, stopped asking him to play with him or come see something or tuck him into bed, stopped hoping that tonight would be the night that they had a family dinner together or watched a movie together, stopped calling good morning and good night through the closed office door. He couldn't stop feeling the pain of his father not even acknowledging his existence, so he made sure his father acknowledged it . . . by doing everything imaginably wrong, bringing a lot of negative media attention to the home, and getting in trouble by creating or submitting to scandal again and again, so that his father would have to acknowledge him and clean up his messes and sit down with him and have a conversation with him (lecture) for the first time since the last time he'd done something wrong. It was the only attention his father gave him, but he never did get over the sting of his father's disappointment and of the idea that his father probably wished he'd never had him as a son.

If his father was aware of his negligence and the loneliness of his only son, he never let it show, never mentioned it, apologized for it, or even hinted at trying to be a better father. But he did continue to pick up John's messes up until the end. He never cut his allowance or kicked him out of the home or followed through with any of his punishments and threats, so maybe that says something. It certainly didn't help John to become more disciplined or more rigid and reputation-oriented like his father.

His father was always so dignified about the image he projected to society, which is why the media never knew how sick he really was, except for small rumors that John had started that couldn't be confirmed, why the media suspected

Claire's affair, and why it was a shocking surprise to America to find that Bill Whitman was dead. Not to mention this great surprise resulting in a significant increase in stocks owned by his father the week following his death. His dad went out with a bang. Which in his dad's world, had to do with money.

Were there any last minute end-of-life conversations and confessions between dad and son? No, because at that point John and he were on not-speaking terms because he'd given his dad the greatest disappointment in the end. "I'll go to hell before I sit behind that desk and run this business. That was your life and your dream, not mine. I want nothing to do with it."

John felt like he'd finally won that one battle, until the will was read and John found out that all inheritance was contingent on his being a major player in the business. He didn't have to completely run all operations as his father had done, as his father had hired and trained additional staff before his departure, even hiring a consultant for John in the decision-making process, but nothing, nothing whatsoever could go through without John's and the consultant's signature. The consultant was given the authority to go to the board and veto a decision John had made, based on John's not knowing anything about what is best for the company, but everything still had to go through John, he still had to attend every meeting, and make and receive phone calls with the consultant on three-way. To John, it's a death wish. Play time is over, his father had said. And this time he finally meant it.

Claire had relayed messages and words that his father had said. One being that he didn't want to die until he got to see his first grandchild. John didn't find any comfort or reassurance in this that his father actually had a heart and perhaps had regrets. Instead, he saw it as just another slap in the face that his father had never acknowledged him and had always been disappointed in him; therefore, hoping there may be a grandchild that would be just like his granddad, and make him proud, as John was never able to do.

The past two years preceding his father's death, when they first learned of his being sick and would probably die within the year, John started down a very different, much more self-destructive path. Claire, originally hired to watch him all the time, keep him out of trouble, and provide a type of nurturing home-environment, which was quite effective in the beginning, began performing more and more work for his father, providing less attention to him, and she practically became his father's personal secretary.

Just when John became accustomed to the mandatory breakfasts, lunches, and dinners Claire forced upon them, no excuses, and their evening board games, movies, or conversations that kept him from going out and getting in trouble, it was all abruptly taken away when his father became ill. Media-suspected affairs became media-suspected drug use and alcohol abuse and prostitutes. Their suspicions were correct. John learned the hard way his predisposition to becoming addicted to alcohol, coke, and heroin, especially in combinations. It was these addictions that led to his being passed out in a back alley in some urban town, when a woman smoking a cigarette caught sight of him and saved his life.

XXX

Slumped in the alley, dark and damp from the rain, John mustered all the strength he had just to try and keep his face out of his own vomit. He was perspiring badly, but could still feel the chill gnawing at his bones. This usually happened when he combined the wrong drugs or drank too much alcohol during his high that made him feel untouchable. Until this happened. Then he had regrets. Regrets about the drugs. Regrets about his life. Regrets about his father, who only now, since sick, actually wanted John to spend some time with him to learn about the business. The business could go down with his old man, for all he cared.

The impact to his ribs surprised him. Then someone was toppling over him with a very feminine shout. He attempted to move his body to ease her fall, but only managed to be the body that kept hers from hitting the hard pavement. She instantly screamed, perhaps thinking he dead.

"Shh, shhh, calm down. Are you all right?"

She stopped screaming. "Are *you* all right?" The flame of her lighter lit up the area covering their faces.

"Well, aren't I the lucky one to have you falling all over me. I'm not usually like this." Then, unable to keep it down, he twisted and vomited again.

"I should take you to the hospital," she said.

"No, no, no, you can't."

"Why not?"

"Um, because the things I'm on aren't exactly legal, and if they know that, then they'll make me stay for a long time and get clean."

"And the problem with getting clean is?"

"I'm John Whitman."

"I didn't ask you your name. I asked you what the problem is with getting clean, because right now you're nothing but a low-life scumbag."

That hurt him.

"No, I'm John Whitman. The only heir of Bill Whitman." Recognition still was not registering. "Bill Whitman, only one of the richest men in this country, aside from Gates."

"So what's Daddy gonna do if he finds out his son is doing illegal drugs? Cut your mil a year allowance?"

"Um, more like the entire world finding out. I love scandals, but this is not one I want found out about."

"Well, that's something you should have thought about before you started using illicit drugs."

"No sympathy? None at all? I'd do puppy dog eyes, but I can't open them right now."

"You put yourself in this mess. That doesn't exactly inspire sympathy," she said.

"I like you," John said, and then everything went black.

He came into consciousness in the hospital while they were pumping his stomach. The pain was grotesque. And all he could think in that moment was, "You stupid bitch. You took me to the hospital."

He wouldn't find out until later that she actually saved his life by taking him to the hospital, because his heart rate and respiration had been way below guidelines. They'd had to put him on a respirator, get his heart stimulated, while simultaneously getting the drugs and alcohol out of his system as quickly as possible.

He'd never even asked for her name, or perhaps he had, and just couldn't remember. John didn't know what his old man was doing to keep this from getting public, or if his old man knew anything at all. It became the last thing on his mind after 48 hours when the real withdrawals began to kick in. He'd never wanted to die so badly in his life, and he couldn't even take that initiative because he was on 24 hour supervision. In and out, in and out, glimpses of him crying, glimpses of him screaming and being very verbally aggressive toward the staff. At one point, he became physically aggressive and had to be restrained and shackled to his bed. How many times he begged and pleaded and shouted and cried for them to, "Let me out, let me out, let me out!"

And then on his seventh day, when it didn't feel so bad, and was becoming just a little bit easier, she showed up. In the florescent lights, he really got to see her for the first time, and thought she the most amazing woman he'd ever met with her cropped strawberry blonde hair, striking blue eyes, dimples in her cheeks and chin, smiling glossy lips. Regardless how casual the clothes she wore, they were filled out very nicely indeed. But her face, those eyes, oh man.

"How ya doin', cowboy?"

"I've definitely been better, but after the past couple days, I can appreciate that."

"I waited until after you were over the worst of your withdrawals. I didn't know if you'd even remember me."

"How could I forget? You saved my life, you know."

"So they say," she smiled easily. "In more ways than one."

"You have no idea," he said, feeling in his voice and star-struck eyes.

"Well, time to go. Just stopped by to see how you're holding up."

"Wait, wait, you're leaving so soon? Wait, what's your name?" She smiled back at him and kept walking. "Will I see you again?"

"Oh, by the way, I took all of your identification and told them I didn't know who you are. They're going to start asking, so you better make up a good name and get some money wired over to you."

And then she was gone.

XXX

Two miserable, sufferable, anxious days went by before she showed up again. John tried not to act too happy to see her.

"Oh, by the way, my name is Bill Junior. I paid cash."

"Well that's very original. How did you come up with that one?" she said sarcastically.

"You look extraordinarily nice again today."

"And you still look like crap. You're starting to get some color back, though."

"Did you bring me anything to eat?"

"I don't start feeding people until I get a few dates out of it first."

"Is that an offer? After I get out of here, I can take you to the finest restaurants with food you'd never imagined could taste so good. We'll spend our evening –."

"Uh, no thank you," she said callously.

"Why not? Do you have a boyfriend or something? Do you love him?"

She laughed a sardonic laugh. "I'll let you figure out why not. I'm just glad that I helped you get the intervention that forced you to come clean. Bye."

"Bye? Just like that?"

And she was gone again.

XXX

"If you don't like me, why do you keep showing up?" John gave her an easy smile the next time she arrived. He felt better than he'd felt in quite a long time. A kind of quiet peace had found him.

"I never said I didn't like you. I don't know you well enough to make that decision. Besides, I wanted to be the one at the center of the humbling of a man like yourself."

"What's that supposed to mean?" he asked.

"Men aren't the only ones who like being the knight in shining armor for a woman in distress. You've obviously been in need for quite a while for someone to step in and save you from yourself."

"No one has ever really cared enough. My father's only concerns are media attention and reputation. His only interest money and the business. Everyone else just comes along for the ride."

"I brought you a book. Two actually. Patterson for entertainment. This for a different perspective."

John very noticeably grimaced. "A bible? Really?"

"Bill Whitman is only your father in the human form, which is flawed. You have another father whom knows and understands unconditional love, who has been watching after you for a very long time. It was through His intervention that I showed up where I did and when I did."

"And was it also through His intervention that he took my mother when I was hardly potty-trained and left me with a father who hardly acknowledges my existence outside his business?"

"People handle their pain differently, John. Perhaps seeing you reminds him of her, what he had with her, and how his life had been with her, and it's too painful for him, so the more pain he feels, the more he throws himself into work. You, on the other hand, rebel entirely against the thing that keeps him going, and perhaps the only thing that could have allowed the two of you to bond in the only way he knows how. Perhaps he feels the only thing he can give to you is his life's work. Yet you want nothing to do with it and cannot appreciate it. You act out your pain through altered conscious, chasing the highs, and destroying yourself in the process. Do you really enjoy that lifestyle? No, you just do it to try to compensate for not being able to have what you really want."

John yawned loudly.

She stood to leave.

"Wait, don't go. I'm sorry. I was just – I was just messing around."

"I'm sorry. I don't find anything amusing about the fact that you almost died. You've been given a second chance, John. Not many people get that." She walked out the door, without even a goodbye.

XXX

John waited three days for her, three very long days. He finished the Patterson book, counted the tiles in the ceiling, manicured his nails with his teeth, plucked the whiskers from his goatee one by one, and used a couple to get an extra meal, until they found him out. There's only so many consecutive times hair can wind up in one's food. He began using the physical therapy room more frequently, spent more time in the cafeteria having random conversations with strangers, and took several walks a day under strict supervision. Night time was the most difficult as he could do none of those things to distract himself. TV's were shut down at 10:00 and he'd gone too long getting accustomed to the night life that sleep was impossible at that time.

Finally, when boredom was so perverse that he was considering biting his toe nails, did he reach to the side table drawer and take out the bible. He opened the cover and several pieces of paper fell out. She had beautiful hand-writing.

I've outlined several scripture to get you started. They hold much relevance to the things you are currently going through and the questions that you have. These are my favorite and have carried me through the difficult times in my life. When you have finished, I want you to write what you think they mean and how they made you feel. Then I will give you the first letter of my name and more scripture and so on and so forth.

Incentive.

When she arrived again, he'd not only finished reading the scripture, but memorized them, wrote 10 pages, and cried harder and longer than he ever had in his life. When he saw her, he could not keep the tears from his eyes. His very own angel, and not worthy of her one bit.

She stayed longer than prior times as they talked back and forth about meaning. They'd take walks, eat outside on the bench in the garden, and read from the bible. At the end of every visit, she would smile at him and give him a letter of her name. Then provide him with more soul-searching homework.

Her visits became more consistent and then daily from 11 to 1. They began establishing their own little routine, something John had little experience with. They'd open their conversation with a brief summary of their time away. Then move to daily bread. From there they'd grab something from the cafeteria, or sometimes she brought food. On nice days they'd eat outside. On rainy days they'd eat in the lounge. While they ate, she'd read what he'd written the day prior. They'd discuss it over coffee. 12:30 to 1:00 was playtime.

They'd speak casually. Laugh a lot. Play a board game. Chase each other in the yard like two young kids. She'd provide him more scripture and then tell him something more about herself.

In this time, he'd learned her name was Angie Ferring. Her birthday was July 16th, 1986. Her favorite color was blue, like the sky on a cloudless day. Her favorite movie was Far and Away with Tom Cruise and Nicole Kidman. Her favorite books Historical Romances and the occasional suspense/thriller. She loved chick flicks and comedies. She hated horror movies because they scared her. She received a Bachelor degree in Social Work and took the courses to being CASAC certified. She worked with children whom have suffered from the abuse and neglect prevalent with alcohol and drug abuse in the home. She had always dreamed of going to Vegas and perhaps Italy, one day. She'd considered missionary work, but was not up for the lifestyle of constant travel, because she's a homebody and family-oriented. Though she'd said nothing in regards to her family.

On the day before his discharge, he yelled to her as she was walking to her car, "I will give you everything you've ever hoped and dreamed for and more. I will marry you, Angie Ferring." She never looked back.

That night he'd awoken to her presence in his room. "Angie, what're you – how did you - ?"

His surprised words were cut short by her kiss. She was different from her usual reserved self. She was free and giddy, passionate, a profound mystery full of surprises. She spoke not a word to him the entire time as she kissed him fully and stripped him of his clothes. As she caressed his body while he frantically removed hers. As she straddled him and welcomed him inside. As her hips rose and fell at an increasing rate and her perspiration dripped on his chest. As she muffled her voice in his chest when they both released. Not one word. She laid there on his chest for quite a while, hiding her face. He noticed her shoulders shaking and thought he felt her warm tears on his chest.

"Angie?"

She stood slowly and began putting on her clothes.

"Hey?"

She grabbed her purse, her keys, not once looking at him, and began walking out the door.

"Angie, wait. Talk to me."

She turned then, and he saw her face, masked with pain and dripping with tears. "What have I done?" and she was gone.

XXX

On the morning of his discharge, he waited for her, expecting her at 11:00 am. Two pain-staking hours passed in the waiting room, as his room had already been filled by another. It was a dreary rainy day. Perhaps the rain would cover his tears or give him pneumonia so that she might want to save him again. He hadn't made any arrangements for a ride, expecting her to be there. He'd been thinking about it for weeks – what they would do together the moment he was released. The very first thing he wanted to do was introduce her to his dad. Then he wanted to spend the whole rest of the afternoon and evening showing her what her life would be like with him, and the type of luxuries and treatment she could expect. After all, was it not every woman's dream to be catered too and pampered and cared for? For the first time in his life, he didn't begrudge this fact. He loved her and actually wanted to spend the rest of his life making her the happiest woman alive.

But now he felt like the loneliest man alive.

He didn't cower his head from the pouring rain, rather lifted it to the sky and allowed the rain to mix with his tears. She'd taught him how to cry. She'd taught him how to feel again. She'd taught him so much. And now she was teaching him loss. The wrenching pain his father must have felt when he lost his wife after so short a life lived together. He walked down the road, having no destination in mind.

Suddenly a car swerved toward him from the other lane. The brakes squealed and the car stopped beside him. "John." Angie opened the door.

He raced toward her, crying openly, feeling heaven just touched his life again. With all the passion of a revived heart, he picked her up and swung her around, kissing her over and over again, all over her face. "I thought I lost you," he cried. "I thought I lost you forever." He embraced her in a fierce hug. Only then did he realize her rigid frame and his unreciprocated kisses.

"Get in the car, John. You're soaked, and now I am."

He did, immediately sobering once hearing her tone.

"Angie, what's wrong?"

"I'm sorry I'm late. I figured with your resources you'd manage a way back home, but to not say goodbye doesn't make it right."

"Goodbye?" his voice cracked. "Why? Why goodbye? Why not new beginnings, like you taught me?"

"I'm going to return you to the place we first met. From there you find your own way. I need you to promise that you will never mention me or my name and my involvement with you."

"I'll do anything you ask of me, anything, I promise. But you need to be straight up with me and tell me what's going on. We have something. We have something wonderful, something people spend their whole lives searching for. You know that, right?"

She shook her head. "No, we are merely a small moment in time, yet one that will remain with us forever. I thank you. I thank you for everything you've shown me."

"No, no, no. You're the one that saved my life. I haven't yet been able to show you anything and to show just how much I appreciate you. It's my turn now. It's my turn to show you. Don't take that away from me. Just give me that chance to show you just how happy we can be together."

"It's not that simple, John. It's complicated."

"Why?"

"Because there's so much you don't know. So much you don't know about me. I got a second chance too, John, and I gave myself over to the Lord. He is the man I vowed my life too, no other, in eternal gratitude for his intervention in my life, and his unconditional love for me that cannot be matched by any human being on this earth."

"Oh, but does he warm your bed at night?" John said sarcastically.

She gave him an icy glare. "That's what got me into trouble in the first place."

"You're being a hypocrite."

"What? Huh-how am I being a hypocrite?"

"Mary and Joseph were married. That did not stop them from living their lives with the Lord. That did not stop God from blessing Mary with the birth of God's son. Did the creation of humans only involve Adam, or did God bless Adam with Eve, because Adam obviously couldn't procreate without her. So perhaps God meant for the union of man and woman, and expected it in his big plan. So by you refusing this union on the basis that you vowed your life to the Lord and no other, then you are being a hypocrite and going against his will."

She smacked him. Hard. The sting he felt was in his heart. "How dare you. How dare you turn his word around and attempt to manipulate me with it? Get out. Get out of my car. God already forewarned me that you were the type of person that would bite the hand that fed it."

"That was not God telling you that. That was your generous, yet untrusting heart. Nor was it God telling you not to share the details of your life. You cannot fully open yourself to God if you've closed yourself to others, including yourself."

"Leave."

CHAPTER 16

John returned home. His whole disappearance and being away fully sorted out with the media. Retreat at some camp for gentlemen. At first he decided that he'd been burned and the best thing to do was forget about her and forget about all the stupid shit she taught him about their being a loving and merciful God whose best interests at heart are the best interests of his children, even if his children may not understand his intentions at the time. He did not, surprisingly, get right back into the swing of things and the lifestyle he had before. Instead, he holed himself in his suite, refusing visitors and phone calls. It was Claire's persistence that finally led him to opening his door to her. It was her patience and calm-demeanor and soft voice that broke down his wall to sharing with one other person what had happened. And he did just that, unable to keep the tears of grief from welling in his eyes.

Afterward, she patted his shoulder and stood. "She went out of her way to save you from yourself. Perhaps it is now your turn to save her from herself."

It took a week, a lot of dead ends, and several monetary favors to finally track her down. A drive past the house showed her vehicle parked in the driveway, confirming he'd found the right Angie, and she was home. It had been nearly two months since he'd seen her.

He performed a U-turn with the intention of stopping at her house, trudging right up to the door, and sweeping her off her feet. Instead, as he neared the house, a sudden thought occurred to him that he hadn't previously considered. What if she's married or had a fiancée or a live-in boyfriend? That would explain *a lot*, especially her freaked out behavior after she initiated love with him. But why wouldn't she just tell him that? She was leaving him anyway, so why not just spare him all the questions without answers and tell him the truth?

John was parked on the side of the road, contemplating all these things, when suddenly he heard voices and laughter. He looked to the right and was struck breathless at the sight of her, almost as though his heart was trying to tear out of his chest in order to get to her. Then he saw the child. Maybe four years old.

"Come on, Mommy. We get the mail," the boy dragged at her arm.

She looked up and saw him before he could maneuver himself away from her privacy, and his violation, thereof. A silence that seemed forever passed as they looked at one another. Different emotional expressions crossed her face. Surprise, a flash of happiness, sadness, anger, something else.

"Go inside, honey. I'll be right in."

"But I want to get the mail."

"I will bring the mail to you. You know I don't like you going near the road. In the house, now."

"But mom, I told you. If a car tries to hit me, I will yell at them and tell their Mommy."

"*One . . .*"

The child scampered quickly into the house. The threat of a car, undaunting. Mommy getting to the count of three. Terrifying.

She slowly walked toward him. "What – uh – how did you – what are you – you weren't supposed to – Dammit, John." She sighed.

He opened the car door, stepped up to her and gave her a quick peck on the forehead, as well as the flowers behind his back. "Well, aren't you going to invite me in?"

"No, John, no I'm not going to invite you in." She was chasing after him as he walked up the small driveway. "We can discuss this from your car."

She'd shown no mercy when it came to intervening in his life, so he had no intention of showing any, as long as his heart could bare it. He entered her home. The boy was standing at the front door, peering through the screen.

"Why hello there, young man," John said in a booming voice.

"Hello," the kid said awkwardly. His attention focused elsewhere. "Mommy, you didn't get the mail."

"There wasn't any. Why don't you go play in your room?"

"But I don't want to play in my room. "

"Mommy has some important business to attend to, so I'm going to ask you only once more to go play in your room. I will come and get you when I'm ready. You didn't forget our plans tonight, did you?"

He scurried happily to his room, thinking about whatever plans they had in mind.

"He's beautiful," John said, watching him go, feeling a surge of something he'd never felt before.

She opened her mouth to say something, but closed it.

"And you're beautiful," he said more softly. "I've thought of nothing and no one but you since I last saw you."

"Why are you here, John?" Her voice was pleading.

"To see you. Why didn't you tell me you had a child? Was that the secret that I didn't know about you, the reason for why you had to say goodbye? You have nothing to be ashamed about, Angie. Nothing to hide from me. I love you, all of you, even if that means you have a child, a psychotic disorder, or Herpes for all I care. I love you and nothing else matters."

"That is probably the most romantic, yet perverse thing I've ever heard," she admitted with a weary laugh. "I told you it's complicated. Please can you go, John. Please."

"Not without an answer."

"I gave you my answer. I gave myself to the –."

"Mommy, I'm hungry."

"You like McDonalds, little man?"

"No, John, don't."

"I love Mickey D's," the boy said with overjoyed enthusiasm. "They got a playground and games and you get a toy."

"No, we're not going to –."

"What's your name, big boy?"

"I'm Henry," he said proudly.

"My name's John."

"Hello John. Are you going to be my Daddy? I've always wanted one."

XXX

"I told you this was a bad idea. I can't believe you used my son to get out of leaving."

"What're you talking about? Look at him, he's having a blast."

"He's just a little boy. He's vulnerable. He's going to get his heart –."

"John, John, look at me. Look what I can do," Henry called.

"All right, Henry. Want to see what I can do?"

"Yea!"

John picked him up, swung him around, and set him atop his back. From there he trampled about the place on his hands and knees.

"You better hold on tight."

"You're a bull. I'm riding a bull. Yeee-haaaa. Mommy, mommy, look. I'm riding a bull. I'm riding a bull. John's a bull."

John observed her pale face moments before she ran into the bathroom.

"Angie?"

"It's okay, John. Mommy gets sick all the time." Henry cupped his hand to John's ear and said, "She's having a baby. I'm gonna be a brother. That's what Mommy said."

And the bull weakened and nearly crumpled. John did the math. He lifted Henry off of him and dashed into the bathroom.

"It's occupied," she yelled, then looked up to see him. She was bent over the toilet, perspiring, holding her gut.

"You're pregnant," he said matter-of-factly, and moved to comb her hair into his fingers and hold it back.

"I'm not-."

"Don't deny it. I know. Henry told me."

"It's my punishment," she said bitterly.

"Punishment?"

"For being promiscuous. Now I must face the consequences, once again, for falling into temptation." She threw up again. He rubbed her back, got her a cold paper towel to place on her head.

"You're wrong. It's not a punishment. It's fate. God knew you'd be too stubborn, too short-sighted to accept his gift, to accept my love, so he planted my seed in you to tell you that I am to be yours and you mine. I can't believe I'm going to be a father. This is wonderful."

"No, as far as I recall, it was you planting your seed. God had nothing to do with that," she laughed a crazy laugh.

"I'm sorry. I was imprisoned against my will in a rehabilitation hospital. Had I known, I would have made sure I came prepared. I assumed you were on birth control."

"Why would I be on birth control?"

"I don't know. Usually when a woman pursues a man in the way that you definitely pursued me that night, and does not ask that he have protection, he is left to assume that she's already protected and it is not a concern. Besides, the thought of having a baby with you, being that I intend on spending my life with you, doesn't seem so bad."

"So you impregnated me on purpose?"

"Excuse me, Angie, for being blunt, but it seems you have some of the facts a little messed up. You fucked me, remember?"

"Oh, God, why do you have to make it sound so disgusting, so . . . awful?"

"Why do you have to make it feel like it was so awful? You pursued me. You knew exactly what you were doing when you showed up at the hospital that night. Then the way you left, the words you said. Can you imagine how that made me feel when I'd been believing that I'd just had the most magical, wonderful, amazing, and profound experience in my life? Then to walk out of my life the following day? Do you know what that feels like?"

"Yes, yes, I know what that feels like."

"But that's in the past. It's all in the past. I'm here with you now, you with me. You're going to have my baby and you have no idea how much that excites me. How unbelievable –."

"It's not yours."

A horrible silence followed as John tried to swallow this very blatant information.

"How do you know?"

"Because I'm only five weeks along, and you and I were –."

"Seven weeks."

"I screw a lot of guys, John. It's a weakness of mine and that which I'm trying to work on with the Lord."

"Now *you* make it sound disgusting and awful."

"Well, you know, sex is sex, 'till someone winds up pregnant."

"I don't know who you are," he said hurtfully, tinged with anger.

"You never did, John. You just thought you knew. You were my good deed."

XXX

It was another two weeks before Claire got the information out of him, to which she responded, "Hmmm, doesn't add up."

"What do you mean?"

"She reacted offended by the assumption that she'd be on birth control. Then she acted like she was a very promiscuous woman. Doesn't add up."

"What are you saying?"

"Promiscuous women who don't want to get pregnant eat birth control like candy. She acted as though she had no reason to be on birth control and took offense to your assuming such. Which means . . ."

"She wasn't having sex."

"Congratulations, John, you've just passed semester 1 on woman's pride and secrets 101. She's got a history, John, one she's been running from for a long, long time. She's trying to save you from herself because she cares about you and doesn't want to hurt you."

"But that's all she's done."

"In the short-term. She's thinking about the long-term. You heard her. She's punishing herself for whatever happened in the past and doesn't think she can have or really deserves someone like you. She probably thinks she deserves to be mistreated."

John kissed Claire in his excitement. "You really are something else, Claire. If I wasn't so in love with this woman, I might have gone after you."

XXX

John showed up at Angie's doorstep the following day, hardly able to contain his excitement and his new-found knowledge. She wasn't home. So he found a position on her porch steps that was comfortable and occupied his time with finding scripture that might open her to her ways of self-punishment and needless redemption. Something happened to her for sure, but John knew, for sure, it wasn't her fault. After all, she was the one raising a four year old child alone and trying every measure to compensate. Punishment comes in the consequences. That which is self-inflicted is shame.

She had hardly put the car in park before Henry was opening the door and running toward him. "John! John! I missed you." John savored the hug from the most innocent of species before conditions are learned. Babies. Toddlers. Children.

"Missed you too, buddy. What do you need to do now?"

"Brush my teeth and get ready for bed."

"Well then you better go do that."

"Will you read me a bedtime story?"

"I sure will."

"Are you going to leave again? It makes Mommy cry and hurts her heart."

"I'm not going to leave if your Mommy doesn't want me to."

Angie had a much less enthusiastic response. She dropped her head into her hand and groaned.

"It's not a good time for this, John," she said, as she entered into the house.

"When's a good time?" he followed her.

Silence.

She moved into, what he assumed, was the bathroom, and got the tub water running. He plopped comfortably on the couch and listened to the sound of a mother and child interacting and going about their daily routine.

He loved the sounds and closed his eyes with a smile pressed to his lips. He was woken abruptly when Henry jumped on him, smelling so sweet.

"You promised a bedtime story."

"That I did. Did you pick out a book you want me to read?"

"No, I want you to make it up in your head."

A little intimidated at first, John laid him into bed, and thought of the similarities. Both of them wanting a father to love them and be proud of them. Both of them suffering from that type of neglect that never quite leaves a person should it not be fulfilled.

"There once was a time when there was a dragon named Emri. Emri was a wonderful, amazing, and handsome dragon. He was always happy and had such joy for the world. He loved everyone and everything, and he especially loved his mom. Everyone thought he the happiest dragon in the world, but what they didn't know, is that sometimes Emri got sad. He got sad because all the other dragons had a mom and dad who loved them very much, or so it seemed, and though his mom loved him very much, sometimes he wished he had his dad.

"See, his dad was away all the time, working, fighting battles, doing what he thought was best, perhaps trying to save the world, perhaps trying to make the best life he could for the Emri he never saw. Emri couldn't understand these things. Emri didn't know his dad loved him or thought of him all the time. Emri didn't know that when Emri was thinking of him, he was thinking of Emri. Emri didn't know that his dad was doing the best he could the only way he knew how, even if that meant being away from Emri. So Emri makes a vow that he will never choose anything over his own son.

"Emri grows up and finds a girl dragon and they have baby dragons. Emri said he'd always be there with his children, but they cry because they're hungry and cold. So Emri knows that he must be there for his children, but he must also keep them fed and keep them warm, so Emri goes out into the world to find a way to feed his children and keep them warm. His children cry that he is gone, but they don't know that he has to be away and he has to work to keep them well and warm and fed and that every minute he is thinking of and missing his children. It's not long after that that Emri hears word that his father is very sick and he must go see him. Emri hasn't seen his father in years. What will he say?

"Emri's father is old and wrinkled. He's nothing like he remembers. He's dying. And he cries and he tells Emri how much he's always loved him, how proud he is at how Emri turned out, and he regrets not having seen Emri grow up and create his own family. Then Emri's father tells him that he spent his life away making sure that Emri would never have to be away from his kids, so that he could be with his kids and watch them grow up. Emri's father dies and leaves Emri with all his life's work. A beautiful home, lots of land, and money, so that Emri would never have to worry again about how he can support his family, because the dad he thought he never had, had made sure that Emri could be the bestest dad in the world."

John wiped the tears from his eyes and tucked the blankets tighter around Henry. He started walking out the door.

"I love you, John. I hope you're like Emri."

"Get some sleep, bud. Dream good dreams."

John found Angie sitting against the wall next to her son's door, in a fresh bout of tears. She'd heard everything. He crouched down beside her and pulled her into his arms.

"This is a cashmere suit, if you can try not to get snot on it," he said.

She laughed and hiccupped and resumed crying. "I'm a bad person, John. I'm an awful, awful person."

"No, you're human and flawed, as am I, and I love you more for just that reason. I'm sorry I left you. Angie, it doesn't matter if the baby is not mine. I love you still. I love

Henry. I love the unborn child, because they are all a part of you. I will raise him or her as my own and never love them any less for it."

"Oh, John. The baby's yours. You're the first man I've been with in almost five years, since I became pregnant with Henry. I wanted you so bad, but I felt so ashamed. So ashamed afterward. Not of you, but of myself. Of my lack of control. I was raised with the law of no sex before marriage, and especially no kids out of wedlock. The world has changed, generations have changed. I have difficulty balancing the two – what I was taught and what I see happening around me and what I feel inside.

"See, it's not just that promiscuity is up. Duty and loyalty is down. Men don't start off pursuing women with celibacy, marriage, and a life-long commitment in mind, like they did back then. Marriage and commitment is the last step on the courting ritual, whereas once upon a time, it was the first. I've spent my life trying to follow my parents' rules, but I can't tell you one man who has proposed to me or vowed his life to me without other conditions being met, such as seeing if we're sexually compatible or seeing if we can even fathom living together for a time before making such a big decision. Except for you, of course. You told me you'd marry me and you knew so little about me and had never even gotten a kiss. Then I screwed it all up because I felt so alone. I've felt so alone all my life, where other people have companions, girlfriends, boyfriends, friends, and I'm supposed to follow this doctrine that tells me to stay away from all that temptation. Friends don't want to go out with a woman who can't have a good time, can't drink, can't have fun with a man without the marriage contract, because that's what they're doing. They're having fun. They're drinking. They're picking up one-night flings at the bar and being proud of their conquest. And seeing this, it does cause me to question whether such an ancient artifact that depicted a society thousands and thousands of years ago can still be relevant today. Society has changed. People have changed. And the rules only work if the majority of citizens follow those rules.

"Besides, I hated my parent's relationship. It was so rigid and authoritative. Dad worked. Mom stayed at home to raise the kids. Mom made every decision around my father, no matter how unfair and even cruel it was at times. We were homeschooled, never allowed friends, or freedom. It was a very monotonous and ritualistic upbringing. Keep your feelings contained and maintain neutrality. Don't cry. Don't get excited. Don't get sad. Don't be happy. Don't sing. Don't dance. Always greet one another and other people with the utmost respect. Curtsy, bow, hold out the skirt, make sure the ankles aren't showing. No makeup. No hair ties. No flirting. I never saw my parents kiss, hug, hold hands, or even look at each other with anything less than formality. I don't even know how they managed to have nine kids," she laughed. "It sounds so horrible, doesn't it?"

"Well, those were the choices they made and lived with. It worked for them. If it doesn't work for you, then you are a free woman in the twenty-first century and you can make your own choices. You remember how the bible tells Adam and Eve created naked as a baby, and there was only shame and self-consciousness when they did what they were told was the forbidden?"

"Of course."

"Shame is not something we are born with. It is instilled. God, their father, their creator, said, 'Do not eat the fruit from the forbidden tree'. They did not listen, were confronted, and were taught shame. Shame because what they felt they did was wrong? Or shame because someone else in a more authoritative role told them it was wrong? In the bible it speaks frequently of obeying one's parents, wives obeying their husbands; thus outlining the patriarchal society at that time. Those who did not obey one's parents, wives whom did not obey their husbands, citizens whom did not obey the social rules and laws at the time, were taught shame through created boundaries of right and wrong. And man is flawed, is he not?"

She nodded again.

"So then doesn't it go to show that the very man to make the rules can make flawed rules out of poor or unenlightened judgment? Then wrongfully instilling shame to those who do not fulfill his flawed reasoning? So then how must one break out of a flawed society? There's always a battle of the generations, one generation finding the flawed reasoning in the others and attempting to either maintain the traditional or break free from it. Unfortunately, society moves a lot more slowly than the generations. It's not that your parents were doing anything wrong outside of their awareness, but it was wrong for you and you've had to suffer a life of instilled shame that you don't quite agree with because of it. How can we truly unconditionally love others if we cannot get past shame over self and self's weaknesses? This is what creates judgmental mentalities and reproduces more shame into others. Which I can so appreciate right now that you are nothing like your mother."

Angie bellowed out loud at this unexpected comment.

"I think religion is an over-rated means for certain persons to subject their authority and judgment on others, because we're a whole lotta people living in the same world, each and every one of us wanting things our own way. Should we have the authority, the resources, the power, to accomplish that, then what is it to stop us from making things our own way?"

"Stop that," she smacked him playfully. "You're making a mockery of it all."

"I am making a mockery of it all. I'm making a mockery of the fact that even though I told you I'd marry you, because you made love to me before we had that contract in our hands providing us permission, you, in your shame, were prepared to completely devastate me, for one, and two, have another child out of wedlock so that you can then repeat the cycle of debilitating shame. Now tell me woman, how does that make any sense whatsoever?"

"Punishing myself, I suppose."

"And punishing me and your children for the fact that you've spent your life punishing yourself for not being able to be what your parents wanted you to be, because your parents always told you what they wanted you to be is what God wants you to be. And here we find the significant similarities between you and I, despite our completely different upbringings. Battle of the generations. And the more inflexible the former generation, the more messed up the latter generation is going to be trying to balance a variety of contradicting demands. So now we have democracy that says every perspective and group and religion and belief is valid, every one has a right to their own opinion, every one has freedom of assembly, which has created warfare within our own communities versus peace and acceptance, because human weakness dictates that we must have something to believe in and we must have a purpose, and our purpose becomes to make the others see our purpose, because we know as much about acceptance and openness as we do unconditional. Which brings us back to our very first concept – we are a very fucked up species. We *are* the cancer that infests the lungs, nodes, blood, and brain of our planet."

"And to think I just thought you a low-life drug-addicted rich spoiled bratty scumbag." She laughed.

"I'm just repeating what a very sweet person said to me. That, and she took graduate level Psychology classes, so she must know something, right?"

"Right." She smiled.

"Now that that's resolved, why don't we drink to our engagement, our wedding in the near near future, and the rest of our beautiful lives together."

All of a sudden, a loud boom struck the door. It was thrown open and four large men grabbed hold of him.

"Hey, get your hands –."

He was struck harshly in the nose. Three women then came rushing in and grabbed hold of Angie as she screamed for John. They took her out of the room, then knocked John into unconsciousness.

CHAPTER 17

John arose on cold ground, damp, dark. His head and face were killing him. He could feel the crusted blood on his face. What the hell happened?

"Rise and shine, sunshine. How's your head?"

He couldn't make out the image of the other person present, though the tone told him he wasn't a fellow prisoner. Perhaps one of the people who put him there.

"This is just protocol. Sorry about the surroundings. They get worse the longer you're here, but should you be cooperative, you won't be down here very long, will ya? Tell me your name."

John immediately thought about using his name and resources to get out of this mess fast. There's no way they would be able to continue to contain him knowing who he was. But he thought of Angie, having no idea what happened to her, and remained clueless as to what exactly he'd gotten himself into.

"Bill Junior, Sir."

"Good, very good."

"And what is your business with Angie?"

"I was a client of hers that she assisted with rehabilitation and bringing me to the Lord."

"And this 'assistance' typically occurred in her home?"

"No, I was in residence over at Grove Hospital."

"So what brought you to her home unsupervised?"

"Unsupervised. I'm a 29 year old man, and as far as I'm aware, she is a full-grown woman with legal rights to do as she damn pleases."

"You said she assisted in bringing you to our Lord. Did she fail to mention the rules of our community and her role in it?" John heard a catch in this man's voice that caused him to suspect this was a lot more serious than he'd ever anticipated. Oh, Angie.

"She ended her assistance once I was released."

"Well that's unusual for a client-therapist relationship. Typically there's several follow-ups to ensure you're sober and haven't relapsed and –."

"She ended it because she noticed my growing attraction toward her," John said.

"So she just cut it off abruptly and left you to your own devices."

"That's correct."

"So how then, sir, did you wind up in her home unsupervised on two different occasions?"

"I believed I'd fallen in love with her. I tracked her down to continue to pursue her."

"Is this usual behavior for you?"

"Not at all. Love does funny things to a person. It is irrational."

"LOVE IS THE GREATEST EVIL," he boomed. "To love is to give our heart and soul to another, and if one gives their heart and soul to another, then they are not giving it to God. It's idolatry. Worshipping something as you would worship him. Did Angie not teach you these things during her ministries of you?"

"You are misinterpreting me, sir. I told you I believed I'd fallen in love with her, which sometimes occurs with patients and those who help them. I showed up at her home to tell her my love for her. A confused man. Angie didn't do anything wrong. Tell me, is she all right? I did not mean to cause her any harm. A desperate man at rock bottom."

"You are a very good liar, but a liar all the same. Tell me, was your and Angie's relationship completely platonic?"

"Of course. I went to her home to propose to her."

"Platonic is as it will always remain with Angie, or is this something else she did not tell you? Did Angie tell you that she is already a promised woman to the Lord? Having a bastard illegitimate child is grounds to be exiled from the community. Angie redeemed herself by making her vows, and swearing celibacy for eternity in order to give herself to God."

John gasped involuntarily. "Angie's a nun?" He could almost feel the man smile.

"So, someone committed a crime here, John. There are markings on her that reveal something less than a platonic nature. So, either she involuntary led you into her home by not telling you of her status, voluntarily led you into her home and allowed you to ravage her, or, as Angie is currently claiming, you came into her home and attempted an intimacy without her consent. Should you confess to the last, Angie will be let go immediately and be free of charges against her, and continue to be a Sister in our community. The punishment to you, on the other hand, will be grave. You do not have to answer now. I will give you 24 hours to ponder it. Food and water will be provided to you per your confession."

XXX

Over the next 24 hours, John alternated between feeling the worst of betrayals that she would accuse him of such and understanding why she had to. She'd said it was complicated, and he had underestimated such complications. Yet she had let him in her home, knowing the consequences. Risked herself for him. Then turned on him. But she had babies to protect. Henry and the one on the way. They would all know once she started showing that they'd been intimate. There was no way out of this without someone being punished. Black and white. The way Angie had taught him of God and portrayed him to be was nothing what he was enduring now and learning more and more about this community. They knew nothing of God.

Poor Angie. How did she ever wind up in this mess? But she betrayed him and could she have done that if she had truly loved him? Or had she accepted the doctrine after all? A loveless heart lonely for company.

By the 22nd hour, John was dry-heaving, having had no food or water in a time period he was not even aware. How long had he been unconscious? He had no watch. No sense of time. No light rising and falling and turning into dark. It was all dark, always, and nothing but one's own thoughts and physical discomforts to occupy one's time. Finally he heard the creak of a door.

"Are you ready to confess?"

"Did you bring water and food?" John said, his voice raw and hoarse.

His neck cracked from the impact of the man's fist.

"I did not ask if you had any questions. I asked if you are ready to confess."

"Yes. I pursued her. Tracked her down. Drove to her house. Let myself into her home when she had told me to remain in the car. She had talked about going to McDonalds with her son, where she left me and told me to leave her alone and to not come back again. I did. I let myself back into her home. Tried to talk to her some more. Then I thought that if I could just show her what I felt …"

John was answered with another crack to the face and the man turned to leave.

"The food and water you promised," John yelled in a hoarse whisper.

The door closed shut.

XXX

On three additional occasions, John assumed at 24 hour intervals, he was violently asked to confess, which he did each and every time, not once changing his story, though he had begun to feel that perhaps his confession was not the confession this man wanted to hear. John was provided only enough food and water to keep him conscious, though he strayed in and out of such consciousness, suffered from the brutal beatings to his face and body, and hardly had the strength and will to move his body.

He was provided a surprise visit in the silence of the night, where there was no light and no sound when the door was opened.

"Who's there?" he said hoarsely, then coughed.

The man did not speak. Rather paced the floor back and forth for several minutes. Finally he spoke, his voice desperate. "Angie has confessed. She is with child. She would not admit that you had raped her. You will be released. You will move on with your life and forget this ever happened."

"Angie committed no wrong. She was appropriate in every way. The sin is mine and mine alone."

"Damn you!" the man barked loudly. "Damn you to hell." Suddenly he sat, his breathing erratic. Silence passed for a great length of time. "Would it matter if I told you that I will torture you and kill you if you do not confess Angie's sin?"

"No, it would not matter. Angie is innocent."

More silence passed.

"I will marry her," John said.

"You cannot. She is already betrothed to God."

"And what are the ways to break a betrothal?"

"One of the parties commits a crime against the community, or each other, or one dies."

"And if one were to wind up missing?"

"We have people everywhere. To just simply disappear is almost impossible. I can't tell you how many have run, tried to escape, and have been found and placed in exile."

"So it is a community that keeps people against their will."

"It's a community that takes its vows very seriously, unlike your world where people marry whomever they please, divorce, and marry another, have faith one day, but not the next.
When one is born into it, then there is little chance of escape." John heard resignation in the man's voice.

"I am Henry's father," he admitted. "Angie refused to marry me, placing us both in the position of exile. She preferred to swear herself into being a celibate nun than to marry me," he said bitterly. "The only way I can be released from my commitment to constant redemption is if it is proven she has broken her vows. It is the woman that possesses the forbidden fruit, but we are punished for accepting it. Should you just confess her crimes, this can all be over for all of us."

"Angie is innocent. My name is John Whitman. My father is Bill Whitman, the second wealthiest person in the United States. We have a lot of resources, and I don't think your community can afford a huge legal battle, regardless of the protections of your religion. Allow me one phone call, this can all be over, Angie will disappear without any opportunity of being found. You'll never have to deal with me again. You'll be freed. And you will receive a sizeable anonymous donation for your cooperation. You can keep it, give it to the church, disappear yourself, whatever."

After a long silence, John received a response.

"I will allow you one phone call under the most discretion. No one is to know of this phone call or anything that follows. I will make the arrangements."

"I thank you."

John received another crack upside the head. "What the hell was that for?" he shouted angrily.

"Forgiveness for your attempts at bribery and making threats toward our Church, and a warning," the man's voice suddenly cracked. "Take good care of my son."

XXX

It felt like several days had passed since his phone call. He had no visitors, but was provided more food and drink at his door, which he ate and drank heartily. Finally, the door opened and he was temporarily blinded by the light.

"John. John, oh God, John, I'm so sorry." He heard the voice of his angel. She ran to him, wrapped her arms around him, felt him all over for broken bones and infected wounds. "Oh, they've hurt you. It's all my fault. It's all my fault," she cried.

"I don't know how in the world you get yourself into these messes, son. Stand up. We're leaving. We must be discreet and quick." His father had personally made the trip down, which John thought, at that time, was done merely to rub it into John's face how he never failed to disappoint him.

"Can you stand? Can you walk? What did they do to you?"

"You must compose yourself and be quiet, Claire. Our success depends on you playing your role perfectly."

"Claire?" John said, aptly confused, because it was not Claire's voice he heard.

John was led out the door. Once in the light and adjusted he turned to her. She was a replica of Claire, except for her eyes and her voice, and he knew in those eyes that she was his Angie. His father, such a clever man. A rock. And John felt a temporary rush of emotion for the man he'd resented and despised for so long.

XXX

John stood before his towering father in the office that had consumed so much of his father's life and love. "I am going to cover for you, boy, and once again let you have what you want. I have seen a change in you, so I do agree that you truly care for this woman and this care has settled you and provided you some peace. I have offered Claire a substantial sum of money to be the one in the spotlight while your lady-love remains completely anonymous. They will go to the same places. Claire is to be the only one seen. They will wear the same clothes. Once within the privacy of such places, you and Angie can enjoy your time together and you may court her as you please.

"Claire will get all the media attention. There will be rumors. She will neither confirm nor deny them. She will do as she's told. She is the greatest asset we have right now, and I know she has acted as a mother-figure toward you as well, watching out for you. You will treat her with the utmost respect as it is she to make the greatest sacrifice so that you can have what you want. You will be able to marry your girl, and the world will think it Claire. Once everything is settled, you wed, settle down, and stop creating so much damn drama, the media leeches will find something else to occupy their stations, and will leave you alone. Understand?"

John nodded, feeling the inferior little boy as he always had sitting before his father and listening to his father speak. He both resented it and admired his father's powerful aura and strength, in spite of being chronically ill and having only months to live. John began to stand.

"Sit down. I am not finished yet."

John did.

"You are my only son, and therefore the son that is going to acquire my life's successes upon my death. I didn't spend the majority of my life building this business off the ground to have it all fall down upon my death. I expect you to carry out the family name, continue to build this company, so that any grandchild of mine may be able to assume it when you retire. Had I had a son that wanted to be financially productive and wanted to do something other than run around, party, and lay in bed all day, perhaps I could have retired at an earlier age and had some peace and relaxation before my death. This is not the case and I will be running this company up until my death."

John's bitterness came forward. "At any time you could have had someone else running the business while you kept ownership. We're not exactly lacking for the funds to afford such."

"No one knows this company like I do."

"Yes, but there are plenty of others more willing to learn than I. You already know my feelings on this. I will not spend every waking hour behind that desk, neglecting my family and the important things in life for a job, for money, as you did and continue to do, even as a dying man. You'd think, as a dying man, you would refocus your priorities and enjoy the things in life that have nothing to do with money and work, but as you said, you will be sitting behind that desk until you die. In fact, that's probably exactly where you'll die, which is really quite fitting."

"You will learn this business! You will be my son and you will accept my life's work!" his father demanded.

"I will not."

"You WILL!" his father shouted, slamming his fist on the desk.

John stood. "You may own a lot of things, but you do not own me. The fact that you're one of the wealthiest men in the world means nothing to me. The fact that you've never been a father to me is something that will forever haunt me. I have no intention of doing that to my own children, and I was really hoping that at the end of your days, this is something that you would actually come to see. You don't even know me. I was raised by your servants. You can rot behind that desk for all I care. I have nothing more to say to you and need no further to have anything to do with you. You may be ashamed that I am your son, but I am equally ashamed that you are my father. Goodbye."

And John had kept true to his word, as it was the last conversation he'd ever have with his father.

CHAPTER 18

John rubs his forehead, papers strewn out all across the cherry wood desk. His father had dotted all his I's and crossed his t's in the efficient running of the company following his death, however, he had never intended on his Chief Advisor forfeiting his life to a drunken car wreck, leaving the company and the company's future entirely in John's hands.

Guilt follows him every second of the day. When home and not working, he can hear his father's words, see his father's disappointment, and mostly see his father's skin-and-bones frame and bluish pallor as he cooled in his death. Had his father wanted to provide closure, apologies, or show his love in the end, John had not allowed it. John had never visited him once in the ending stages. Never held his hand. And especially, never told his father how he really felt.

Now he is constantly burdened with the whys, what ifs, maybes, and if onlys. He had become very much his father's son, equivalent in the inability to share one's emotions and feelings, to feel something so strongly within, yet never let it seep toward the surface. If this was the case, then his father had always loved him and expressed it in working seven days a week, 18 hours a day. Not working for himself or his enjoyment of such, but working non-stop until the very end to be able to leave the grandest empire behind. I don't love you this much. I love you this much. I have made you the second richest man in the world. That is how much I love you.

John is haunted by these thoughts night and day, and thus plagued by all the ways in which he'd hurt his father, disrespected him, and never cared for all that his father provided, for all his father had done, just because he'd had a father that didn't know how to hug, hold, kiss, or scruff his head. *People show their love differently,* he remembers Angie's words from seeming so long ago.

John now recognizes his father was an amazing man. Yet John, probably the only person his father had cared to want appreciate him and admire him, did not. Only in trying to fill those shoes does John acknowledge that he cannot fill them by half. He is working constantly, yet striving just to keep the company afloat and the vultures away.

A gentle knock on the door alerts him. "Come in."

Claire enters, working as late as he, a priceless asset and responsible for a lot of his life's enjoyments. "It's your wife. Line 1."

"Shit. Will you tell her I'll call her back in a little while? I've just got a few more things to do."

"No, you can tell her yourself. Just trust me from a woman's perspective."

"Claire, come on. I pay you well enough, don't I?"

"You're sounding like your father," she says. "I'm going home, John. I'll see you on Monday."

"Monday? No, I need you to work Saturday. I've got a –."

"Saturday is Christmas Eve, John, and Sunday is Christmas. Perhaps you ought to write it down in your schedule so that you'll remember. Goodnight."

John groans, pours himself a double shot of Brandy, then picks up the phone with dread. "Hey there, Angel Dove. I was just thinking about you."

"If you were thinking of me, you'd be here," John listens over the phone. He notices her voice is tense.

"I'm sorry, honey. I'm working late at the office tonight. Trying to get everything done before Christmas so that I can spend it with my family. Is that so bad?"

"I'm sorry, John. I don't recall the last holiday we spent together. Ever since your dad died –."

"Please, not right now, Claire." He realizes his mistake immediately.

"What did you just call me? Did you just call me Claire?"

"It was a simple mistake, Angie. It's because I was just talking to her, and her being my assistant and all . . ."

"I'm sure you were just *talking* to her, and both of you just happen to be working at the office until 11 at night. What secretary works until 11 at night?"

"Claire is not a secretary. She is my executive assistant and my advisor."

"Oh, I'm so glad you're prepared to jump up and defend her, but you don't defend my accusations."

"What accusations, exactly, are you making, Angie? Is this really where you want to go with this right now? Are you accusing me of having an affair?"

"Is that what it is? Are you having an affair? You're never home. Always at the office. You can take so many potential clients out on a date, with Claire, of course, but you don't have enough time to take me. I did not plan for this, John. Had I known, I never would have married you. Henry lost another tooth today, but you wouldn't know that, would you? He stayed up as long as he possibly could for you to get home so that he could show you his tooth. And Lucas –."

John hangs up the phone. He doesn't mean it, though has no intention of calling her back or answering the phone as it rings. In fact, he pulls the plug right out of the wall so he doesn't have to listen to it ring. When did she become such a nag? She didn't bargain for his working all the time, but he certainly didn't bargain for her witching all the time.

He's doing the best he can. They want their luxurious livelihood, then he's gotta work. He has to have something to offer his children, and perhaps it will never be as profound, as accomplished as his father, but it will at least be something. He can't just let this company bury itself into the ground or be overtaken. The only way to continue to be accomplished is to remain on top. As long as he stays on top, he is secure and untouchable. Why can't Angie understand this? She should be proud of him.

He has to set an example for his kids. Life is not about play beyond 25 years old. The first 25 years, your loving parents provide you the opportunity to live your life and make the most experiences. After 25, it's time to be the loving parent and provide that opportunity to your kids.

John pours another glass of brandy and stares out the window, resenting the simplicity of other's lives.

XXX

John is awoken abruptly with a cry, and sees Claire standing above him, a glass in her hand. He is soaked and very cold. Next thing he recalls she is placing coffee in his hand and ibuprofen down his throat.

"Swallow it," she says. "I had a feeling I'd find you like this."

John's back creaks and cracks with every movement. He'd been sleeping on the hard floor and age was reminding him of the consequences.

She comes behind him and begins rubbing his shoulders and back. It feels amazing. "I scheduled you an appointment for the chiropractor on Monday."

"You know Monday's are my busiest days, Claire."

"He'll come to you."

"That feels so good. Can you – a little harder? – Yes, perfect." He closes his eyes and enjoys the sensations of her fingers on his back, kneading his muscles, making him feel so good.

"Did you have a fight with Angie?"

"She thinks I'm having an affair. She's been on this thinking for a while. I suppose according to her the only way a man can be working late is if he's having an affair."

"I presume she is pointing her fingers at me?"

"Of course. Every wife is jealous of the female staff he works with."

"Well, you do spend more time in a day with me and more time communicating with me. You can't blame her for that."

"You understand me."

"I understand her too."

"Does Paul suspect anything? Does he believe you to be having an affair?"

"An affair? No. But he would like me home more often and reminds me frequently that the money is of no consequence as he can provide for me."

"Then why do you remain? Why do you do the work you do for me?"

"Because you need me."

"You're unique, Claire. So very different. Loyalty is unheard of now-a-days, but you –."

"I'm going to assume that you're still feeling the effects of last nights' drinking. Go home, John. It's Christmas. Your family needs you."

"I love them so much."

"I know you do."

"But there's so much work that has to be –."

"Go home, John. The work will still be there Monday morning."

"I don't know what I'd do without you, Claire."

"You know the right thing to do, John. You are your father's son, but you are not your father. Go home to your family. They're waiting for you as mine is waiting for me."

XXX

John watches his family enjoy their Christmas. He feels like an outsider, a stranger peering in through the window of a loving home. When did Lucas start walking? When did he stop wearing diapers? Henry can ride a bike without training wheels and he's got a mean curve ball. A pitcher. And John knows that he can't take credit for any of it, as he hasn't been there.   Angie is now six months along with their third child. He pictures her in the earlier days, so small and frail. A size 3. Beautiful. He hadn't been the only one to change. They had both changed. Were they growing apart? He couldn't speak with her about work. In fact, she had set a house rule that there was not to be any talk of work while he was there. How can you not share with your life partner the very thing that dominates your life, the only thing in his life? That leaves nothing to say, really, except for idle chatter.

A face once so joyous and full of smiles and love is now etched in worry, unhappiness, and hopelessness. She no longer greets him when he comes home. He misses having her jump into his arms the moment he stepped through the door, the excitement in having a homemade dinner on the table for him and wondering how he will like it. She would sit in the chair, hardly able to keep still, and watch him with those big blue eyes as he took his first bite. So hopeful. So devoted to his happiness. So innocent.

He opens a gift from her. It is a beautiful framed photo of their rare moments of family fun. Angie looking at him with such loving eyes. Her arm around Henry. Lucas on his lap with a drooling smile. A lazy contented grin on his own face.

"You can put it on your desk at the office, so you won't forget. Maybe sometimes you'll remember to look at it," she says, her tone edged with bitterness.

He swallows his come-back, kisses her, and says, "It's beautiful. And this is for you." He pulls a small box out of his robe pocket. She opens it without enthusiasm. Stares at the Cerulean blue studs and heart-shaped pendant. "Claire has very good taste, for people who like that kind of thing. I'm sure it will look very beautiful on her," she says with an emotionless tone. Then she tosses him the box and walks out of the room.

XXX

Come Monday, John couldn't be more pleased to be back at the office. It had been a sufferable two days and a Christmas he'd rather forget, as even his own children did not give him pleasant grateful hugs, rather issued cold emotionless thank yous for the gifts he'd bought. A Playstation 4 for Henry and a battery-powered jeep for Lucas. How is he supposed to handle the demands and expectations of a career and a family, when such demands often conflicted with one another? Both of them wanted a significant amount of his time and he just doesn't have enough of it. Perhaps he's his father's son after all and should never have thought that he could be any different.

John stares out the window, sipping spiked coffee at 9 in the morning, when Claire arrives, always chipper and looking fantastic.

"Here, you can have these," he offers her the box.

"But I bought these for you to give to your wife?"

"Yes, I guess it's not her thing, or whatever she said. She told me to give them to you because they'd look more beautiful on you. And I'd have to agree."

"I'm sorry, John. I told you I'm not very good at shopping for people. What *is* her thing? You told me to just go and get her something nice and that made me think jewelry. What does she like?"

"Christmas is over. Better luck next year. I don't know what she likes or what pleases her. Sometimes I feel that there is nothing that can. In fact, sometimes I feel like I don't know her at all. She's changed so much. Here, let me," he stands to help her with the jewelry.

He stands behind her. She lifts her hair so that he can clasp the necklace. John notices the smell of her hair, the creaminess of her skin, her closeness to him, their proportioned heights, and savors the smell of her perfume. When was the last time he'd made love with his wife? But even that thought doesn't seem too appealing. He finds himself wondering what Claire must be like. Soft and gentle? A firecracker? Full of passion?

"You've been so good to me, Claire," he whispers.

"You smell like you've gotten into the drink already, and it's hardly 9:30." She steps away from him. He notices her voice is shaky. Does she feel it too?

They both turn at the guttural sound of someone's pain and watch Angie flee from the office.

XXX

John pounds on the door. "Angie, come on, don't lock me out. I want to talk about this. It's not what it looked like. I was just helping her put the necklace on. You said you didn't like it."

"You're drunk again, John."

"I'm not drunk. I just had a few drinks. You have no idea what it's like, Angie. The pressure. Having the whole weight of the success of this company on my shoulders. This is only a milestone. It's not forever. I told you that. As soon as I can find someone who is qualified, then I can start to distribute the responsibilities."

"You've been saying that for almost three years, John."

"Yes, and it has taken me that long to learn the company and the market. I can't sufficiently train someone if I myself don't know. I didn't plan for this but it's going to get better. And then we can be a family again. I'll be home more often. I'll help you with the kids. We'll go out and do things together like families do. Don't do this, Claire. Son of a —."

"You did not just call me by her name again." She begins to cry.

"Angie, please, you need to stop this. I love you. You. I married you. I chose to spend my life with you."

"But all you can ever think of is Claire. Why don't you go hit her up for a place to stay? I'm sure she'll be more than happy to share her bed with you."

This enrages him. "You know what, Angie. I might just do that. You think I'm having an affair with her anyway and nothing I say or do can change your mind about that, so I might as well make it true."

CHAPTER 19

John is in and out of conscious awareness, reality and dreams a line he can't separate. For all Angie's life-saving techniques to get him on the right path, he's back to a life of being unloved and unwanted. He'd spent 30 years longing to have what he had now with his deceased father, and his wife just didn't understand. Claire understood. After all, it was Claire who was there when his father was sick and dying. Claire that was there when he was getting in one scrape after another, trying to get his father's attention. Claire that saw how deeply it had wounded him to lose his father without any last words, because of his stubborn refusal to acknowledge his father in death and dying, as his father refused to acknowledge him in life.

He kept his office door locked, refused even Claire's presence, unhooked the phone, and dabbled in the drugs and alcohol that were once his escape from this reality. At one point he heard Claire knocking and yelling through the door. The next he's seeing her ethereal face floating above him, just her face.

"It's time," he hears her say, her neck twisted to the right, before he returns to his oblivion.

The next time he comes through he is no longer in his office. This wouldn't have concerned him enough to waking but for the straps on his ankles and wrists imprisoning him to a chair.

"What the - ?" His first thought is that he won't be able to abstain from withdrawals while strapped to a chair, causing exactly that to double him over where he retches on the floor. The room is pitch black, which he notices as soon as the withdrawal passed for the moment.

"Hello! Hello! Can anyone hear me?" he yells, or more or less croaks. His mouth is parched.

"I'm here, John."

"Claire? Claire, what the hell is going on?"

"I'm helping you," she says, but her voice, though Claire's, is oddly cold and strange. He cries out when she yanks back his head and he feels a sharp prick in his neck. His withdrawals instantly disappeared.

"Oh, thank you, thank you, Claire. You've always been my favorite. I should – I should have married you, not her. You've always understood. You've always been so nice. You've always known what I needed."

"Oh, shut up, John," she snaps. "The only thing you've ever cared about are your own needs. Just like your father, you think of no one else's but your own. Given a second chance at life when you found that girl. Everything your father and I went through so you could have that girl, and you're throwing it all away. And now, even though you don't deserve a third chance, you're being given the gift of your third and final chance, but it's going to cost you."

"Cost me?"

"You've been chosen, John. You've been chosen by *Him*."

"*Him?* None of this is real, is it? How long have I been high? I'm dreaming or hallucinating. The Claire I know doesn't sound like you. So sweet. So kind. So gentle. So much like my mother."

"ENOUGH!" a low male voice resonates loudly through the room. "I am *He*, and you have been chosen. I offer you my gift, a very rare and precious gift indeed. I offer you a glimpse into your future for a million dollars that you can certainly spare."

"Who are you? Wha-where are you?"

"Behind you, in front of you, surrounding you, and inside you. Are you willing to pay the price for this gift, your third, and your final chance? I have chosen you, because I have seen your future, and it is grim, John, but in giving you the power to hold the future in your hands, you can change it if you're so willing."

John tries to will his eyes to see in the dark, but all he can see are glimpses of a black silhouette, seeming nowhere and everywhere at once.

"There's no such thing as a man that can tell the future. Impossible."

"*I AM HE!*" the voice roars. The room shakes and trembles, and suddenly the floor is no longer beneath John's feet. The floor opens up to a white rectangular light. John's eyes tear over as he tries to keep them open against the blinding light. His eyes adjust and he finds himself looking at Angie's downcast head, her beautiful red hair drawn over her face and her shoulders. Her shoulders are shaking.

"Angie! What did you do to my wife?!"

Harsh laughter echoes throughout the room. "This is not what I did. It's what *you* did." Zooming out, he sees that Angie is sitting at his desk in his office. On the desk before her are his empty liquor bottles and used needles. Suddenly, as though somehow aware that her private moment is being shared, she looks directly at John, her beautiful blue eyes shining with tears, her face profound with devastation. Abruptly all goes black and his feet return to the floor.

"NO, no, no! She wasn't supposed to see. She wasn't supposed to see. I just needed a few days to get my head straight, that's all."

"You haven't been home in two weeks, John." Claire's voice.

"Oh no! What's – what's going to happen now? I'll go back to the hospital. I'll get clean again. I can't lose her. I just *can't*! Tell me. Am I going to lose her?"

"Are you willing to pay the price?"

"Yes, yes, anything. Please, just please tell me I won't lose her."

"That is in your power and your power alone, John. I can only show you what your future looks like right now, from this moment. You will pick a time in the future, and you will see as long and as far as you can bear to watch."

"All I need are four more years. That's when contracts can be renegotiated. Then I'll have all the time to spend with my family, and be the father and the man they need. Show me. I want to see five years from now."

"As you wish."

The room shakes and trembles as it did before. His chair lifts and his feet leave the floor as it did before. John stares into the place where just moments again a bright light illuminated the devastating image of his Angie, but nothing happens. The floor doesn't open. Nor is there light. He waits, his breathing heavy, two minutes, five minutes.

"How come nothing's happening?"

"It is, John. It is happening," the voice is somber.

John hears Claire shriek and begin to cry.

"What? What is it, Claire? Do you see something?"

"No, John. I don't see anything. Because five years from now, you don't exist."

XXX

John wakes slumped over in his office chair. His first thought being that he is going to die within the next five years. His head screams at him for his recent behavior and he feels the severe nauseousness from withdrawal.

As the fog uncoils from inside his brain, he understands he'd been dreaming. Withdrawals can cause such fierce nightmares. If he can just lift his head, and get just a little fix, things will make a lot more sense. His hand strikes an empty bottle and it clatters to the floor. In a pile on his desk, just like his dream, are the collection of empty bottles and the evidence of his recent drug use. Behind it is a framed picture of his family, Angie and the two boys. He is not in the picture.

His only consolation that causes him to cry in devastated relief is the note that she left in her beautiful scrawl.

```
I'm not giving up on us yet. I
believe in you, and so does the Lord. Get
clean and come home, John. I never should
have accused you of such awful things, so
I take responsibility in your relapse.
More than ever, you need our support. I
love you, John. Please come home.
Love Angie
```

Thrilled, he grabs for the phone to call her, to hear her voice, to tell her he isn't giving up on them, either, but he hangs up after the second ring, because the only thing that he can hear in his mind is that he is going to die, but he doesn't know how or when. He dials Claire's number instead.

XXX

"John, I can't just get you another appointment with him. He came to me, on behalf of you, and scared the hell right out of me in the process."

"I need to know what it all means, Claire."

"Jesus, isn't it obvious, John? If someone told me that I was going to die within the next five years, I'd be living my life to the fullest. That's why he called it a gift. In showing you death, he gave you the gift of life."

"No, he said my future is up to me, and he can only show me what my future is at this point in time. He said that in giving me the power to hold the future in my hands, I can change it if I want to. I need to find out when and how I die. If I can know that, then I can avoid it from happening."

"Your life, John, you can change your life. You can't change your fate, though. You sound just like your Dad, who believed he could avoid death if he never went to sleep, as he'd known he would die in his sleep."

"Claire, listen to me. I'm 32 years old. My children are only two and six and I've got another on the way. 20 years I'd grudgingly accept my fate, but not ten and especially not five. I refuse to leave my children without a parent, as I was left without one. I don't believe in fate. If my mother hadn't died when I was little, my life would have been completely different, and so would have my future. I don't care if he's God or the Grim Reaper or both or neither. I refuse to die before my children are grown. There's a reason he came to you to help me, and your faith is so much stronger than my own."

"Then perhaps that is something you'll have to change, John."

"If I believed, then I'd have to believe in a God that stole my mother away from me, Claire. I started to believe again when Angie came into my life, but it's going to crap. What kind of God does that?"

"I'm not having this conversation with you, John."

"Okay, okay, fine. Research churches and see if any of them are having mass today, and you can take me and show me how to believe."

There was a long silence on the other end of the line. "Have your wife take you. I'm not your mother, John. Nor do I work for you any longer."

"What do you mean you no longer work for me?"

"I put in my resignation two weeks ago. You were too busy drowning yourself in misery to notice, apparently."

"Claire? You – you can't leave me. You can't just – I need you." But he is talking to dead air.

XXX

Two weeks later, Claire is happily filing the passport in her purse when her phone rings from an unknown number.

"Yes?"

"Claire?" a distraught voice says over the line.

"Who is this?"

"It's Angie."

Silence.

"I'm sorry to call you like this, and I know I haven't been very nice to you, but I need your help. Have you seen John at all? Have you spoken with him?"

"No, Angie, I haven't. You know I no longer work for him, right?"

"I know. I just thought that maybe you knew where he was. He's been so strange the past couple weeks. I mean, at first, I can't tell you how happy I was when he came home to me and the kids, and told me he'd been enlightened, and wanted to find his faith, and that everything was going to be different from here on out. I'd thought that he would begin attending Sunday services regularly with me and the kids, but it's obsessive, Claire. Before he wasn't ever home due to work, and now he's never home because he's at one church or another. It's been three days. I haven't seen or heard from him. I think he needs to see a Doctor, and you're so resourceful, Claire. Do you know anyone that might be able to help him?"

"I'll see what I can do," Claire says, heavy with exasperation, tears prickling her eyes.

"Well, that confirms it." She turns to Paul once getting off the phone. "We're not allowed to have our life, or the future we planned, because it's so caught up in this mess. How many times I've gone back and wished I'd never answered that ad. Even billionaires can be completely unhappy and ridiculously messed up. It didn't work. He's not going to stop until he gets his answer."

He wraps his arms around her, pulling her distraught face into his chest. "Then that's exactly what we're going to have to give to him."

XXX

John had fallen asleep, still on his knees, before a life-like statue of Jesus hanging from the cross. He's been here for three days, and has fasted for three days to show that he is ready, willing, and committed to giving his life to *Him*. He wakes with a strong breeze that darkens the chapel as the candles he'd lit blow out, and a sharp pain in his neck.

"Get up off your knees," the voice booms.

"Oh, it's you. Oh, thank God. Thank you. Thank you Jesus."

"Why have you not used the gift I gave you?"

"I – I have. It returned to me my faith. My life is in your hands now. I just need to call upon your mercy, not for me, but for my children – whatever price I will pay for my children, whatever it is you ask of me. I will do anything to be there with my children until they're grown. Even if it is the price of my soul."

"Then why are you still not there for your children, you idiot. While you've been seeking me, they remain without you."

"Umm, I – ."

"Never mind. Did you bring the money?"

"Yes, of course, but why money?"

"Would you prefer I ask you the sacrifice of your newborn child?"

"You couldn't?" John gasps.

"I was making a point. DO YOU DARE CONTINUE TO QUESTION ME?"

"I'm sorry. Can I – just – one more question?"

"What?"

"So I know you can't give me the answers, and you can only give me a glimpse of a time in the future of my choosing, but, just in case, is there an easier way of trying to reach you if –."

Abruptly the candles relight and the church becomes empty but for John. The briefcase remains untouched on the pew.

XXX

Now one might find it very odd, and very stupid of the person who walks around 24/7 carrying a briefcase filled with a million dollars cash, but it has become a way of life for John as he waits. He sleeps with it under his pillow, places it on a chair beside him for his meals, brings it to the park when he takes his kids there to play, keeps it on his lap at church, and even brings it grocery shopping with him.

He displeased this giver of future and chances, and knows he is asking for far too many chances to get it right. Every week he adds a million more to prove his sacrifice. Angie, though grateful that he is home more often, would say that he is constantly on edge and distracted. Only once did she ask him why every night before bed he prayed for *Him* to return to him, pleading for just one more chance.

He happily agreed to going to a psychiatrist, but he'd also seen every other specialist there was, where he'd been told that other than high blood pressure and stress, he's healthy as could be. Angie would tell him that he always seemed elsewhere and she couldn't reach him there, and she was right. After two months, she urged him to go back to work, fearing that she had asked too much of him, blaming herself for his collapse. Then she had begun leaving multiple messages with Claire to please see him. Then one morning, when they're eating Sunday brunch, following another huge donation to yet another church, a text message comes through to his phone. An address.

His entire face comes to life and he dashes out of the chair and out the door with joy, leaving Angie to peer at his phone to wonder what caused his sudden liveliness.

John steps into the middle of the road to grab the attention of a taxi, and has it racing through traffic to get to the destination as quickly as possible, for which he pays very well for the cab driver's endangerment. He doesn't notice his surroundings, only the lone chair in the midst of the room. With tunnel vision he walks toward the chair, but the more he walks, the further the chair is away. He begins to jog, then sprint, yet no matter what, it remains out of his reach. Sweating, wheezing, and every muscle of his body screaming, he finally lunges for the chair. The chair disappears and he lands harshly on cement floor.

"In my briefcase is 10 million dollars, a million for each chance. If I find my answer before the 10 million runs out, you can keep it. Money no longer has any meaning to me. It is my life I ask for. Before I asked to see five years into the future and now I ask to see four years," John yells.

"As you wish," the darkness whispers.

John stares up, then down, then concentrates on all four surrounding directions, yet there is only black, the absence of light, the absence of life.

"One year," he calls.

His body lifts so that he comes to be sitting on a chair. In front of the chair appears his dining room table, then Angie at the far end of the table, his two sons on either side. No one is talking or looking at each other. Forks scrape plates. Everyone seems so sad, so somber, and looks so unhappy.

"What's wrong?" he tries to ask his family, but it is only the room that hears his voice, and nothing changes in the image. No one looks up or responds to his voice. "What's going on? Why is . . . ?"

Something fierce hits his gut. A year he asked for. Angie is no longer pregnant, but where is the daughter they were supposed to have had?

"Where's Gizelle?" He turns his face in the direction of *His* presence, and the image instantly evaporates.

"No, this can't be. I want to see a year at 8:00 pm when Angie and I tuck the kids into bed. Maybe she was just taking a nap."

He remains in the chair, but instead of a table before him, it is his office desk.

"No, why am I at my office? I should be home. I should be home with my family. I should be tucking my kids into bed. I want to see my daughter."

The office door opens and Claire appears, wearing only a shirt, one of his shirts, carrying two glasses of wine. A cigarette dangles from her mouth. Giggling, he watches her sit on his desk and bend toward him, the shirt opening to reveal her braless chest. The vision moves toward the desk, to a drawer, where his hand retrieves a lighter. He lights her cigarette, and she brings the glass of wine to his lips.

John pulls away from the image. Again, the image fades to darkness.

John wracks his brain, trying to remember his wife's due date, but he doesn't even know what month it is.

"Can I see two months from now, please," he says desperately.

The image reveals he's on a light blue couch, one he's not familiar with. He tries to look around him to see where he is, but the image remains facing the couch. The couch moves and he looks up. It is Claire again, sitting beside him on the blue couch, looking sadly upon him. She is wearing light pink pajama bottoms and blouse, and her blonde hair is down across her shoulders. Why is she looking at him so sadly? Where is he?

"You've had enough. How about having some coffee instead," she says to him. She pries the Jack Daniels and the empty rocks glass out of his hands.

"You have always been there for me, Claire, when I've needed you the most." He hears his voice say.

"There, there." She opens her arms and his head moves toward her chest. The imagery is so strong, he thinks that he can actually smell her. For a moment, in reality, he feels comforted. She is nurturing him, like the nurture she used to provide before Angie. He'd so much missed that nurture these past months when she'd gotten cold with him, and the more he'd told her he needed her, the more he pushed her away. It was good to know that in two months' time they would return to being the friends they once were.

But suddenly the room is blasted with light and he hears Angie's yell. It came from behind him, and not from the image before him. He twists and sees her horrified face, standing in a doorway. Then, just as quickly, she turns, closing the door, placing him in darkness again, but not before he gets a glimpse of the now familiar blue couch he saw in the image.

Confused by what is present reality and future imagery, he hears the squeal of tires, a horn beeping, and a scream. Angie's scream.

"Shit," he hears beside him, and even as his world grows even darker, the type of darkness that only unconsciousness can bring, he knows it was Claire's voice.

CHAPTER 20

Paul feels the sharp sting of her slap. "How could you?" Her voice is shrill, hysterical. He's never seen her in this state before. He's so far into his own grief, he doesn't know how to respond. "No one was supposed to get hurt, Paul, you promised that what we were doing was to help people, not, not hurt them."

"I'm sorry. I'm sorry. That wasn't supposed to happen, Claire."

"But you specifically told me to text him the address. Why Paul, why? There's a thousand other ways we could have given him the message."

"How was I to know he would rush out the door without his phone and that she would read it and come here? How was I to know that she would run out into the street at the precise moment our next store neighbor was going to pull his motorcycle out into the road?"

"You tell me, Paul. You're the mastermind. You're the one that can see the future."

"I can't – Claire, seriously, you know how this works. Do you actually believe that I can see the future?"

"You've been spot on, Paul. Everything you predicted with the other two happened. You said it was for the good, but you got one guy who is homeless and one in prison, and now . . . now . . .? Oh God, a child is dead, Paul. I need you to be honest with me, completely honest, Paul. How did you know the child would die? We never discussed that. And why didn't you do anything to stop it if you knew it would happen?"

"I'm – I'm not God, Claire, I can't –."

"No, you certainly are not, because God does not create destruction. Evil does, but it lures people into believing that what is evil is not, like you lured me. You didn't just know the baby was going to die, you set it up so that it would happen."

"Please don't lose faith in me, Claire. Please don't leave me."

"How did you know I was going to leave you, Paul?"

"I didn't foresee this happening. I promise you that."

"Then that's too bad. Messing around with the lives and futures of others while completely ignoring your own. Typical Doctor. But here's common sense from a laywoman, you can't help anyone else if you can't first help yourself. I believe in fate, and you believe that people make their own future, so now you can sit here and ponder the mess you made out of your life while I can be secure in knowing that this simply just was not meant to be. Goodbye Paul."

XXX

TWO MONTHS LATER

Claire is reading a book, curled up on her couch in her pajamas when she hears a knock at her door. For a moment her heart picks up, thinking maybe it's Paul. He disappeared, just simply vanished, two months ago. She'd intended on staying at her sister's, but he had told her he would be the one to leave, as it wasn't right for her to leave her home because of him. He left, not taking a single thing with him, clothes, phone, money, nothing, so she expected he'd be back to at least get his stuff. After taking the time to cool off and be able to make the right decision without all the emotion, she realized that he'd been right in that there was no way he could have made events happen as they did, and he hadn't actually shown the child as dead. He could have simply just forgotten that Angie was pregnant and forgot to include the child in the visuals. He never came back. She couldn't locate him. She had his phone, so there was no way of contacting him. He just vanished.

"Who is it?" she calls through the door, but is answered only with more incessant knocking. Deep inside she knows Paul is too much of a gentleman to knock that like, but she still hopes as she opens the door, and still feels crushed when she meets blue eyes instead of brown.

"Juh – John, what're you doing here?"

He stumbles past her, weaves this way and that before plopping down on her light blue sofa. Deja-vu smacks her in the face as he's carrying a half empty bottle of Jack Daniels in one hand and a glass in the other.

"I walked here, Claire. I walked here. I had to see you."

"John, it's 13 miles from your house."

"I had thish keepin' me company," the contents of the bottle splash.

"John, you're completely drunk. Let me – uh – I'm going to get you some coffee."

"She'sh gone, Claire. She'sh gone."

"Angie?"

"My daughter, Claire. My daughter. She'sh gone."

"You've had enough of this," she says gently, taking the JD from his hand. "Have some coffee."

"Angie. She'sh not there. She blame shme. S'my fault. But you, Claire. When I need you the mosht, you have alwaysh been there. I'm dying, Claire, I've never felt thish bad before, not in my whole entire life, not even when Mom pashed, and I got no one, Claire. I got no one."

"There, there." She goes to hug him, for his head to fall on her shoulder, but he curls his head and lays it on her chest. She rocks him, running her hand through his hair, as he cries. "Ssshh, ssshhh, it's okay. It's okay," she says. She feels her own tears wanting to fall. "I'll – uh – let me drive you home, John."

"No! No, I can't go back there. Not yet. Not like this. Angie's a mesh. I have to be there for her, have to be there for her. It sh'all my fault. She hates me, cush she knows I love you."

"That's not true. John. You know that's not true. You love Angie."

"I doo. I doo love Angie, but it'sh different. And I love you." Claire feels the touch instantly, but has to look to be sure to know that yes, he is touching her.

"O-kay, time for bed, John. You shouldn't have come here. Come on, let's get you laid down," she slowly moves her body until he is laying down. "Will you shleep with me, Angie? Will you shleep with me. It'sh been so long sinsh you shlept with me."

"All right. All right. Let me just get a blanket and a pillow."

When Claire returns with the blanket he is sleeping soundly. She covers him with it, and sits on the floor with her back against the couch. Quietly she surrenders to her own grief and loneliness. *Why didn't you come back, Paul? Why did you disappear? Did you never love me at all?*

"Don't cry, Claire. Don't cry. I'm here," he says, placing a heavy arm around her shoulder. "Come back to work with me. Will you come back to work with me? Do you promise?"

"I promise," she murmurs, as she lays her head back into the crook of his arm and falls asleep.

XXX

"We need to talk."

"Can it wait? I've got some things I'm right in the middle of doing."

"No, we need to talk now."

"All right, I'm on my way, but I've got this thing that I really can't miss, so you'll have to tell me on the way."

He picks her up and knows instantly that he had missed her, but she is a mix between distraught and happy, and this makes him anxious.

"So, what did you need to talk about?"

"I'm pregnant."

He looks at her. She's facing forward. Suddenly her face contorts in horror and she screams at what she's seeing in front of her. He looks, but it's too late, and everything goes black.

XXX

9 MONTHS LATER

Claire had called him here to meet her tonight, and dinner had been somber because they knew he was going back to the office, having only come home for dinner, just to leave again, but this is something he has to take care of . Something he has to do. He now knows what needs to be done, but it had cost everything to get there. He just wants to get it taken care of quickly, so when she comes through the door wearing only his shirt, with a cigarette dangling from her lips, he feels annoyed. But he had been given the gift, had he not? He'd already seen this play out before. And he knows the consequences. When she sits on the desk, he patiently lights her cigarette, but this time when she tries to feed him the wine, he takes the glass from her hand, and places it on his desk.

"This is completely one hundred percent inappropriate, Claire. I know I owe you a lifetime of gratitude for everything that you've done for me, but it's time I draw the line. You need to find yourself another job."

"Your – you're firing me?"

"You've left me no choice. I've told you a hundred times that I'm not having an affair with you. I love my wife, my children. I've put up with your behaviors for nearly a year, because I felt I owed you for all your kindness that you provided me throughout the years, but I've had enough."

"But you said you loved me. You said you needed me."

"I do love you, and there were times I needed you, yes, but I loved you like a mother, Claire. Nothing more. I am so sorry that I took so many years of your life out of neediness for a mother-figure, and I used you for that. But that's all it was. I – um – I don't need that any more. I've got a family now, Claire. A wife that adores me and that I adore in return, and two sons that feel the same. Angie and I, we've been discussing, possibly – uh – trying to – trying to have another child, you know? Hopefully a daughter. And I'm sure, Claire – uh, positive, that there's some great guy out there for you. "

Oddly, she smiles at him. "So have you told her yet?"

"Told her what? Nothing, nothing ever happened between us."

"I mean about you being bankrupt. That's why I called you here tonight. I apologize for my attire. I spilled coffee on my suit, so it's being laundered. You now have all the time in the world to spend with your family, because the billion dollar business that your father built is dead."

CHAPTER 21
TWO YEARS LATER
(10 years after it all began)

Michael is sitting outside The Cave, which continues to be his hotspot, because people from long ago that remember him can't get through the door without knowing that there was once a person that they knew, that they fed off of, like thirst to water. He gave them hope and now he gives them pity, which they pay for. A number of them had tried to get him off the streets, tried to help him out, but he had humbly declined, because he'd been given the gift of seeing his future, unlike all the rest of the poor souls out there, and he embraced it.

He has nothing to his name, yet he feels more free than any man alive. People so often would look on him with pity or disgust or fear, and he'd just smile with the knowing that once upon a time he had been there. So long ago, it didn't even seem possible that it had been his own life. Now, he just sits here or there, and watches and pities all the people running around, suits and ties, skirts and blouses, rushing to work and from work, stress and anxiety lining their faces, dying hope in their eyes that today might be the day, competing, and trying to overcome all the pressure. Just trying to make it and give their lives purpose and meaning.

He feels like he knows a secret that no one else knows, other than those like him. He feels special and unique. So many looking upon him with a variety of feelings or non-feelings, and none of them realizing that he has the greatest freedom there is. He wants to share it, but because they are all so disillusioned, who listens to a homeless guy who is happier than they'd ever felt in their lifetime.

Just another man wearing a suit and tie, carrying a briefcase, blunts his vision, which he expects to pass, but the man's shadow remains standing over him.

"You mind getting out of my sunlight, kind sir? It could well be the last of my heat for the day and I'd like to enjoy it for as long as I can."

The briefcase is placed in front of him.

"Interesting keep sake for a homeless man," the man with the briefcase points out Michael's wedding ring. "You'd think you would have pawned it years ago."

"The only good memory I have of my times back then. I was once a married man, you know."

"I do know," says the man. "I know all about you, Michael. I also know you still have a wife and a child out on Grand Park Avenue. You've seen your future, Michael, and now you've endured it. So I leave you with this to decide the rest of your future."

Michael recognizes the briefcase, as his name is still engraved on the handle. He gasps. "You." And lifts his face. No one is there. Looking left and right and scouring the streets of New York City, there are nameless hundreds wearing that same black and white suit, allowing invisibility to anyone who just wants to appear no different from the crowd.

Inside the briefcase is a million dollars.

Michael mourns the best friend he'd ever had, who had passed last winter on a particularly cold night. He would have had a hoot. They would have gotten the most expensive room there was and been a sight to see, two homeless men sharing the wealth of their million dollar fortune. But that wasn't to be, because his old friend was gone.

He travels all day to get to Grand Park, eating only a sandwich tossed by just another restaurant goer whose eyes were bigger than their belly. He sits to rest at the bench in Grand Park, kicking his feet with two grimy toes sticking out of his brown shoes.

"Hey, you can't be here. No homeless wanderers in Grand Central Park. I don't want to catch you here again."

Michael stares fondly up at the Officer. "I just come to see my wife, Susan Taylor, to pay some overdue child support."

The Officer gets a chuckle out of this. "Yeah, the likes of you married to the famous actress. That's the best one I've heard from your kind. Get going."

Michael nods and begins walking in the direction the Officer's eyes had looked when he'd spoken Susan Taylor's name. On the pretty mailbox is engraved her first name and his last name. He walks the front steps, and places the briefcase in front of the door. He's just about to ring the doorbell and run, when the door opens.

It is like seeing an angel he never thought he'd have the blessing to ever see again.

"Michael!" she gasps.

"This is a little awkward. You weren't supposed to open the door until I was gone."

"Well isn't that just like you to find me then leave me without saying goodbye."

"I brought something for you and the child. I haven't been a good man, and I especially haven't been a good father, but hopefully this makes up for it. So nice seeing you. You look more beautiful than I remember." He tips his head and begins moving away.

"Michael Scully, you get your grimy dirty behind in this house and get yourself cleaned up. You've had enough of your homeless pity-me act. It's time you be a father to your son."

"But I – I didn't intend on – I -," Michael stutters, something she was always good at making him do.

"You think I'd just let you come here and watch you walk out of our lives again? NOW, Michael."

"Yes Ma'am." He jumps and runs into the house, feeling properly scolded.

XXX

Jim is brought into another room, a stern square-faced woman behind the desk. He hears the rattling of keys, then blessed freedom as his hands are uncuffed. He rubs at the indentation on his wrists.

"Sign here saying you've received everything we confiscated from you seven years ago."

A single solitary gold wedding band is placed on the counter.

"Keep it."

"Pawn it. It'll buy you a pack of smokes or a beer or a decent meal." He places it in the pocket of the clothes they were nice enough to provide him with, so that he wouldn't have to leave wearing the hospital gown he'd come here in.

He is escorted outside and on the other side of the gates.

The gates are quickly closed and locked behind him.

"Jim," one of the guards call. "Don't come back here."

"You don't have to worry about that. I'm never getting married again," he shouts good-naturedly.

Jim walks to the curb and just stands there, breathing in the fresh air, and looking out over the expanse of his freedom. Seven years of his life was gone, seven years he'd never be able to recover, but even he knows it was the best thing to have ever happened to him. Confinement in a jail cell had freed him from a lifetime of imprisonment. He looks left. He looks right. The whole world in front of him, and all he needs are his two feet and a random direction to get started.

No place to live, not a dime to his name, or a friend to call. New man, a fresh start, and the hindsight to know he'd never make the same mistakes.

A black limo pulls up beside him, suddenly, and the window cracks down an inch. "Jim Piersall?"

"That's me."

"Get in."

"Who are you?"

"Your new future."

The door is opened and he steps inside the dark interior, but there is no one there but for his old brown leather briefcase.

"Well I'll be," he grins.

"Where to, sir?" the chauffeur intercoms him.

"The only place a man would go after seven years in prison. Hot beach, beautiful girls, where the alcohol flows like the suns' sweet rays."

XXX

A tap sounds at John's office door, which was previously the master bathroom in their new downsized home. Angie steps in, her red hair shining and her face aglow. "You almost ready, sweetheart? We don't want to be late for Lucas's first football game."

"Wouldn't miss it for the world," he smiles at her. "Five more minutes to finish up Mr. Lawrence's IRA transfer, and my work will be done for the day."

Following the bankruptcy of his father's company, they had lost everything. He had been laughed and scorned at by the press for not filling his father's shoes, and managing to bankrupt a billion dollar corporation more quickly than it had taken his father to get it started, but moreso had it become publicly known that the majority of his millions had gone toward church donations and charities around the world to help those in need. It was no longer money that made his fame, but what he had done with it, aside from the 22 million dollar price he had paid for the priceless gift of being able to avoid his demise.

Angie had taken the news of their bankruptcy with a thrilling smile and girlish giggle. She admitted she had always hated the money, the big house, the four cars, and with the support of all those churches he had donated to, they were given a doublewide on a half-acre of land that suited them perfectly. He started his own business, in his name, and not his father's, and for the first time no longer feels the towering presence of his father. Now he feels him at his side, working alongside him, whispering in his ear his uncanny predictions of the stock market.

John keeps a small caseload of clients, and works on his terms, on his schedule, from the comforts of his home. Unlike his own upbringing, Angie and his children are free to come and go, and the office is never locked to them. He enjoys them every morning, every evening, every weekend, and every holiday. But today is especially special, for a few reasons, one being that he'd be finally attending his son's games, rooting him on from the sidelines.

"All right, I'm going to get the car ready. There's something I want to talk to you about on our way there," Angie says, an odd note in her voice.

"Actually, sweetheart, it's such a beautiful day out. I'd prefer to walk."

The second reason today is special is because it's the day he was supposed to die.

"Well then we'd better go now if we're walking. It'll have to be a fast walk."

She screams in laughter as he lifts her off her feet and carries her to the door.

"Oh, wait, don't forget your briefcase."

"Briefcase?"

"Yeah, I'm assuming you put it by the door so that you wouldn't forget it."

He hasn't seen that briefcase since a whole different life ago. He sends up a silent prayer.

"Open it," he smiles.

She gasps, "John – what - ? How much is in there? Where did you - ?"

"We're going to need it to build the addition to the house."

"You knew? How could you know? I just took the test this morning," she giggles.

The third reason today is so special is that he'll be alive to raise their two boys and the new child his beautiful wife now carries in her womb.

He steps out on the sidewalk just in time to catch a glimpse of black turning the corner.

XXX

Glasses clink together and a toast is made.

"To an extraordinary life and a brilliant man," Claire smiles at her new husband.

"To a honeymoon that lasts a lifetime," Paul answers back.

The boat cascades over the waves into a seeming endless expanse of ocean. Seemingly limitless and without boundaries, like the future to the young, where anything is possible, and life is what you make of it.

"Come here, you little squirt," Paul says after their two year old little girl who, fortunately, is as beautiful as Claire.

He limps after the giggling child and scoops her up in his one arm not holding the cane. He will always walk with a limp and will always need a cane, due to the accident, when Claire had tracked him down and surprised him with the news of their pregnancy, which was the very ending they had needed to, not just turn John's life around, but to fix their own.

This isn't the future he had ever planned for, and he is glad of that. Fate had stepped in when he needed it, booting him abruptly to rock bottom, and changed his perceptions and choices he thought he'd had. It was in those new choices that provided him more than he could have ever even hoped for. Choice led him to his decisions, but fate intertwined all their lives and futures together. Just one glimpse at a hopeless future was powerful enough to change their entire trajectory paths. There's a secret to it, in that everyone has that ability, but Paul will never tell. After all, would you pay a million dollars for a glimpse of your future?

Almondie Shampine lives in New York with her two children and their animals, and has been writing professionally for 14 years. She's a proud author of 'Monster Down the Street' in Linden Hills *Beyond Time and Place*, 'My Son' in a teenage anthology, 'Intrusion', an adult e-book, as well as a variety of short stories, poems, and articles, four of which were contest winners. She received a Bachelor of Science degree in Psychology: Applied Behavioral Analysis, which has inspired a lot of material for her psychological thrillers. You may also find her recently published book, *The Reform*, which is the first book in the Modules Series featuring the brilliant, yet unruly Catina Salsbury. Check out www.almondieshampine.com for instant access to releases and promotions or find her on Facebook.

Sample Chapter

She was losing blood, too much blood as it spilled out of the wounds on her chest, her stomach, her sides, her legs, her arms. Too many holes, too much blood, too much pain, too much weakness, too little time.

All odds were against her, yet she continued to fight the unconsciousness that simply wanted to absorb her in its bleakness, its blackness, its painlessness, with a primal, animalistic intent . . . survival.

She left a trail of red on white as she dragged herself through unpacked snow, burying her face in it here and there to quench the severe dryness of her throat.

She was dying from a succession of 17 merciless stab wounds from a six inch hunting knife. She would die. It was inevitable. Yet she continued her painstakingly slow crawl toward some kind of life, all the while continuing to hear his agonizing shouts playing over and over and over again in her head like a broken record.

"I love you. Oh God, I love you. I love you so god damn much!"

****

The alarm clock blared, arising Burton to that particular abrupt awakeness that occurs when one's slumber is suddenly disrupted. He looked at his wife in wonder – that she could continue to sleep completely undisturbed despite the beeping at 75 decibels directly beside her ear. Once leaning over her and swatting the snooze button, his head returned to its indentation in the pillow, but then he was harassed with a new awareness to raw heat of nude parts emanating off of his significant other. Completely unguarded in her sleep, Charisma was a beautiful specimen. It was this moment every morning for the past five years that Burton was in complete awe of the woman he had married.

The whole of her 5'8" frame was curled in fetal position, her porcelain pale face unmarked by anything bothersome buried in the long, black, silky hair pulled over her left shoulder. Her lips curved slightly upward in that constant small smile he'd first fallen for, like a woman in love, like a contended child. There hadn't been any bad dreams since the night before their honeymoon. To watch her so innocent in sleep, it would have looked completely natural to find her thumb between those soft child-like lips. . . . But he'd rather it be his tongue between those lips as despite the vulnerable impression of her child-likedness that made one react with nurture and a fierce need to protect, her aura displayed woman with all her fiery passion and hormone-driving phermones mixed with a delectable combination of maturity, knowledge, and wisdom.

She was neither the intelligent, cold, and nerdy prude, nor the impulsive, foolish, bodacious bimbo. Rather she was a mixture of the two, an intelligent bodacious babe that could be spontaneous while maintaining a healthy climate of modesty, humility, and dignity. But she was never cold, by God, cold Charisma was not. She carried warmth from the deepest portion of her soul to the satiny surface of her skin and outward. Her inner warmth warmed his soul where her outer warmth set his body aflame.

He admired her.

How many times in these past five years had strangers thought they newlyweds?

How many eyes had looked upon them with envy?

How many pessimists had scoffed, saying it would dull and fade once the new wore off?

And how many others had turned to faith in hopes that they may be blessed the same with such a perfect and unburdening love?

Had they been blessed? Absolutely. And never would they stop counting their blessings. They'd inspired many and they'd insulted many with their deep and undying love.

Despite having grown up in the same small town of Camillus they'd never crossed paths prior to the tragedy that had brought them together. He was non-denominational, and she had been strictly Catholic, making them as diverse as Black and White, though ironically believing in the same God. Six years ago, Charisma was left beaten, broken, and pregnant amidst a religious group and family that couldn't understand how Charisma could possibly want to keep the greatest reminder of her tragedy. Where Catholics are typically strictly pro-life, they deemed the child in her womb a spawn of one of the devil's demons that needed to be exorcised rather than aborted or terminated. Like society, like government, morality, rules and regulations, and laws are everchanging in the eyes and hands of the beholder, and the people, once provided poor premises from authority they trust and respect, go along with it as though it had always been the way.

When Charisma refused to rid of the child in her womb, they turned her away and shut her out of their world of truth and enlightenment and right. She had been completely closed off from her portion of society and life that she had always known, always loved, always believed in, because she believed that all children were good in the eyes of the Lord, no matter who or what they came from.

She had come to Burton's church a stranger, confused when she could not find the confessional box, a foreigner to a different world. She'd had her back to him when he first gently approached her. Her shoulders were hunched, and she quite resembled the Virgin Mary herself with the cloth that wrapped around her head and body to keep out the chill of a dying winter.

"May I help you?" Burton had asked her, carefully moving closer.

Her shoulders jumped and straightened. "I'm here to make a confession," she had said.

"Okay," he had said, not familiar with this approach. Normally people just asked for his help. "You can come into my office if you would like. I can make you some coffee or some tea."

"I don't drink coffee or tea. It's a –"

"So you're going to freeze to death in the name of our Father?"

And suddenly she giggled, realizing then how ridiculous it all was.

"I suppose you're right." He could hear the smile on her lips. After long hesitation she turned toward him, "I wouldn't suppose you have any hot cocoa in that office of yours, would you?" And that's when Burton had lost his heart to the one woman he would ever love.

"Only if you like it overflowing with marshmallows."

She nodded, a shy smile on her lips, and a small struggling rebellious flame in her eyes that processed her potential to go against all she had ever known.

"Come on." He had grabbed her hand, feeling oddly boyish and giddy. "My office is filled with every sweet and fulfilling beverage and morsel a person could ever want. I have a confession to make myself, and it has to do with this unnerving sweet tooth of mine that can never be sated. The children love me because they know I will share all my goodies."

"Well, for having such an avid weakness for sweets, it obviously has not affected your smile any."

"Ah yes, sugar and sweets will rot your teeth. It's all in the genes dear, all in the genes and body composition. There are those who never touch sweets, yet their teeth are weak and decaying, and then there are those, like myself, who eat sugar all three meals daily as well as a mid-day snack, evening snack, and midnight snack, and have not a problem in that regard."

Burton had seated her comfortably on the small recliner in his office with a steaming cup of cocoa overflowing with bobbing marshmallows. Whether the hot cocoa or the space heater or himself, she came to be warmed and relaxed quickly, and he found something even more beautiful than the phenomenal acoustics of the church resounding in chorus, and that was her laughter echoing all around him, as he made her laugh time and time again with the purely selfish desire to hear her laughter. He made a vow that day after secretly vowing that he would marry this woman, that he would always make her laugh. He found one other glorious thing that night aside from Charisma and love . . . Father Burton Faulkner had found God with the enlightenment of one of his greatest miracles of true love.

They talked and they laughed until the birds began to chirp the following morning. Disowned by the parents with whom she'd been staying, Charisma was homeless. That the woman could still laugh after what she'd been through was a miracle in and of itself. From spending three weeks in intensive care progressing from a mere two percent chance of surviving to 65 percent, she was transferred to recovery where she spent another month of her life. It was at her six week stay when they realized she was pregnant. After two months of hospitalization, Charisma had returned home to a whole congregation of Catholics, not to welcome her back, but rather to pressure her into ridding of the child in her womb. And now three months after her brutal victimization that she just barely survived, friends and family alike had cast her out as though she were the criminal and to blame.

Burton had welcomed her into his home, into his church, into his family and friends, into his life, and into his heart.

Society had then turned on them both, calling it a scandal. She was called a child then at 17 years old and he a pedophile at 28. He'd moved into the scheme of the stereotypical pastor and that's all they saw him for. His job was jeopardized, his reputation to the people, and he and Charisma alone, once the most respected people in society, had stood up to them all, had taken the blows, . . . and had forgiven. Martha Lampshell had started the food-throwing at the church to get the Pastor off of the podium, but when Martha Lampshell's house burned down, it was Charisma and Burton that took her into their shared home while supporting her and providing her with all those things needed to get her back on her feet.

When they'd gone on their honeymoon, consummating their love for the first time after having lived together for a long and sufferable six months, the church had been desecrated horrendously for their return, and without a word, Burton and Charisma had fixed it up.

Not a single person arrived at the hospital when the child was born, and when it was time to baptize the newborn child, the holy water was found to be contaminated with salt. Patiently Burton had locked the doors so that no one could leave and with Charisma at his side, they drained the basin and refilled it with pure holy water.

"If this child is to pay for the sins of his father, then may God make the water burn him," Burton had exclaimed, and everyone had held their breathes, expecting just that. Not only didn't the child burn, but he came up from that water laughing and gurgling ga, ga, ga, ga which to highly alert ears sounded very much like God, God, God, God!

It was that day that Burton had given one of his most prominent and remembered speeches. "Mary was called a whore because her child was not conceived in the traditional way of procreation of a man and wife. Everyone turned their eyes away and shut their doors on their faces. Mary gave birth to God's only son, Jesus Christ. Years later when Jesus was a man and trying to spread the word of God, their were many that betrayed him and turned their backs. They tortured him with their words before they tortured him on the cross, because they were ignorant and close-minded. We are born sinners, but let us not be so ignorant and close-minded that we do not see the truth. God has already given my family his blessing , just like God's blessing was already bestowed upon Jesus Christ. God's blessing was enough for the suffering Jesus Christ just as God's blessing is enough for my family. I quote Jesus's words, 'Father forgive them, they know not what they do.'

He had stormed out of the church that day, carrying the newborn he loved as his, and holding the hand of his gentle wife.

Gradually in six months time, the congregation, save a few souls, had given them their belated blessing. And six months after that with Charisma and he just as much in love and a pretty average baby boy, many had come to him to ask, "Father, how can I earn what you have been rewarded with? How can I find what you have found?" Like a mother will tell her children to eat his fruits and vegetables and he will grow big and strong, Burton would tell them to do good things and follow the righteous path and to keep their eyes and minds open to the opportunities that come about.

Now five years later, Burton touched her heart-shaped face with profound adoration. He traced the curves of her expressive high-defined cheekbones, her kid nose ... and suddenly Charisma abruptly jumped out of bed, startling him.

"What is it?"

"Baby's up," she said, hurriedly covering her nudity with a peach robe.

"I don't hear -" And sure enough there were the little baby goggling sounds barely audible from across the hall. An alarm clock a foot from her ear hadn't awoken her. Burton's warm touch hadn't awoken her. But a sound that could only be heard through intense concentration had woken her immediately. Amazing. She was wide awake now, her full breasts ready to nourish their dependent six month old baby girl; their first and their last addition to the family.

"I was having some very detailed, juicy dreams. Wanna hear?" she said to him while pushing her feet into peach slippers.

"Yeah, tell me every detail and maybe I can replicate it."

"Maybe later." Charisma winked at him before scooting out the door. Burton went for a swipe at her rear, but missed. He thought of that rear in the palm of his hands, enveloping his face. Forgive me father for I have sinned, but that's a hell of a temptation. You enjoyed every minute of making that mold.

Charisma scooted into the room closest to her and Burton's bedroom and patted her son's rear. "Come on, Bun Bun, time for breakfast."

She moved on to the next room across the hall. "Good morning, baby doll." The precious babe suckled air, giving a visual of where her mind was at the moment. Charisma quickly lifted her, planting a kiss on her forehead before patting Bun Bun's bun bun once again, and gliding down the stairs on tiptoes.

Charisma popped a nipple in the suckling baby's mouth and threw some butter on the heating frying pan. One-handed she cracked the eggs on the skillet, laid out strips of bacon on another, and placed some bread in the toaster. She flipped the eggs, the bacon, buttered the toast, laid out two plates and distributed breakfast onto them just as a bedraggled six year old Sonny entered the room followed by his lesser bedraggled adoptive father, both yawning and letting their noses do the walking. Charisma got out the cups and poured the freshly-brewed coffee into two cups and the orange juice in the spider man cup that had a color-changing straw.

As though merely a football, Charisma moved the baby to curl into the other arm and latched her on to the remainder of the meal before returning upstairs and grabbing her son's school clothes and backpack. The baby content and dozing, Charisma hurriedly changed and dressed her, placed another kiss on her forehead, and laid her back down in the bassinet. "Sweet dreams, love," she sang as she closed the door and moved to her dresser to get her clothes for the day.

Sonny met her in the livingroom as she returned downstairs with his clothes and backpack, as well as her husband's tie and briefcase. "Can I watch cartoons?"

"As soon as you put on your clothes."

The dirty dishes soaked in a sink full of hot suds that Burton had filled. He laid his paper down and pulled out a chair for her in front of her already-made up coffee. They held hands across the table as they sipped off of their lives' fuel and discussed their plans for the day.

He stood. She helped him with his tie. He put his shoes on. She made up a fresh mug of coffee. He wrestled with Sonny's jacket as she tied Sonny's shoes.

"Bye mom, love you," Sonny said, grasping his father's hand.

"Love you too, sweetheart, have a good day at work."

Burton wrapped his arms around her in a big bear hug. "Bye sweetheart, I love you."

"Love you too, have a good day at school."

Sonny giggled as they kissed.

Burton grinned at him. "What? What's so funny?"

"Mom says yer going to school and I'm going to work. Mom's silly."

"Silly-lookin'," Burton said, causing Sonny a riot of laughter.

"Yeah, we'll see how silly-lookin' I am when you crawl into bed tonight."

"Is that a threat or a promise?"

"Both."

"Until my guy comes out growling, we'll see who's screaming," Burton said.

"What guy? You mean a … a monster!?" Sonny said excited.

"Oh yeah, a big hairy scary monster," Burton said.

"Oh wow!"

"Not that big. It's a little monster." Charisma showed Sonny with two fingers three inches apart. "So small you can bite its head off."

Burton grimaced. "Ouch, dear, very big ouch."

"Come on, Dad, you're making me late for school."

Little Sonny dragged a reluctant Burton out the door.

Charisma waved from the tall window until the Green Taurus was but an ant on a hill, allowing herself that small moment of sadness that they were gone, before getting to work on all the baking she needed to do today for the bake sale. The bake sale's profits would go to the children's wing at the hospital, where Charisma had to go after the bake sale, as she'd volunteered to paint the wing's walls a nice cheery yellow as bright as the sun as were the children's requests. From there she had the church choir as they were preparing for the Easter Mass Concert. She would see her husband on and off all day. He wouldn't be there at the bake sale as he had his own prepping to do for Easter Sunday, but he would be there to help paint the children's wing, and then despite supposedly being locked up in his office, Charisma would find him peaking around the corner of the door at her as she sang in the choir.

At 3:00, as Charisma rushed around to clean up the eight rooms and two bathrooms in their Victorian-style home, Sonny came running through the white picket fence in the front yard, full of the energy only a child can have.

"Mom! Mom!" he cried. "I been lookin' out the window all day and seein' the sun and I want to go swimming. I want to go swimming."

She laughed. "Well then what are you waiting for? Go get your trunks."

He scurried up the stairs as Charisma hurriedly changed herself and Jewel for an afternoon of swimming. Charisma was slowly making her way down the ladder, baby Jewel in her arms, when Sonny did a running cannon ball, spraying cold water to all those places not yet used to its cold.

Charisma laughed. "Don't splash, Sonny, it's getting on your sister."

"Put her in bed. Let's play me and you, mom, then we can splash all we want."

"It's not her nap-time. She's been sleeping all day. For once she's finally wide awake."

He dragged on her arm. "Hold me, hold me, hold me."

"I can't hold you, sweetheart. I'm holding your sister."

"Throw me, Mommy. Pick me up and throw me in the water like you do sometimes."

"Not now, honey. I have your sister."

He squinted his eyes at her, furrowed his eyebrows, tightened his lips. Charisma held her breathe.

"I don't want a sister. Take her back."

Charisma laughed. "I can't just take her back, silly. And when she gets older, you'll like her a lot more because you'll have someone to play with."

"Can she swim like me, Mommy?" He frantically did the doggy-paddle.

"Nope, that's why I have to hold her."

"What if you dropped her?"

"She would fall in the water."

"Would she drown?"

"Until I got her back out of the water."

"Would she die? Would it kill her?"

Charisma gasped. "Sonny, where do you come up with these things? I won't be dropping her which means no, she won't drown, nor will she die."

He seemed to contemplate this for a moment and then grudgingly concluded, "Good, cause then I won't have a sister no more."

Jewel giggled in delight, throwing her little hands at the water.

"We can play with the beach ball. Do you want to do that?"

"Yeah!" Sonny exclaimed excitedly. Back and forth they hit the ball until he tired of that game. Then they played bumper boats with their floaties. They were having so much fun that time passed quickly and

Burton arrived out on the deck, home from his day's work with a dinner not yet even started.

Burton admired his family unaware before diving into the deep blue waters to the screams of the rest. He surfaced, gliding his hand from Charisma's calf, up her thigh, touching her most privately and then plopping a wet, dripping kiss on the baby's mouth, and a longer, hotter, lingering, passionate one to his wife's lips already aquiver from the small pleasure he'd aroused in her. Going back under he chased Sonny's paddling feet to his son's shrill delight.

"You got this while I go in and start dinner?" Charisma asked, but their fun play was answer enough. With a silent smile she boarded the deck, laying Jewel on a towel while wrapping her own around her waist. She caught her husband's admiring eyes and his glint of disapproval when the towel covered all her curvy delicacies. He was a wonderful man. Truly a wonderful, wonderful man.

He was a full-blooded and full-bodied Italian with dark thick hair at the moment wet and plastered to his head, a few strands curling over his forehead. He wasn't huge but his frame was large, big-boned, and somewhat fleshy around his torso and chest area. He had a round head with pink cheeks and navy blue oval eyes. His lips were a natural dark pink, something Charisma envied him for, as well as his long thick lashes. He was covered in black hair in the front, but fortunately not too absurdly in the back. He was a good-looking man. Not gorgeous, not pretty, but good-looking, handsome in his suit and tie, sexy in his navy blue swimming trunks.

Burton had a way about him that made him the perfect Pastor. People wanted to talk to him. People wanted to confide in him, despite the intimidation of their being judged because of his cloth. He was mild-tempered and soft-spoken. He did all the smiling with his intense eyes and the crow's feet surrounding them. He never yelled. He never had to. His power, his authority, his control came from within. He was the type of man you never wanted to disappoint because although a word wouldn't be said on his part, he would have that look, and that look would cause the most merciless to squirm in their pants with a conscience newly-developed. But when you pleased him, boys, girls, adults, the elderly alike would feel that pride the child feels when they've made their father proud.

And Charisma loved him. She loved him for the helping hand he'd so willingly provided six years ago. She loved him for the stand he'd taken against the congregation for her. She loved him for the acceptance of a child that wasn't his. She loved him for everything that he was and everything that he wasn't. He'd taken her in. He'd supported her while she completed college. He was there for her every step of the way, no matter how thick. He'd won her heart, married her, adopted her son, bought them this house, and finally given her his child, the baby girl. If he'd accomplished all this in only six years, Charisma couldn't imagine the blessings 20 years from now would bring.

While the meatloaf and potatoes baked, Charisma called them from their play. Together they set the table. Charisma poured their wine as Burton filled the sink with suds to let the dirty dishes soak. Jewel was placed in her highchair, clapping her hands in delight. Sonny took his seat on the booster in between his mother and father. They all held hands as Sonny spoke their dinner prayer.

Burton mmmed and aaahed over the meatloaf.

Sonny declared how much he hated meatloaf.

Charisma lectured him not to use the word hate.

Jewel scarfed down her applesauce and pureed green beans.

Charisma critiqued her meal saying she should have used more of this and less of that.

Burton assured her it was perfect.

Once the subtleties were out of the way they spoke of their day, Sonny overpowering any sort of conversation with his wild tales and exhilarating excitement.

Burton cleared the plates and put them in the sink as Charisma set her son up at his desk so that he could do his homework. Only upon its completion could he have dessert, providing the motivation to hurry up and get it done. Jewel went down for more sleep. Burton filled their wine glasses one more time as they now had the opportunity to speak one on one in quiet voices.

He gripped her hand and lovingly caressed it. "Darling, I must confess. I have been cheating on you with my eyes. There is this woman who sings in the church choir and her angelic beauty and voice stand out from the rest of the choir. She wears the mandated maroon robe but every time I look at her, I find myself wondering what she is wearing beneath the robe and I picture her not wearing anything at all."

"Burton, to have such thoughts in church, under God of all places."

"I know. I cannot help it. She is just too beautiful."

Charisma flushed with his compliment. "Well then I, too, must confess that I see this man peering at me as I sing, looking so handsome in his starched suit and tie and my thoughts tend to wander in the want of taking hold of that tie in my hand and wrapping it around my wrist and pulling him to the nearest pew and—"

"Daddy!" Sonny called.

"Hold that thought, dear. Our son needs higher intelligence, hence his calling for his daddy rather than his mommy."

"He just wants to ask you how to spell pig."

Charisma went through the dinner mess as Burton helped Sonny with his homework. Once completed Burton came in with Sonny at his side. "Can I have my dessert now?"

Charisma scooped both of them a brownie with vanilla icecream and then woke Jewel to take care of the evening feeding and a quick bath. Sonny was next in the tub, and then they all sat down together for their nighttime reading. With Burton's deep resonant voice, it's power and ability to change characters, he was the perfect story-teller.

At 8:00 they tucked Sonny into bed and Burton gave the night-time prayer. Love you's were exchanged and the door was shut very very slowly.

Suddenly Charisma bolted down the stairs, Burton not too far behind her. She threw the shower on as he rapidly undressed her, then ridding of his own clothes he joined her in the warm spray. Each taking turns with the soap they lathered it over one another's bodies and alternated positions to rinse. He brushed his teeth as she washed her hair and then he washed his hair as she brushed her teeth. She wrapped the towel around her hair and took off naked toward the stairs as he followed dangerously close snapping a towel at her rear.

"Quiet, you'll wake the - "

He tackled her as she squealed in a face-plant on the big bed. His hands hurriedly roamed her backside as she flipped herself over. Their lips clashed hotly as they prepped one another, their hands moving over one another. Charisma arched her hips as he slid smoothly inside her. They moaned and murmured, never tiring of the dance they'd begun five years ago and continued to do on a three to four days a week basis. He lifted on his knees and took both her cheeks in the palms of his hands and slid her over and around him as he grinded against her, awaiting his favorite climax-causing moment of her gasping, "I'm gonna – Ahhhhhh."

Settled into and on one another, they kissed until their contended end. Gathering her up in his arms, Burton rolled off of her and they fell to sleep with her head at his shoulder, her hand splayed on his chest, their legs entwined, his arms wrapped around her and holding her hand.

Life was good.